A Lady's

DECEPTION

Haslemere Men Series

A Lady's

DECEPTION

Haslemere Men Series

PAMELA MINGLE

Entangled Publishing, LLC
2614 South Timberline Road
Suite 109
Fort Collins, CO 80525
Visit our website at www.entangledpublishing.com.

Select Historical is an imprint of Entangled Publishing, LLC.

Edited by Erin Molta
Cover design by Erin Dameron-Hill
Cover art from Period Images and
Deposit Photos

Manufactured in the United States of America

First Edition August 2017

For my sister Janis
Sharing our love of books since childhood

Prologue

Hugh Grey stood in the shadows at the Haslemere assembly, as far from the light as he could get and still make out the dancers. For November, it was oppressively hot inside. No surprise there—the room was packed with revelers. Too many sweating bodies crammed into a space barely large enough to contain them. He was present for one reason only.

To catch a glimpse of Miss Eleanor Broxton.

Hugh had nearly concluded she was not in attendance, and his patience was on a short tether. He had business to take care of. In two days, he would board a ship for North America. Canada, to be precise, if one could be precise when it came to such a vast breadth of land. Not for him the battlefields of the Peninsula and the never-ending war with Napoleon. He wanted something new, and the colder climes of Canada suited his temperament.

A blond head flashed by. Not Eleanor, devil take it. When the dance ended, and Hugh had yet to spot her, he began to move toward the anterooms. She'd stayed away, proving she was wiser than he by half. It was difficult to progress quickly through such a crowd, but because of his size, people moved aside for him. And emerging from a sea of bodies, there she was.

Hugh stopped cold, flummoxed. "Miss Broxton."

He bowed, and she offered her hand. "Mr. Grey. You're not leaving?" He loved the cadence of her voice. So caressing, wrapping her words around him. And could that be a spark of pleasure in her eyes?

"I was, yes." Hugh was still holding her hand. Reluctantly, he released it.

"So soon? It is early yet."

He hadn't intended to do anything more than feast his eyes upon her, but he said, "If you will dance with me, perhaps I'll stay."

"I—" A handsome young buck approached, full of himself. How easy it would be to grasp him by the collar and send him on his way.

"My dance, Miss Broxton." She spared the boy a glance before turning back to Hugh.

"The next, then," she said. He nodded and watched her walk away with her partner. After a moment, she looked back at him. Not once, but twice, the second time a hint of a smile curving her lips. Something clutched at him, just under his ribs, and would not let go.

Should he wait and hope to claim his dance? If she hadn't looked back at him and smiled, he probably wouldn't have. He worked his way over to stand with those who were not dancing. And that's when Hugh spotted Sir William, Eleanor's father, his cold and forbidding eyes staring at him. Challenging him.

Hugh got the message. As long as the man drew breath, Eleanor would be off-limits to the likes of him. Even though his brother, Adam, was Broxton's man in the House of Commons, Hugh still wasn't good enough. He should never have come here. Why was he tormenting himself?

Instead of waiting for his dance with Eleanor, he made his way to the entrance, all the while counting himself a fool. Nothing had changed, nor ever would, if Sir William continued to believe the worst of him.

• • •

Eleanor, for once, was glad of the general chaos that was an assembly ball. It limited interaction with one's partner. If her eyes roved around the room, said partner would probably not even notice. Or care. She took full advantage of the situation, especially after they'd gone down the middle, to find Hugh in the press of people.

Since he was taller than most of the men present, she had no difficulty spotting him. To her dismay, it looked as if he'd decided to leave. *No.* He'd asked her for the next dance. Well, she had been the one to do the asking. He'd simply nodded his assent. But when she'd looked back at him, his eyes had gleamed out at her from the dimness. He had *wanted* to dance with her.

Eleanor made a rash decision to follow him. Assemblies were less formal than private balls, so excusing herself wouldn't matter. Much. It didn't matter to her, in any case. "Mr. Buckley, I'm feeling a bit unwell. Pray excuse me."

"But—"

"No, I'll be fine. Please stay and find another partner." A perfunctory curtsy, and she made her escape before he had time to balk any further.

In truth, she was feeling, if not unwell, strangely agitated. She hadn't felt that way since the house party at Deborah Grey's country estate earlier in the year, where she had met

Hugh. Like a fool, she'd initially set her sights on his brother, Adam, only to discover he was enamored of someone else. But Hugh had swept in and somehow managed to take her mind off Adam. In fact, he'd captivated her. He'd taught her how to shoot an arrow—his big body surrounding her—even though she'd been hopelessly inept at it… The memory had never left her. And the night of the ball, before its abrupt end, he had walked with her in the garden and stolen a kiss. Remembering the feel of his lips on hers sent a thrill right to her core.

She was desperate not to lose sight of him. Nudging, and in some cases shoving, merrymakers out of her path, she set a course for the entrance. The room was dimly lit, and she prayed her parents wouldn't be on the lookout for her. Recalling where they'd been standing when she'd last seen them, she veered away from that part of the room and ducked her head. Their vigilance was suffocating. Out of their range at last, she glanced up, searching for Hugh. But he was nowhere to be seen. He must have already gone.

That didn't deter her. Grabbing her shawl from the pegs near the door, she threw it around her shoulders and ventured out into the cold. She would find him.

Icy sleet lashed at her, and she wrapped her shawl close around her, dodging puddles and piles of dung. Carriages were lined up along the street, the coachmen huddled around fires, drinking and laughing. She kept to the shadows to avoid their notice. Hugh would be heading for the livery to claim his horse for the ride back to Longmere. Her eyes were beginning to adjust to the darkness, and she lifted her skirts and picked up her pace.

Thud! She slammed into something that felt like a wall, and the breath whooshed out of her. The wall turned and grasped her arms. "Eleanor."

It was Hugh, wearing a heavy greatcoat. And now that

she'd found him, she had absolutely no idea what to say.

He reached for her hand. "Let's get out of this deuced weather."

That suggestion held promise, though it was also fraught with danger. But she allowed him to lead her. When they reached the stables, Hugh opened a swinging door on the far end of the building and drew her inside. They were in a storage area, with bales of hay piled in neat stacks. Tack hung on the walls and rested on long plank tables. The air was redolent with horse, manure, and saddle oil. He seemed to be familiar with his surroundings, unerringly finding a short stack of bales for them to sit on and pulling her down next to him. Warmth immediately surrounded her.

"I'm afraid it's not as elegant as you're accustomed to, but it's the best I could do on such short notice." His teeth flashed white in the darkness. He found this situation amusing, did he? Eleanor tried to think what, exactly, she wanted to say, but he spoke first.

"Why did you follow me?"

Why indeed? Through the neighborhood grapevine, she'd heard he had bought a commission. What if she never saw him again? She wanted to be near him, hear his laugh, his soothing voice. And she craved more than that. She desperately wanted him to touch her. Kiss her. Hold her. Do everything a man does with a woman. *Oh God.* She couldn't possibly say any of that.

"I heard you were leaving. I wanted to say good-bye."

"The gossips have done their work, then." He chuckled, a low, provocative sound in the dark. "I should thank them."

Eleanor sighed. He'd wanted to see her, too. "Why didn't you stay for our dance?"

"Your father looked as if he might call me out, if I dared speak to you. I thought it best not to goad him by dancing with you."

Her father again. Would he never allow her to live her own life? Decide for herself what was best for her? Defiance reared its head, spurring her to be rash. "I'm not answerable to him. To them." She had to include her mother in this, since she was worse, in many ways, than her father. She expected— demanded—Eleanor's absolute obedience to whatever directives were set out for her, and Eleanor had had her fill of it.

"I can hardly believe that."

He was right. Until she was married, she was dependent on them. It had been a foolish thing to say, but she felt daring tonight, and a twisting, bunching feeling down low in her belly made her reckless. "Where are you going, Hugh? When will you be back?" And then, hesitantly, she said, "I wish you weren't leaving."

• • •

Damn. Why did she have to say that? His cock stirred, and he was glad of the darkness. Grasping her shoulders, he drew her close. He shouldn't take such liberties, but here they were, in this secluded place, alone. It was so dark he could barely make out her features, so he traced his fingers over her face. He explored her cheekbones with his thumbs, finally skimming them across her lips. She gasped, whether from shock or desire, he couldn't say and didn't care. And then he did what he'd been longing to do since their first kiss that night in the garden. Lowering his head, he set his lips on hers.

At first Eleanor didn't respond, receiving his kiss in an innocent, untaught way. When he whispered, "Open your mouth, sweetheart," she complied without hesitation. After a moment of simply soaking up the pure joy and sensual experience of his open mouth on hers, he plunged his tongue into the warm moistness of her. He wasn't sure how she would react. To his everlasting delight, she threw her arms around his neck, pressing her breasts into his chest. Hastily, Hugh shrugged out of his coat. Hardly knowing what the hell he was doing, he got to his feet, dragging her with him. His arms went around her, but he couldn't hold them still. He was beyond that.

He ran his hands up her sides, pausing at her breasts, pressing his thumbs against the fullness overflowing her stays. His swollen length was crushed against her with unmistakable urgency, something even an inexperienced girl would recognize. Downward his hands moved, until they cupped her magnificent derrière. He filled his hands with it, aware he should stop, but also knowing he wouldn't unless she demanded it. But she didn't. On the contrary, she welcomed every onslaught he made against her innocence.

Operating purely on the pent-up desire raging in him since last spring, he slid her skirts up so he could touch her with no impediment. He hesitated for a beat, allowing her the chance to push him away, to call a halt to what they were doing. But she did not.

• • •

Eleanor was floating in a haze of sensuality. Never before had she experienced anything like this desperate need that now held sway over her. She couldn't have denied it even if she'd wanted to. Which she most decidedly did not. When Hugh stroked her inner thighs, above her stockings, she purred with pleasure.

He spoke softly into her ear. "I want to see your breasts, Eleanor. Feel your breasts. Will you let me?"

God help her, she wanted that, too. She tugged her dress down over her stays, so that the tops of her breasts were exposed. Hugh pushed the straps of her chemise off her shoulders, and her breath caught when he slid his hand underneath and found the tip of one breast. He rolled it between his fingers, delicately pinching, until she moaned, "Oh, God, Hugh. Oh, God." And then he pulled up her skirts and returned his attention to her thighs, moving ever closer to her most intimate place.

Suddenly, before she could find her moorings, he was stroking her there, the most sensitive part of her. She felt as she had the one time she'd been to the sea and floated on the buoyant water, the feeling joyous and surprising. When the pleasure grew so intense she thought she might lose her mind, Hugh pulled her down onto their makeshift bed. She was too far gone to even consider stopping him.

He pushed up her skirts, and in the darkness she saw him fumbling with his falls, felt him pressing against her entrance. But just as she was on the verge of exploding, he hesitated. "Eleanor—"

"Don't say anything," she said, putting a finger to his lips. "I want you, Hugh Grey."

And then he was pushing inside her, little by little, and sliding back out, giving her time to accustom herself to his invasion, then thrusting forward again. She felt no pain, only a sense of fullness and an incandescent joy that he was now a part of her. When at last he broke through her barrier, she barely noticed, because she was focused on the one thing that truly mattered: release from this torture, this agony of bliss she was drowning in. Hugh thrust a hand between them and found her center once again, and Eleanor dropped over the edge at last, crying out fiercely. He followed her, emitting a primal grunt of release, then dropping down to cover her body with his.

• • •

Two thoughts occurred to Hugh as he lay there in the warm cocoon of Eleanor's body. His backside was damned cold, and second, what the hell had he done? Taken advantage of a chaste girl by stealing her virginity, that's what, all for the sake of satisfying his uncontrollable urge to have her. And worst of all, he'd ruined her, if anyone were to find out. It was that last thought that spurred him into action, even though he'd much prefer lying on the hay bales with her in his arms for hours more. He sat up and buttoned his falls, then fished in his pocket for a handkerchief. He found Eleanor's hand and set the square of linen in it.

"Eleanor, you must get back to the ball. Your father will be wondering where you are. If we were to be discovered—"

He couldn't see her expression clearly, but when she spoke, she sounded like a thoroughly pleasured woman. "Nobody will discover us. And I'm not concerned about my parents."

Hugh smiled at her bravado, then leaned down to kiss her once more. "That's foolish, and you know it. Up you go, you must be off." He stood and brushed himself off while she cleaned herself. When she rose, he made sure no telltale strands of hay marred her skirts.

"My shawl," she said, when they were nearly to the door. "Where is it?"

Hugh glanced around, finally spotting it, a splash of darkness against the hay, and hurriedly wrapped it around her shoulders. He did not let go.

"You must return on your own, Eleanor. We can't be seen together."

"I'm aware. This is good-bye, then," she said, her eyes wide.

He nodded, unable to speak. What could he say? He refused to apologize for making love to her. He knew her well enough to believe she would have called a halt if she hadn't wanted him. But there was a huge difference between what two people wanted and what was prudent, and they'd crossed that line. He wished to hell he'd never bought that commission, but it was too late now. Besides, nothing had changed. Broxton would never countenance a union between him and Eleanor.

So he said the one thing that seemed to make sense. "You've given me a precious gift, Eleanor. Thank you."

She nodded, and he opened the door, peering into the night to make sure nobody was lurking outside. And then reached for her hand. They walked together until the lights of the assembly rooms might have revealed them. There was one thing that must be said.

"You will inform me if there are consequences. Adam will know how to get word to me."

Nodding, she said, "Good-bye, Hugh. Be safe." Rising up on her toes, she brushed her lips across his.

When he could see that she'd entered the building, he returned to the stables and asked for his mount. He rode home to Longmere in a persistent, icy drizzle, half buoyant, half miserable. He'd just made love to the woman of his dreams, but was soon to be separated from her for God knew how long.

What a damned mess he'd made of things.

Chapter One

Surrey, April 1815

Sir Hugh Grey huddled inside his greatcoat, tugging the collar up as far as it would reach. Even so, he could not prevent droplets of rain from sliding down his neck and saturating his shirt and coat. If he had a good reason for lingering at his father's grave, he might be able to justify soaking himself to the skin. But the truth was, he didn't know what held him there. There was no explanation, except he'd missed the burial and was sorry for it. And that he had always been, and probably always would be, inextricably bound to his father. By blood, by character, by reputation.

"The Grim Reaper came calling, and even you couldn't turn him away," Hugh said aloud, staring at the gravestone.

His words went unremarked by the denizens of the church graveyard, including his father. The weather reminded him of the day he'd left England more than two years ago, although rather than a spring rain, November sleet had accompanied him on his journey to the coast. He'd been in British North

America until six weeks past, when his brother, Adam, had sent word of Benjamin Grey's death. Hugh had been ready to sell his commission by then, anyway. It had been time to come home.

Home to what, remained an unanswered question. Estranged from his brother and mother, Hugh had nobody he considered family. His father had left the country estate, Longmere, where Hugh had grown up, to him. It had been in a sad state before he left, and he dreaded seeing what further damage two more years of neglect had wrought. After another moment of wasted contemplation, he spun around, passed through the lych-gate, and climbed into the carriage he'd purchased in London. The estate owned no such conveyance, and he suspected he might have need of one. Hugh had also bought four Cleveland Bay carriage horses, with strong, capable shoulders. A newly hired coachman sat on the box, and a groom rode at the back, by the boot.

On the drive to Longmere, they passed the approach to the Broxton home. He wondered if Eleanor were there right now, reading, perhaps, or working. She liked to sew, he recalled. Design things. Gowns, and dresses. Then it struck him that she may not live there any longer. She may have wed. Hell, she may even have children. And with that jarring thought, his mind traveled back to the last time they were together, when he'd taken her virginity in a frenzied, heated passion. Visions of that night were what had sustained him through the first year in British North America, during the cold, ceaseless winter. Kept him warm and comforted him. While the mystique of it had faded somewhat, the memory had not. Making love to Eleanor had been, against all odds, the best moment of his life.

She had drawn him from the first. They'd met at his mother's country home, at a house party he'd reluctantly attended because she had entreated him to do so. Eleanor had been the one bright spot in an otherwise lonely week. Her loveliness was only part of it. There was something about her...her reserve, perhaps. Her reluctance to reveal herself, despite the fact that her every emotion shone out of those radiant eyes of hers. He had found out later that her father had hoped to marry her to Adam. Thank God, Adam had already been in love with Cassandra Linford, whom he'd since married.

Though Eleanor had been reticent with the others, Hugh had drawn her out, and he'd sensed her ease with him. By the end of the week, there was no denying their attraction was mutual. Still, making it known she had wanted to dance with him at the assembly ball, then following him and making love to him with abandon had taken him by surprise. He hadn't expected her to be so daring. So ready. In a mere few months she'd matured, changed. Known what she wanted and wasn't afraid to go after it. After him.

But in more than two years, how else had she changed? Hugh didn't know, but he intended to seek her out and discover the answer for himself.

• • •

Three weeks later

The day was waning. The gradual loss of light was Eleanor's enemy. In her north-facing work area, it became too dim in the late afternoon to continue sewing. Not if she expected the highest quality of work from herself and her assistants.

Discouraged, she sighed and pushed herself away from her worktable. "Let's be done for today, Jane."

Needing no encouragement, Jane dropped what she was doing and said, "Yes, miss." She neatly folded the gown she'd been working on, jabbed her needle into a pincushion, and placed her thimble and scissors into a box. Eleanor, who worked best when the tools of her trade were organized, was grateful the other girl followed her example in this.

Eleanor stood and stretched, then hunched and released her shoulders a few times, trying to work out the knots in her muscles caused by too many hours bent over her work.

"Are you eating dinner with your parents tonight, miss?" Jane asked.

"I told them not to expect me." In truth, she was simply too tired to walk up to the house, nor did she wish to be subjected to her mother's belittling comments. "You should be on your way. Your mother will be needing you."

"Nan is there today. She'll help."

Jane had many siblings. The fact that her family needed every penny each one of them of working age could earn was no secret. One of her brothers had been lately looking for work. "Has Simon found employment yet?" Eleanor asked, hoping for good news.

"Oh, aye, didn't I tell you? He's working for Mr. Grey over at Longmere. Or I suppose I'm obliged to say 'Sir Hugh' now, aren't I?"

The box of thread Eleanor had been carrying to the cupboard slipped from her grasp, narrowly missing her toes. Spools of all colors popped out onto the floor and rolled around the rug. It was like a children's game. She and Jane dropped to their hands and knees, scooping up the wayward spools and safely stowing them back in their container, which happened to be an old hatbox.

Eleanor sat back on her heels. "How long has he been home?" She tried to sound indifferent, but she didn't know if she succeeded. How could Hugh have been back for weeks and she not even aware? Was she so closed off from the world? Shut away in the cottage every day, she supposed she was.

Jane rose and donned her bonnet and shawl. "Near

a month now, I'd say. He's rebuilding the place, and he needed laborers for the job." She tied her bonnet strings and continued. "Simon thinks he must be rich. He hired himself a top architect from London to draw up the plans for the new house. Simon and the rest of the crew are pulling down the old place meantime."

"I see," Eleanor said, even though she didn't see at all. Clinging to a chair for support, she got to her feet.

When Jane had finally gone, she put the kettle on. Hugh was home, and he'd made no attempt to see her. The cad. The wretch. The complete rogue. She wanted to throw something, but couldn't risk damaging her very small, necessarily tidy work area. Instead, exhorting herself to be calm, she poured her tea, added milk, and wandered outside to her garden.

Her cottage had been constructed on reclaimed meadow, and so her garden bloomed with lady's-smock and buttercups; she had added heartsease and cowslips. It was a small space, dominated by the flowers, which had to be continually thinned or they would, like spoiled children, take over. No room for grass, but there was a flagged area, where she'd installed a bench. It invited her to sit, and so she did.

Why was she so angry about Hugh's lack of attention to her? After all, she'd heard nothing from or about him in all the time he'd been on a different continent. And now he was "Sir Hugh." And, according to Jane, he was rich. A military commission wasn't so lucrative, was it? Amazing that whatever exploits he'd undertaken to gain himself a knighthood hadn't reached her ears, although she'd had other things on her mind since he'd been gone. Given her situation, it was far better that he stay as far away from her as possible. And yet, she yearned for him. She had thought there was genuine affection between them. And for more than two long years she'd romanticized their one night together, the night of the Haslemere assembly. She had relived it, dreamed about it, and no doubt exaggerated its significance. To him, it apparently had meant little. It was different for her. For her, it had changed everything.

A wet nose tickled her ankle and she looked down at her pup, Bobby. Eleanor picked him up, holding him aloft to examine. "Who were your sire and dam, little one?" Her guess was spaniel and border collie, and her father, who knew about dogs, had agreed. The dog had wandered into her garden one day looking lost, probably abandoned, and she hadn't had the heart to turn him out. Probably because he was the most adorable creature, save one, she'd ever seen, with his black and white curly coat and floppy ears. She drew him close, and he licked her nose and face until she put a stop to it.

"Time to feed you, Bob, you bothersome imp." She set him down, and he followed her excitedly into the cottage, where he knew he'd find sustenance and generally a special treat.

• • •

The following morning

Hugh stood, hands on hips, monitoring the progress on the tearing down of the old Elizabethan manor house he'd grown up in. He reckoned they had another week's worth of work before it was complete, and then a second week disposing of the remaining rubble before the builders could start on the new place.

He hadn't wanted to take down his childhood home, but the architect he'd hired, John Ridley, who had spent a week in Surrey thoroughly going over the house and working on plans for the new structure, had recommended it as the only sensible—and safe—choice. Parts of the house were rotting away due to improper guttering and a roof that had leaked for years. Other sections were infested with termites. Ridley deemed some of the beams and supports so weak, the place was no longer fit for habitation.

Fortunately, the stables were in far better repair than the house, so the groom, coachman, and footman he'd hired could lodge there temporarily. They'd moved most of the furniture—the pieces worth saving—out there. Without a kitchen, he couldn't feed anybody, including himself. Every day, Hugh purchased cheese, bread, and meat pies from the local shops for his own staff and all the other laborers working on the property. In his experience, well-rested and well-fed men made the best workers.

Hugh was staying in an old tenant's cottage. Unlived in for years, it remained in surprisingly good condition, much better than the manor house. It had been locked, which was a good thing, because it had forced Hugh to search for the estate key ring. He could picture his father, back when he still cared about the place, wearing it over his broad forearm. He'd finally found it in a drawer of Benjamin Grey's desk. Hugh had moved his bed, an old wooden chair, and a small table into the cottage, and it would meet his most basic needs for now. The mere where he and Adam had swum as boys would serve for bathing.

Most days, he labored alongside the other men. Hugh was no stranger to hard work. In the past, he'd often helped tenants with repairs and rebuilding and had done what he could to patch up the manor house with what little money he'd had. And the army had taught him much about putting in long days. But not today. This morning he was traveling to London to meet with the family solicitor. He wanted a list of his father's outstanding debts so he could settle them. He was also meeting with Ridley to finalize the building plans and construction schedule.

That evening, he would be dining with Adam and Cass. He'd reluctantly accepted the invitation and scheduled the other appointments for the same day. His nephew had been born while he was away, and Hugh was looking forward to meeting him, if not spending time with his brother. He hoped to God, Deborah, his mother, wouldn't be there. According to Adam, she was frequently away, in the company of her devoted admirer, Freddie Cochran.

Hugh's attention was drawn by something rooting about in the rubble, a little creature, probably a weasel or a squirrel, and Hugh walked over to chase it off. But no, when he drew closer, he saw it was a small dog. A pup, really. A little black and white ball of fur. Quickly, he reached down and grabbed it. "Hey, little scamp, you must go back from where you came. It's not healthy for you around here." He called to his men. "Anybody know whose mongrel this is?"

Simon Weeks laughed from his perch on a ladder. "That must be Miss Broxton's dog. My sister told me she's got a new pup. Do you want me to take him home before he gets himself killed?"

Hugh assessed. "No, I'll do it myself." It was just the excuse he'd been looking for to see Eleanor. Dressed for Town, he was more presentable than on most days. He set off on a path through the woods toward her cottage, thinking about why he'd delayed this visit, since he'd found out, his first day back, where she was living and what she was doing. Gossip traveled fast among the countryfolk. No, he blamed putting this off on his expectations, or lack thereof. Would she be happy to see him? Would the two years he'd been gone fall away, and she would be eager to hop back in his bed? Or back on top of his hay bale, as it were. Or would she despise him for making love to her and leaving for North America without a word since? Surely, she knew he'd returned. Wouldn't she be wondering why he hadn't called on her?

These disparate thoughts clashed in his mind until the dog distracted him, nuzzling into his coat, probably drooling all over it. "Does your mistress hold you like this, old boy? Does she snuggle with you? God, how I'd like to be in your shoes…paws. You're a lucky devil, eh."

. . .

Eleanor had departed the cottage for the garden to escape from the hurt feelings she'd caused. She'd had to spend the better part of an hour ripping out stitches, and Minnie, her second assistant, blamed herself. As Eleanor had patiently explained, it was the poor light that was at fault. From now on, both she and Jane must tell her if they couldn't see well enough to stitch. Ripping out could ruin expensive, delicate fabrics. And so on. They'd discussed all this before, but the two girls, Minnie especially, still seemed to think haste was better than fine workmanship. The three women were acutely aware of the large number of orders they'd been receiving and worrying about how they would be able to fill them. The Season would be ending in a few months, and ladies wanted new gowns for the final entertainments.

She stooped down by the flower beds and began pulling weeds. The garden needed more attention from her, but she hadn't the time to spare, except erratically. Like now. Muttering to herself, she tugged unmercifully at the damnable, pestilent things, working without pause until her hair came loose and fell around her face. Eleanor didn't notice. She was too busy complaining out loud.

Why hadn't some clever person invented a source of artificial light? Why couldn't she have a larger work space, so she and the girls weren't elbow-to-elbow all the damn time? Why was it so hard for them to understand that the highest quality work, along with her designs, was their stock-in-trade? Their reputation for both was what kept them afloat.

It was then that a pair of booted feet caught her attention, and she ceased her grumbling. Staring at the boots, she inferred two things in short order: they were beautifully made top boots, probably from Hoby's in London; and second, nobody in the immediate vicinity would be wearing such boots. Which caused her to look up at last.

Into the devastatingly handsome face of Hugh Grey. Dazzling dark eyes, prominent nose that screamed arrogance, beautiful male physique boasting wide shoulders and muscled chest. Oh, God, how she had missed him. All six-plus feet of him.

She toppled over onto her haunches and saved herself from tumbling completely backward only by planting her palms on the ground. Was that a chuckle she heard? Before he could help her, she scrambled to her feet.

"Hello, Eleanor," Hugh said.

She must look a fright, with her unkempt hair and her worn day dress. And here he stood, looking like a plate out of *Ackerman's Repository*. Forest green coat, immaculate shirt, silk waistcoat. And those boots.

She said the first thing that came to mind. "Aren't you a bit overdressed for the country, Sir Hugh?"

He laughed, a deep sound emanating from his chest. And then he said, "Aren't you missing something?"

A stab of fear hit Eleanor in the gut, and she could barely catch her breath. *He knew*. How? It was the best kept secret in all of Surrey. And then she saw that he was talking about Bobby, and she could breathe again. "That's my pup you're holding."

"So I'm told. He was nosing around my property, and it's not safe for him there. Nails, broken glass, big male feet. Bound to get hurt." The pup wiggled, and Eleanor gathered him into her arms.

"He's called Bobby."

Hugh smiled, watching her. "It suits him."

Eleanor cast about for something to say. "My condolences on your father's death." She was sincere in the sentiment and hoped he didn't dismiss it as mere pleasantry.

He nodded his thanks, and they stood there awkwardly. He had put his hands behind his back, and his coat pulled snugly against his chest and shoulders. The man could fill out a coat. His tailor must love him—no padding required. And his britches. She shouldn't even think about his britches. Was she staring? Oh God, she was. Gesturing to the bench, she said, "Will you sit down, Sir Hugh?"

"No, thank you. I'm off to London on business this morning." He glanced at the cottage. "You are residing here now?"

There was no censure in the question. "No. Working here. I live with my parents." That was a half truth. She slept at her cottage many nights. Sometimes it seemed easier. When he didn't respond, she explained further. "I have a dressmaking business. I work primarily for the London set, although I do have some local custom." He could make of this what he might. She didn't care.

Smiling, he said, "I recall your love of creating your own designs. It must be demanding work."

A breeze ruffled her hair, and she brushed it off her face. "It is. I have two assistants, girls whose families needed the extra coin. They're good workers, and I try very hard not to take advantage of them."

"I can't imagine you would do any such thing." He nodded toward the cottage, then said, "Is there enough room for the three of you to do your work in such a, well—?"

"Ridiculously small space? Barely, but so far, we've managed."

A brisk nod, and then he said, "I must be off, if I'm to make my appointments in Town." He held out his hand, and what else could she do but offer hers? For a moment, she thought he might kiss her fingers, but he simply gave her hand a gentle caress and let go.

"I'll count the days until we meet again, Eleanor."

He spun around and was gone before she thought of replying.

Chapter Two

Hugh rode his bay mare up to Town, reflecting on his awkward visit with Eleanor. She was far lovelier than he'd remembered. Odd, that, because memories usually magnified the pleasure of a thing. But in this case, the reality far surpassed the memory. Her hair had darkened to a light brown, with blond streaks threading through it.

He'd had to use all the self-control he could summon not to slide one of those wispy strands through his fingers. And her lovely hazel eyes, more green than brown today, were a perfect complement to her hair. When Eleanor first spoke, asking if he wasn't a bit overdressed, the cadence and lilt of her voice had nearly felled him. And her mouth. Sweet perfection. How he longed to taste it once again.

Yet he could detect no answering pleasure in her. She'd barely smiled. Not that he'd given her any reason to smile. But everything about her seemed to say, "Don't come near me." Avoiding anything personal, she'd concentrated on telling him about her work. She had invited him to sit, but it was merely a gesture of politeness, so obvious that he'd refused.

Why was she being aloof with him?

Hugh could think of two reasons. First, she might be embarrassed, even ashamed, of the fact that she'd surrendered her virginity to him in the stables. But given her manner that night, he couldn't accept that. If anything, she had been the seducer, not him.

Possibly she was angry with him for not communicating with her while he'd been away. But he'd had no means of doing so. Her father would have confiscated any letter he might have written to her. In retrospect, Hugh might have asked Adam to smuggle a missive to her, but he wouldn't have wanted to involve his brother.

There was a third reason. Considering he'd been back at least three weeks, he should have called on her before now. He'd been afraid of his reception, and with good reason, as it turned out. Clearly, she needed time to feel at ease with him again. It had been more than two years, after all. He would pursue her, but gradually, and he'd have to command all the self-discipline he could muster to hold to that. To wait until she once again warmed to him.

There was one thing about Eleanor that worried him. Her eyes held traces of sadness, and her expression seemed strained. He didn't think it was due to his unexpected presence. By God, he'd find out why she was unhappy, and he'd fix it.

Hugh reached Southwark late in the afternoon. He stabled his horse there and took a wherry across the Thames to the City, where both the solicitor and the architect maintained offices. The meeting with his father's solicitor, Stewart McBride, was brief and perfunctory. Hugh had first met the man years ago, and he was now quite up in years. His hair had faded to gray and he was slightly stooped, but he sprang to his feet like a young man when Hugh entered.

"Sir Hugh," McBride said. "Good to see you. Please, be seated." He hadn't lost his Scottish accent, even after all the years he'd lived in London. Hugh loved the burr and the curious Scottish phrases that sometimes crept into the man's conversation. Like "keep the heid" when he was urging calm, and "Ah dinnae ken," when McBride was puzzled about something.

He sat, and the solicitor informed him that he'd followed Hugh's instructions, paying off various creditors with what money had remained in his father's estate. He summoned his clerk, who handed him a paper. After a quick glance, he passed it to Hugh. "This is what remains of the debts."

After a cursory scan, Hugh said, "I don't see Broxton's name on here." Benjamin Grey had been deeply in debt to Sir William, Eleanor's father. It was the one obligation Hugh wanted to settle without further delay.

Mr. McBride shifted in his chair, his bushy gray eyebrows knitted together. A young man entered pushing a tea trolley, and McBride waited until the refreshments were laid out before responding. He spoke while pouring. "Your brother came to see me shortly after your father's death. He was most keen to pay off the debt to Sir William. I told him what was owed, and he sent me a bank draft to cover it. I didn't think you would object."

Indeed. Yet Hugh did object. He was the heir; his father's debts were his responsibility, not Adam's. He'd sort it out with his brother later. After drinking tea and partaking of sandwiches and apple tarts, Hugh shook hands with Mr. McBride, thanked him, and left.

A short walk later, he'd reached the offices of John Ridley, Architect, located in an unprepossessing redbrick building. Ridley was expecting him. They went over the plans for the new house one more time. Hugh was keen to pin the man down as to a starting date for construction, but as usual, Ridley managed to dodge a firm commitment. "Depends," he said, with his usual brevity.

"So you've said. My patience is wearing thin."

"The contractor I hired is finishing a job in Kent. You can't predict with any certainty when that will be completed. Then there's all the materials. The stone must be brought in from Sussex."

"There's no reason to delay that," Hugh said. "I've laborers there every day. Hell, *I'm* there nearly every day."

Ridley said, a hint of irritation in his voice, "This business works on its own schedule. You know that. But I'll set things in motion, with shipments of stone and other materials and supplies." He consulted a paper on which, Hugh could see, every line was filled, and even the margins were annotated. "The workers you've got demolishing the place. Any of 'em got experience building?"

Hugh nodded. "Some do, not all. I've a good feel for who can be kept on."

"Excellent. And the rubble will need to be hauled away to make room for everything else."

"Already doing that. We cart it away every few days." Hugh paused, not wanting to aggravate the man further. He liked Ridley, and they had a friendly relationship so far. "Could you at least give me an approximate date?"

Ridley inhaled a deep breath and released it, puffing out his cheeks. "Let's say one month from today. But don't hold me to it," he said wryly.

Patience, man. "My thanks," Hugh said.

• • •

In the late afternoon, Eleanor walked toward the Broxton home on the footpath, Bobby scampering along at her heels.

She had been in an ill humor ever since Hugh's visit. And her mood would not improve during an evening spent with her parents.

After Hugh left, she had tromped back inside and resumed her work, first cutting out a cloth pattern for a walking dress she'd designed for a local customer, and later working on sketches for new gowns. At least she'd made some progress there, poring over the latest issues of *Ackermann's Repository* and *La Belle Assemblée*. Her father had given her subscriptions for both journals as a gift. Even though he didn't approve of what she was doing, he often helped her in small ways that actually made a great deal of difference. She frequently found designs in one of the magazines and adapted them until they became originals. EB Creations. That was what she called her business, and she took an inordinate amount of pride in it. Even though the work was more daunting than she'd ever imagined.

Throughout the remainder of the day, thoughts of Hugh had disturbed her concentration. Damn the man for looking so devilishly handsome. It wasn't just his appearance, though. It was his bearing, too, far more assured than she remembered. Hugh had always carried the stigma of being raised by Benjamin Grey. In the past, her own father had referred to the man as the Libertine of Longmere, and he wasn't the only one who had. Many people in the neighborhood had put Hugh in the same category, quite unjustly. Although Eleanor had to admit, she knew nothing of *that* side of his life. When she had first met him at the house party, three years ago now, he was darkly good looking, obviously intelligent, but somewhat hesitant in his manner, especially approaching her. As though she might have turned him away. Even the night of the fateful Haslemere assembly, he'd been unsure of himself. He'd left after her father had stared him down, and she'd had to go after him.

No longer. This morning, he'd exuded confidence and... for lack of a better word, boldness. From his expression, she gathered he'd found her entertaining, in the way a child might regard a new toy. Something that ignited a spark of amusement, but quickly flickered out.

Oh, Eleanor, you're reading way too much into such a brief encounter.

Calling to Bobby, she picked up her pace. She had to bathe and dress before dinner, and she hadn't left much time for it.

Eleanor wondered what Hugh would do if he knew the truth. If he knew that while he'd furthered the British cause in North America, she had given birth to his child, a daughter named Lili.

• • •

Hugh arrived at Deborah's townhouse, where Adam and his family also resided, around seven o'clock. The home had belonged to his father, but, as McBride had informed Hugh, he'd left it to his estranged wife in his will. Deborah had lived in it for years, ever since she'd parted from her husband, taking Adam with her and leaving Hugh behind. He'd never been able to forgive either of them.

A few years ago, before Hugh had left for North America, Adam and Cass had married. Hugh thought his brother had been a lucky devil after his wartime service to meet up with her again and persuade her to marry him. It wasn't Cass with whom he had any quarrel.

The butler announced him, but before the words were even out, Adam, Cass, and a rambunctious infant hurried into the entryway to greet him. The child slid to a stop when he reached Hugh, staring up at him and looking puzzled. Hugh immediately stooped down so that his size didn't intimidate the boy. "You must be Christopher," he said.

The child's eyes, the same deep blue as Adam's, fixed on Hugh's face, but after a moment, he turned, shoved his fingers into his mouth, and looked for the reassuring presence of his parents. Adam dipped down and scooped him up, holding out his other hand to Hugh.

"We call him Kit." Adam's eyes crinkled at the corners. "Welcome home, Hugh. It's good to see you."

A part of Hugh wanted to express the same sentiment, but the words stuck in his throat. So he simply shook his brother's hand and nodded. Cass broke the awkwardness by kissing Hugh's cheek and then inspecting him.

"You look wonderful, Hugh. North America agreed with you."

He shrugged. "I wouldn't go that far. I'm glad to be home."

"Why are we standing here?" Cass said. "Let's go to the drawing room."

"Is anyone else joining us?" Hugh asked as they climbed the marble staircase.

"Not tonight," Adam said. "Deborah and Freddie are visiting one of his daughters."

Hugh was relieved that he wouldn't have to see his mother. Even though he'd attended a house party at her home in Surrey a few years ago, when he'd first met Eleanor, he hadn't spoken to her in any meaningful way before or since. Or during, for that matter. She'd cut him out of her life when she'd left him with his father, and he didn't see any point in the pretense of a relationship.

Adam poured brandies for himself and Hugh and sherry for Cass. To Hugh's dismay, his brother raised his glass in a toast. "To Hugh and his safe return."

"To Hugh," Cass said. "We are so happy to see you again."

Hugh smiled, but before he could take one swallow, Adam lifted his glass again. "And to your knighthood. You'll have to give us the particulars."

Christ, that was the last thing he wanted to discuss. "It was nothing," he said. "Completely undeserved."

"Come now, brother, knighthoods aren't passed out for nothing."

Hugh demurred. "I'll tell you about it another time. Let's not spoil the evening with talk of war."

"Fair enough."

"Now," Hugh said, "I'd like to become better acquainted with my nephew. Would he let me hold him?"

Said nephew was currently sitting on the floor, playing with a key ring, inspecting each key, and every so often, gleefully shaking the ring so that the keys clanked together. Each time that happened, he looked up at them and smiled. He looked positively angelic.

"Never mind holding him," Hugh said. He lowered himself to the floor before Kit, stretching out and propping his head up with one elbow, and waited to see what the child would do. In short order, he was edging closer to Hugh, who held very still. "Ah, see, I'm not such an ogre, am I?" Hugh asked. In a trice, Kit was crawling all over him. Hugh flipped onto his back and set Kit on his thighs, bouncing him up and down, until the boy was laughing out loud.

"All right, I believe that's enough excitement for now," Cass said. "Your trousers will be ruined!"

"Your mama says we must cease our fun, Kit," Hugh said, grasping the little boy in his arms and rising. A nursemaid was standing in the doorway. She, Adam, and Cass were all three smiling as though something very funny had just happened.

"What?" Hugh asked. "Have I done something wrong?"

"Not at all," Cass said, collecting Kit from Hugh's arms and passing him to his nurse. "Not at all."

"Have you seen Eleanor yet?" Cass asked during the soup course.

Although the question seemed innocent enough, Hugh sensed more than a polite interest. And it presupposed that he would see her at all. He was quite sure both his brother and sister-in-law were aware that, nearly three years ago, around the time of their own courtship, Hugh had been interested in Eleanor. He'd have to tread carefully, be noncommittal. The last thing he wanted was Cass quizzing Eleanor about him.

"Just this morning. She has a puppy. He was poking around my building site, and I carried him home before he got hurt."

"You went to the Broxtons'?"

Hugh swallowed a final sip of the excellent turtle soup before answering. "No. She's a dressmaker now. Did you know?"

"I'm one of her clients," Cass said. "Her work is beautiful."

"I don't doubt it." Conversation ceased while the next course, poached fish, was served. "She and two girls ply their needles in a small cottage, which is where I returned the pup. It must be exhausting work."

Cass looked nonplussed. "Foolish of me, but I hadn't thought about that aspect. I've been recommending her to other ladies who've admired my frocks." She paused a moment, as though gathering her thoughts. "Eleanor seems quite set on increasing her business."

Hugh knew he probably shouldn't ask, but the words were out before he could reconsider. "Do you know why?"

"To get out from under her father's thumb, of course," Cass replied.

"We don't know that, Cassie," Adam admonished. Setting his wineglass down, he said, "Sir William is very circumspect when it comes to his daughter. Never speaks of her unless I ask him a direct question. His answers don't reveal much of anything, and he changes the subject before I can follow up."

"Eleanor's situation seems highly irregular to me," Hugh said, "but then, it's none of my concern. The sauce on this fish is delicious, by the way. What is the herb? Fennel?"

Bidding Hugh good night, Cass left the brothers alone with their port. "I must check on Kit. Lovely to see you, Hugh."

As soon as she'd gone, Hugh said, "Remember when I told you you'd be a damned lunatic if you didn't marry Cass?"

Adam chuckled. "I think it was 'bloody lunatic.' How right you were. We couldn't be happier. I highly recommend marriage — to the right woman, of course."

"Naturally. Maybe someday."

"How are things coming at Longmere?"

Hugh smirked, knowing how Adam hated the place. "Our boyhood home is no more. One of the reasons I came up to Town was to see the architect and finalize everything, but I can't pin him down on a starting date. He's a wily bastard, says they don't keep a normal schedule, unlike the rest of the world. I got him to agree to a month from now, but he asked me not to hold him to it."

"You'll be living in the cottage for a while longer, then? Cigar?"

Hugh shook his head. He hated the things. He didn't know when Adam had adopted this vile habit, or how Cass put up with it. "Looks like it."

"How are matters proceeding with the tenants?" Adam asked.

"Slowly. I've been so preoccupied with demolishing the house and all that entails, I've had little time to visit them. Which reminds me, I need a steward. Someone to survey the property and work with the tenants. With your vast knowledge of the citizenry, can you recommend anybody?"

There was a silence while Adam lit his cheroot and puffed. "Edward Martin would be a fine steward. He's been employed in various industries—ironworks, tanning, that kind of thing. But husbandry is his passion. You'll find him at his parents' tavern in Haslemere. He's helping out there while he's between jobs."

Hugh nodded. "I'll pay him a visit."

After a pause, Adam said, "You've come into some money, brother."

"Yes." Hugh's finances were none of Adam's business. He felt no need to elaborate.

Adam eyed him cynically. "Felicitations. May I ask how this good fortune came to pass?"

Hugh sighed. Not that he owed his brother, or anybody else, an explanation, but he supposed it wouldn't do any harm to tell him.

"Have you ever heard of the North West Company?"

"Can't say I have, no. Something you came across in North America?"

Hugh nodded. "You must have heard of the Hudson's Bay Company?"

"Everybody's heard of them. Biggest fur trader on the continent."

"That's right. The North West Company is their chief competitor. A friend of mine—a Scot in his cups most of the time—gave me a tip. I took advantage of it."

Adam chuckled. "I never pegged you for a genius at speculation."

"Far from it, I'm afraid. I asked around, sought advice from other people, and took a chance. It paid off, is still paying off, in spades." He paused for a swallow of port. "They were growing, subdividing the shares and bringing in new partners. I invested all the money I'd saved, and then some. And speaking of money, McBride told me you paid Father's debt to Sir William. I wish you hadn't done that."

Adam shrugged. "I'm his man in the House of Commons. It was awkward conferring with him on various subjects, having that hanging over us. I wanted it finished."

"How much do I owe you?"

He waved a hand through the air. "Don't worry about it. Deborah and I covered it."

Hugh had felt the slow burn of his temper flaring, and now it exploded. "God damn it, Adam, our father's debts were my responsibility. Not yours, and definitely not Deborah's. Tell me what I owe, and I'll see to it. I know it was a significant amount."

"You won't let this go, will you?"

Hugh got to his feet and threw down his napkin. "Why should I? I'm his heir. I'll handle anything to do with him and his estate. You'll do the same for Deborah someday."

Adam rose, too. "You want to keep us separate, don't you, Hugh? You on one side of the road, and Deborah and I on the other. No meeting in the middle."

"That's right, except our divide is much wider than a road."

"We're your family, Hugh. Is it so awful to contemplate a reconciliation between us? Between you and a mother who breaks down in tears whenever your name is mentioned?"

"I've heard enough," Hugh said. "McBride will tell me the amount, and I'll send you a bank draft."

When Adam started to follow him to the door, Hugh said, "Stay where you are. I'll see myself out. My thanks to you and Cass for dinner."

On the way back to his lodgings, after his anger had petered out, he thought about the conversation at dinner. He'd said Eleanor was none of his concern, but he knew that was a lie. He wanted to keep his distance from his mother—but he'd like nothing better than to become closer to Eleanor.

Chapter Three

The next morning

Eleanor and her father sat in companionable silence in the breakfast room. He was perusing the morning papers and giving her little tidbits of news every so often, mostly amusing bits of gossip. "Lady Henley's garden party was interrupted by a marauding bull. A certain intoxicated Miss L. jumped into the fountain at Lady Sheridan's ball and had to be rescued," and the like. Eleanor sipped at her chocolate and then helped herself to eggs, scones, and fresh strawberries. At this rate she might have to give up modeling her new designs.

Last evening had gone better than she'd expected. A neighbor and his wife had dined with them, so her mother was constrained as to the nature and tone of her comments. After the guests left, they had all three retired. Eleanor had slept like the dead, exhausted from her day's work. It seemed every day was like that.

Her mother entered the room and called for a fresh pot of tea. As was her habit, she refused any breakfast.

Eleanor sometimes wondered how she got by without more sustenance. She was thin and, as far back as her daughter could remember, her figure had been slender bordering on skeletal.

"Good morning, Mama."

Her mother eyed her suspiciously, as though her greeting carried some sinister meaning.

"Aren't you eating?" Eleanor asked. Of course her mother would not be eating, but Eleanor couldn't resist needling her about it, just as she knew her mother would needle her back regarding the great quantities she was consuming.

"And I see you have the usual full plate. *Tsk, tsk.* Nobody will want to buy their gowns from an unfashionably fat girl."

Sir William dropped his paper at that. "My dear, Norrie is far from fat. In fact, she could stand to gain a few pounds."

"That won't be a problem if she continues to eat so much."

Eleanor slathered butter onto her scone and bit off a huge piece, relishing the disapproval on her mother's face. She recalled all the days she skipped meals because she was too busy to eat. Or simply too exhausted. Work was her raison d'être at present, because all she cared about was saving enough money to support herself and Lili. When she reached that point, she could leave Haslemere and purchase a modest home somewhere else. And she and her darling girl could be reunited under the same roof.

"I suppose you are hurrying away as usual this morning," Lady Broxton said with her customary reproving tone of voice that so grated on Eleanor's nerves.

"You know I have a business to run, Mama. I'm not off having fun."

"Yes, you are in trade now. Heaven forbid you might want to enjoy yourself occasionally. I thought perhaps you could attend the Jensens' reception with us this afternoon. It is in honor of their son, who's returned from the Peninsula."

Her mother periodically threw eligible men her way, even though she must know there was no chance Eleanor would show any interest. "I'm sorry, that won't be possible. I am hoping to visit Lili this afternoon. We have three gowns almost completed, and I think I'll have time after we finish putting the trim on them." Eleanor paused a moment to consider what she was about to say, then plunged ahead. "Would you accompany me, Mama? You haven't seen her in a long while."

Her mother's face flushed with anger. "No. Were you not paying attention? The Jensen reception is today."

Eleanor's father was watching them, looking uncomfortable. "We could make an appearance there, leave early. Those affairs are so tedious, my dear."

"Wonderful idea, Papa! It would mean so much to me if you both came with me. I don't want her to forget you."

"Absolutely not. We can't be seen at the home of those people."

"'Those people,' as you call them, were handpicked by you and Papa to be Lili's foster parents. And who would even notice?"

"It's out of the question, Eleanor. What is the point? Lili will never be our granddaughter in the usual way. She's a bastard, after all."

"That's enough, Kitty!" Sir William said, rising from his chair.

Eleanor, stunned, remained motionless, as though stuck to her chair. "You go too far, Mama."

Her mother went on as though neither her husband nor daughter had admonished her. "And then there's the matter of your father and I not knowing who sired her. I can understand," she said, scrutinizing Eleanor, "why you would wish to protect the girl's father. It is different here than in London. Among the *ton*, many men have by-blows. Some men acknowledge them; some do not. But here in Haslemere, it would cause a scandal. It is not simply your reputation at stake. If it became common knowledge, your lover would no longer be accepted in polite society."

In a strained voice, Eleanor said, "What is your point, Mama?" *I'm certain you have one.*

Her mother leaned forward in her chair. "Simply this. You must tell your own parents who the child's father is. The secret would be safe with us."

So this was basically another attempt to learn the identity of Lili's father. It was more egregious than usual. Never before had she called Lili such despicable names. *Bastard. By-blow.* Eleanor would never give her the satisfaction of learning the truth. She blinked back a hot rush of tears, refusing to let her mother sense any weakness in her. Pushing her chair back, she got to her feet. "If you'll pardon me, I must be off." On the threshold, before she lost her nerve, she turned and said, "Rest assured, Mama. *I* know who Lili's father is." Her voice broke on those words, but she wasn't made of stone, was she?

"Will we see you tonight?" her mother called after her retreating form. She didn't answer.

After leaving her parents' home, Eleanor made a spur of the moment decision to visit Lili first, before she began her workday and grew too tired. Too many days to count, she'd postponed a visit because of exhaustion. She didn't want that to happen today, and perhaps that was due to her mother's attitude about Lili. How could she withhold love from such a precious child? It ignited Eleanor's protective instincts and made her love Lili all the more.

Without permission, she asked one of the grooms to hitch up the gig for her. It would take too long to walk, and nobody used the small conveyance anymore. At one time, her mother had driven it for fun, back when she'd *had* fun, and Eleanor had sat up on the seat beside her as they tooled around the countryside calling on friends. What had happened? When had her mother become so joyless and cold? And unforgiving?

Bobby sat on the seat beside her, the wind ruffling his coat. Poor puppy looked frightened and edged closer and closer to her. It was a short drive to the Abbots', who lived on the road to Haslemere. Eleanor half believed her parents had chosen them to be Lili's foster parents because the approach to their home was long and therefore out of sight. She pulled up in front of the house and handed the reins to a young boy. He helped her down, and, after tucking Bobby under one arm, she made for the house. Before she even reached the door, it swung open. Jacob Abbot stood there with his usual sneer.

"The child's sleeping," he said, before Eleanor had a chance to greet him.

"Good morning, Mr. Abbot. I'm here to see my daughter, and since I can clearly hear her voice, I think you must be mistaken."

He remained where he was, glaring at her. "You should notify us before you come. It upsets her routine."

Eleanor's hands fisted in her skirts. She tried to be polite, but this was wearing on her. Lately, every time she visited, he had tried to put her off in some way. Thus far, he hadn't denied her entrance, but she felt it might come to that. The man had no right. "Come, Mr. Abbot. That was not part of our agreement."

He was a bear of a man, and the odds were against Eleanor being able to force her way past him. Finally, he opened the door and stepped aside.

"Mama!" Lili spotted her and came running. Eleanor bent down so the child could pet Bobby, whom she adored.

"Hello, my beloved."

Lili smiled up at her while her little hand stroked Bobby.

"Goggie," she said, with a jolly note in her voice.

After a minute, Eleanor said, "We'll play with Bobby later, love." She set the dog down and gathered the child into her arms. Dark-haired and lively, she was pure joy to her mother, from her soft skin to her milky smell and sweet voice.

Carrying her daughter, Eleanor walked toward the kitchen. Lili's foster mother, Edith Abbot, could normally be found there. The woman was hard at work, as always. "Good morning, Mrs. Abbot." And then, "Oh, heavens, should you be doing that?"

She was on her hands and knees, a bucket of water at her side, scrubbing the floor with a brush. It wasn't the first time Eleanor had felt concern over the daunting tasks Edith Abbot undertook. She was with child, which was becoming more obvious now. About five or six months along, Eleanor estimated. Judging from their home, dress, and possessions, the Abbots should be well able to hire some help for Edith. With Jacob Abbot's income as a carpenter, plus the funds the Broxtons were providing for Lili's keep, they couldn't be short of money, especially since they had no children of their own yet. Abbot was probably just too miserly to provide something he would consider a luxury.

Lili wiggled in Eleanor's arms, eager to be set down. Eleanor let her go and squatted down herself, wondering why the other woman hadn't spoken. When Edith looked up at last, Eleanor understood. Her face was bruised along one side, an ugly smear of black fading to purple. Eleanor sucked in a breath.

"Morning," Edith said softly.

Lili plunged her hand into the water and then pretended to be scrubbing. Eleanor let her do it. "What's happened, Edith?"

"Oh, this," she said, pointing to the bruise. "It's nothing. I fell on the steps and landed on my face."

"I help," Lili said, oblivious.

"Yes, sweet." Eleanor didn't believe Edith's explanation for a minute. Jacob Abbot was in the drawing room still, or possibly in the hallway, listening to Edith's account. Eleanor didn't want to endanger her further. "I'm sorry. It looks quite painful. But should you be doing this kind of work in your condition?"

"She's pregnant, not sick," Jacob Abbot said, stepping into the room. "Edith's always been healthy and strong."

Eleanor rose. "We all have our limits, Mr. Abbot. I would be more than happy to find a girl from the village who can help her with this kind of heavy work."

"Oh you would, eh? Would you pay her, too?" He took a step toward her, and for a moment she thought he meant to strike her. But she held her ground. She would not allow this man to bully her.

Apparently, he thought the better of it. "Keep out of our business, miss. Because we look after your girl doesn't mean you can tell us what to do."

Lili was fussing now, possibly sensing the menace in the room, and Eleanor bent down and scooped her up. "It was merely a suggestion." She turned toward the back entrance, snapping her fingers at Bobby. "I'm taking Lili outside."

Later, on the way home, Eleanor agonized over her arrangement with the Abbots. She hated leaving Lili at the end of her visits, but today had been worse than usual. Because now she'd discovered that Jacob Abbot was capable of physical violence. Yet, Lili did not seem frightened by him. She didn't shrink from the man, though she'd started fussing when he'd picked his fight with Eleanor. How she regretted the day she'd given in to her parents' demands that her child be fostered out.

After Lili's birth, when Eleanor had returned to Surrey with an infant, she'd had little choice. Sir William had personally selected the Abbots and claimed to have thoroughly evaluated their fitness. She and her mother had given Lili directly into their care as soon as they'd set foot back in the county. Eleanor had allowed it, because she could not raise a child on her own. She had no money and nobody to rely on, other than her parents. And her mother reminded her daily that she would be ruined if word got out. That their family would be ruined. For a few months after Lili had gone to the Abbots, Eleanor had nearly been overcome with sadness and despair. Only after she'd attended a soiree one evening, at her mother's insistence, and several ladies had complimented her on her gown, had she begun to think of becoming a dressmaker.

And that occupation was now all-consuming. Locally, word was getting out about her designs. In London, too. That was largely due to Cassandra Grey, for whom Eleanor had designed several gowns greatly admired by Cass's circle of friends. The end of the Season was not far off, and Eleanor was receiving new orders every day. In fact, it was time to schedule a trip to Town, to confer with clients on the designs, take measurements, choose accessories. She could ill afford the time away from the actual sewing, but it could not be helped. Visiting the clientele was part of her work. And her work was everything. Her sole means to earn the money she needed to bring Lili home—although she didn't yet have a home. But that was what drove Eleanor, pushing her to the brink of exhaustion most days.

She needed more help, but at present could not afford to hire another girl, and sewing wasn't the only task she needed help with. The cottage required improved lighting. There must be a way, but Eleanor didn't have the solution. She could also use a bookkeeper, since she had neither the time nor head for figures. Her father would help her if she asked. But she hated to ask when she knew he disapproved of her endeavors.

She left the gig at the Broxton stables and walked the footpath toward her cottage. The trail wound through woods interspersed with small clearings. Bluebell season was nearly over, and wild garlic now ruled, covering the ground so thickly it looked like snow and spread right down to the banks of the nearby lake. Eleanor loved the pungent smell of it.

Passing the lake, she heard a splash. Perhaps a fish had jumped. But then she heard a yelp, and unless fish had recently developed vocal cords, she didn't think it had come from one of them. No, this sound was distinctly human. And male. There it was again. Perhaps someone was in distress?

She hurried over to the edge of the water, skirted by trees and low-growing foliage, and saw Neptune himself rising from the water. Minus a trident, but possessing other attributes. Quite impressive ones. God above, it was Hugh Grey, in all his naked splendor.

When they had made love, she hadn't really seen any of him. It had been all touch and taste, scent, and sound. She stared without shame or guilt. He was holding something, and she quickly realized it was a cake of soap. While she stood rooted to the spot, he began to run it over his body. Slowly, sensuously, almost as if he knew she was watching him. Over his neck, and those magnificent shoulders. His sculpted chest and taut belly. And, yes, even *there*, his male parts. He dipped into the water to rinse himself. No yelping this time, so he must have gotten used to the water temperature, which certainly would be quite chilly. Eleanor stepped behind a tree. Hugh's clothing and drying cloth were lying on the ground near her hiding place.

He bobbed back up, and glory be, he'd turned around so that his back was to her now. Slowly, he moved the cake of soap over his firm buttocks and thighs. He raised his legs in turn to wash them, and then ducked into the water again.

Eleanor felt warm, wet at the apex of her thighs, and knew that if anyone saw her, they would think she'd just come from an orgy. Her head canted to one side and her mouth hung open. After a moment, she came to her senses and saw that Hugh was swimming to shore, in smooth, long strokes, directly toward where she was concealed. Not very well concealed. She backed up quietly, right into something prickly, and whimpered loud enough to be heard. Hugh stopped swimming and rose partway, looking toward the shore. She did not move.

"Is someone there?" he called. "Who is it?"

Oh, good heavens. She couldn't be caught. So she did the only thing possible. She turned and fled, running full-out and holding up her skirts so she wouldn't trip. She did not stop until she reached her cottage.

Chapter Four

Hugh threw the soap aside and rubbed himself briskly with the towel. Christ, the water was freezing, even though it was a sunny, mild day. He supposed it wouldn't warm up until June, at least, so he was doomed to bathe in cold water until then.

He chuckled to himself, wondering who had been watching him. He'd caught a flash of blue before she'd gotten away. Was it Eleanor? It might have been one of her assistants, but she was the one more likely to be on the path leading to the Broxton place. Tempting her with his body wasn't beneath him. In fact, Hugh wished he'd known she was there. He could have treated her to so much more. He pulled on his shirt and britches and made his way back to the tenant's cottage. Once there, he donned a cravat, waistcoat, coat, and top boots, and set off for Eleanor's cottage, determined to find out if she'd been the one spying on him.

When he reached her door, he heard voices. And then laughter. Dare he eavesdrop? They were probably talking about him. He waited, and they finally resumed their conversation.

"Your bubbies are bigger than hers, miss," a voice—not Eleanor's—said. Giggling ensued.

"Minnie, don't speak so." That was definitely Eleanor.

"What I mean is, like, whether it fits *you* isn't a good estimate of how it will fit *her*."

"You're right. Help me out of the blasted thing." Eleanor again.

They weren't talking about him at all. That took him down a peg. Or two. He knocked and heard a good deal of scampering around while he waited.

Eleanor opened the door, wearing a diaphanous rose gown that barely contained her breasts. Her assistant was correct—it didn't fit her at all. *Thank the Almighty*. Hugh enjoyed the view until one of the other girls tossed Eleanor a shawl and she covered herself up. "Mr. Grey. I mean, Sir Hugh. I wasn't expecting you." Her cheeks were as rosy as the gown.

He held back a grin. "I gathered that."

She stepped out and closed the door.

Damnation! He'd hoped to be invited in. How would he see if she'd been wearing a blue dress before she'd changed into this gauzy thing?

"May I help you with something?"

He should have come up with an excuse for calling, but he'd been too single-minded. And now he couldn't think of a plausible reason. Or any reason. "I, er, that is…I was merely passing by."

Folding her arms across her chest, she eyed him skeptically. She was having none of it; that was obvious.

"May I see your workroom, Eleanor?"

"Why?"

"Why what?"

She rolled her eyes. "Why do you want to see where we work?"

Hugh leaned forward, placing his forearms on the gate, and smiled his most winning smile. "You mentioned you had a small work area. I thought perhaps I could suggest a way to create more space."

"Oh, really? You know about such things, do you?"

The ends of her shawl had separated after she'd crossed her arms, affording him a view of her breasts. He remembered how they'd felt in his hands, like two soft, inviting pillows. Oh hell, it would have been wiser if he'd remained behind the gate.

"Very well, come through then." She led the way. After cleaning his boots on the footscraper, he followed.

Her two assistants were seated at a worktable pushed against the windows, both with needles in hand. They leaped up when they saw him and bobbed curtsies. Hugh bowed and said, "Good morning, Jane. And…?"

"This is Minnie," Eleanor said. "Sir Hugh wants to see if he can help us devise a way to increase the size of our work area."

Now that he was inside, and Eleanor was out of his line of sight, he could concentrate. What he saw troubled him. He estimated the entire space to be no more than five paces by four. The windows were north facing, which allowed little light, especially in the afternoon. On the opposite wall was the hearth, with the requisite coal bucket, wood carrier, and tools close at hand. A small window was to his right, near the door. On his left was one storage shelf, with stacks of boxes piled beneath it. There was a row of shelves on the back wall as well, along with a door to another room. Curious, Hugh moved toward the second room, but Eleanor blocked the way. One of the girls tittered.

"That is a private space."

Hugh stopped. "My pardon." He stepped back, but not before he'd glimpsed a bed with a blue dress thrown across it. He smiled.

"Do you find this amusing, Sir Hugh?" Eleanor asked.

"Of course not. I find it appalling. Your lighting is inadequate, you lack sufficient storage space, and your work area is cramped and smells of smoke."

"Well," Eleanor said, sounding flustered. "We do the best we can. We keep the door open in warm weather. That provides more light. And airs out the place."

He'd offended her, but she must know the truth of what he'd said. He softened his voice. "You would see a great improvement with a few small changes."

"Nothing I could afford!" He'd really gotten her back up now.

"Not true. I could—"

"So kind of you to stop by, Sir Hugh." She was ushering him to the door, dismissing him. "You've given me much to consider. I'm sure your time is too valuable to waste on our simple endeavors, but I do thank you for your concern."

She hurried outside, as though to make certain he was truly leaving. He took his time, bowing to the girls, bidding them a friendly good-bye. "My brother likes working up at Longmere, Sir Hugh," Jane said.

"Ah. Good to hear. I'm glad to have him. Simon is a hard worker." Slowly, he made his way outside. Eleanor stood there tapping her foot.

Hugh walked right up to her, crowding her. She stepped back, and he leaned forward, raising his brows. "Why won't you listen to reason?"

She had a petulant look on her face, and he didn't like it. Nor did he understand what was causing it. "Because I don't need your help. We're getting along fine on our own."

"No, you're not."

"And how would you know? We're completing our orders on time, we've plenty of new clients, and they pay promptly.

Those things add up to a good business."

He thought she might stamp her foot.

"I've been in your position, Eleanor, that's how I know. I've worked under less than ideal conditions, with poor light, not enough supplies, no elbow room." He was jabbing a finger at her, to emphasize each point. "You and your assistants have to work twice as hard as you might, were your working conditions improved even slightly."

He gazed at her, her beautiful mouth beguiling him. He'd never noticed how perfectly shaped it was. Bowed, but not too small. He could stare at it forever. He pulled his gaze up to her eyes, which seemed to hold a world of sadness, and then he felt like a brute. "Look, I wanted only to help. My apologies if I overstepped. I'll be on my way." He sketched a quick bow and walked through the gate.

Just as he gained the path, he heard her say, "And we have adequate supplies, thank you very much."

Hugh knew he shouldn't, but he couldn't stop himself from striding back. She was still standing right where he'd left her. "Glad to hear it. I almost forgot to mention, that was a very becoming blue dress you were wearing earlier today. I hope you enjoyed what I was wearing. Good day, Eleanor."

• • •

Damnation! Hugh had worked out that she was the one watching him at the pond. How dare he bring it up? She didn't like his new authoritative manner, although she could not deny it made him even more attractive. *Blast!*

He never used to be like this. He was…he had not been so imposing, before. Eleanor didn't need another man in her life telling her what to do. She was stuffed to the gills with bossy men, not to mention her mother. And besides, if she gave Hugh an inch, he'd take a country mile. She could not allow that, which was why she could not tell him about Lili.

Her parents and the Abbots already organized her time with her daughter, controlling what she could and couldn't do, placing all sorts of restrictions on her. Hugh had been off in the wilds of North America when she fell pregnant—or at least when she'd realized she had—and even though he'd asked her to let him know if there were "consequences," how could he possibly have helped? He may as well have been a million miles away.

She didn't know what he would make of being a father. Or of her lying to him, by omission. Would he demand rights? Would he take Lili away from her? If she'd had more than a brief acquaintance with him before she'd recklessly slept with the man, perhaps she'd be a better judge of what he might do under these circumstances. But as things stood, she simply had no way of gauging his reaction or what actions he might take once he learned the truth. No, she could not risk telling him.

Her reasons were largely selfish, resulting from her fear that Lili could somehow be snatched from her. What her mother had said this morning further confused the issue. If Hugh were forced to acknowledge he had a child, a scandal might ensue. Just at the time he was rebuilding his home and his standing in the community. Obviously, both meant a great deal to him. She didn't wish to ruin his prospects.

If only the matter weren't so complicated.

And now she must get back inside and change out of this gown before she burst the seams. When she entered the cottage, the two girls, who'd had their heads together whispering, looked down and resumed their work.

"Help me out of this, Jane, if you please."

Jane first retrieved Eleanor's dress from the back room, and then helped her slip out of the gown intended for one of their London clients. After Eleanor was dressed, she turned to her assistants and said, "Out with it. What were you whispering about just now? And don't tell me a bouncer. I'm very adept at working out when someone's lying."

Jane and Minnie cast each other guilty looks, and then Jane spoke up. "We were wondering why we couldn't take Sir Hugh up on his offer to help us."

Eleanor rubbed at her forehead and gave them her back. How to explain it? She spun around and said, "Because when someone offers to help, there are always strings attached. I don't want to be obligated to Sir Hugh in any way. Do you understand?"

"Can't say I do," Minnie said, coming over to stand near Jane. "Sir Hugh's a nice man. What would he want from us?" Jane was scowling, looking like she wanted to throttle her mistress.

"What is it? Speak up," Eleanor said.

"You're not thinking Sir Hugh would ask us—or you— to do something *improper*, are you? He's a good man, miss. Simon says he feeds all his workers tea and meat pies every day, and what's more, gives them a long break, doesn't he? Aren't many bosses do that."

Perfect. Just what she needed, to be the object of gossip regarding Hugh. She had to nip this in the bud. "Not at all," she said firmly. "I believe him to be an honorable man, in every way. It's not that."

"Then what?"

"It's just that I don't want anybody telling me what to do. Now, can we end this and get back to work?"

"Yes, miss, but if he could help us with lighting and extra space and such, why not let him?"

The discussion had gone far enough. "I'll give it some thought," she finally said, even though she had no intention of enlisting Hugh's help with anything.

Bobby curled up at her feet, Eleanor spent the remainder

of the day composing letters to London clients to arrange appointments with them. The last time she'd gone up to Town, she had stayed with Cass and Adam Grey and hoped to do so again. Since Adam was Sir William's man in Commons, they no doubt felt obligated. But they'd made her feel welcome and comfortable, and she and Cass had developed a friendship of sorts. Eleanor was also fond of Christopher, their baby son.

Eleanor shooed the girls out when the light dimmed. The fire had been banked, and she fanned it back to life to ignite a few spills. From these she lit candles, leaving one in the main room and returning to her desk with two more. She continued working, making lists of other places she'd need to visit while in Town. Layton's drapery shop on Henrietta Street and Harding, Howell and Company in Pall Mall. If necessary, she would call in at Wilding & Kent, on New Bond Street. They were far more expensive, and rarely did Eleanor feel the extra money was worth it. Some of her clients were quite extravagant and didn't mind the extra expense to achieve the right look, but others were so parsimonious, you'd think they were about to be sent to the Marshalsea.

After giving it some thought, Eleanor made up her mind to hire a man of business to handle her bookkeeping. Adam could most likely recommend someone. She added that to her list of things to accomplish while in Town. She would need to make sure her accounts were up to date before her trip. *Ugh.* Although tempted to put it off, she would sleep better if she tackled it now.

On her tiptoes, Eleanor reached for her ledger book. Why was that blasted shelf hung so high? Stretching her hand out a little farther, she made a grab for it. Ah, there, she had it. And then her hand slipped, and the heavy tome fell and hit her squarely on the bridge of her nose. Eyes watering, she sank back onto her chair and gave into a full-fledged bout of weeping. This day had been almost too much to bear.

First, the hurtful conversation with her mother and then the unpleasant confrontation with Jacob Abbot. And Hugh's unexpected visit, in which he had accurately summed up all that was wrong at the cottage. Her fatigue. She used to love designing and sewing clothes, but lately it had become drudgery. Eleanor felt like Atlas, attempting to hold up the skies on her shoulders, though she hadn't his strength or endurance. After a moment, she blotted her tears and blew her nose. Feeling sorry for herself was an indulgence she could not afford. She must be strong in her resolve to work hard, save money, and eventually provide a home for herself and Lili.

Eleanor's stomach rumbled. Not surprising, since she hadn't eaten a bite since breakfast. Her mother would probably say that was for the best. How she would soothe her hunger pangs, she didn't know. She'd been planning to spend the night at the cottage, and she didn't keep any food here. Thank goodness she had a tea caddy and a kettle. There was nothing for it but to venture outside and fill the kettle from the water tank behind the cottage. She nearly tripped over a basket that rested on her front step.

"What on earth?" Eleanor set the kettle down, picked up the basket, and walked back inside, her curiosity getting the better of her. She placed her candle and the basket on the worktable and spread open the cloth covering. The tempting scent of meat pies wafted toward her. And there were also a jug of tea and a small bowl of fresh blackberries. *Heavenly*.

Then she saw the note. It was resting against the side of the basket, and she'd nearly missed it because its cream color blended with the cloth. Turning it over, she held it next to the candle and read: *My apologies for presuming to advise you on your work arrangement. I hope these victuals will assuage any offense I caused. Yrs, H.*

Damn the man. Why should he believe his words would

have the power to hurt her? Another presumption on his part, thinking she cared what he said.

Nevertheless, a smile tugged at her lips, and when she tucked into one of the pies, it wasn't simply the rich flavor, or the fact they were still hot, that caused warmth to flood her belly. It was something else altogether, and well she knew it.

Chapter Five

Later the same week

On Friday, Hugh rode into Haslemere to purchase the daily ration of food for himself and his crew. But he had another task to attend to first. He needed to talk to Edward Martin about the possibility of becoming the Longmere steward. He found the tavern on the outskirts of Town, the King's Head, and ordered an ale. When the man working the taps placed it before him, Hugh said, "Are you Edward Martin?"

"Aye, that's me. Who's asking?"

"Hugh Grey." He hadn't gotten used to the "Sir" honorific and felt pretentious using it. "I'm looking for a steward up at Longmere, and my brother, Adam, said you might be interested."

Martin, possessed of a high forehead and a crop of unruly chestnut hair, stood a little straighter. His eyes were an unusual pale blue and lit up at the mention of the job. "I might."

There was little custom at this time of day, and Hugh invited the man to join him at a table for a few minutes.

When they were settled with tankards, Hugh gave him the particulars. "It won't be an easy job. My father neglected his tenants for years. It's likely most of the cottages need repairs, and the tenants will need help with drainage, enclosure, clearing the land, and the like." Hugh downed a few swallows of ale and said, "Tell me about yourself."

"I've worked a variety of jobs, but my true calling is the land. I'm single-minded about it. For five years I was Mr. Compton's steward, up at Hillsdale Farm. We made great strides with enclosure, especially. When he died unexpectedly, his son wanted his own man. I decided to help my parents here at the inn until another opportunity presented itself."

Hugh liked the man. He was eager, but not overzealous. He had an open, friendly countenance and a genial way about him. "Tenants can be demanding know-it-alls. How would you deal with that?"

Martin thought a moment. "Tact, but with some bite to it," he said, and they both laughed.

"The job is yours if you want it," Hugh said, rising and holding out his hand.

Martin clasped it with a firm grip. "Yes, sir. When can I start?"

"Call me Hugh. Can you be ready by Monday?"

"Say the word, and I'd be ready tomorrow. But Monday's fine. Gives me a chance to help my folks find another man to fill my place here."

Hugh nodded. "I'll be at the site. We're still hauling away rubble."

He turned to leave, and when he reached the door, Martin said, "Everybody calls me Ned."

"Ned it is, then. I think you and I will get along fine."

• • •

The following Thursday

Hugh glanced again at the invitation lying on the oak table in his cottage. It was from Cass and Adam, inviting him to a dinner party next week. He'd been debating whether to accept. If he attended, there would be no avoiding a meeting with Deborah. Surprisingly, when he mulled it over, Hugh's primary feeling regarding his mother was indifference. He no longer hated her—it expended too damn much energy. He simply had no desire to reconcile with her.

On the bottom of the invitation, Cass had written, *Eleanor and her parents will be there. C.* He pondered over the reason why Eleanor would be in Town, then recalled she'd said she had London clients. Hugh didn't relish seeing Broxton and his wife. Would Eleanor's father treat Hugh any differently now that he'd been awarded a knighthood? He doubted it. Broxton still outranked him, since he was a baronet. Hugh recalled Eleanor's mother from the house party, where she'd acted as chaperone. In his memory, she was a thin, humorless sort of woman. Perhaps that assessment was unfair. He'd not spoken more than a few words to her, nor she to him.

A quiet knock interrupted his thoughts. "Yes, enter."

Ned Martin stuck his head in. "Can you spare a minute, Sir Hugh?"

Hugh had given up on getting the man to drop the honorific. Clearly, Ned felt more comfortable calling him Sir Hugh, as the laborers did. Hugh pointed to the only chair. "Sit down, Ned. What can I do for you?"

"Can you come over to the site? Deliveries are starting to arrive. Bricks, the stone from Sussex, even glass for your sash windows. We need to sort out where to put everything. And to rig up something to protect all of it from the elements."

"I'll be there as soon as I finish up some correspondence. You shouldn't have to see to things at the building site. That's my job."

Ned flushed, and Hugh regretted his words. "Not that I don't appreciate it, but I want you to start visiting tenants." He scratched at the stubble on his face. "In fact, we should do that together. Let's take care of the deliveries, and then we'll ride out to survey the land and begin seeing tenants."

"I've already done some surveying and I've been jotting notes. We could go over them together when you've got time."

Hugh sighed. Suddenly it seemed there was much more to oversee than he had the time for. "I need to post a letter in Town and pick up today's food before I do anything else. But we'll get started as soon as I return."

"I could do that for you."

While Hugh was thinking it over, Ned said, "It would give you time to organize things at the building site. When I'm back, we can head for the farms."

Hugh gave a decisive nod. Why not? The daily trip to Town was becoming tiresome, and if Ned was willing to help with that, well, he wouldn't look an eager gift horse in the mouth. "Give me five minutes to write a brief note. I'll see you at the site."

Ned left, but Hugh delayed, ruminating. After a moment, he composed a brief missive accepting the invitation.

• • •

Wednesday, the following week

Hugh, keen for a speedy ride to Town, drove there in a rented curricle and found lodgings not far from Deborah's townhouse. Knowing Adam would be out on Parliamentary business, Hugh paid a call on Cass. The last few weeks, whenever he thought about the evening he'd spent with his brother and sister-in-law, and how it had ended with him losing his temper and shouting loud enough for the entire household to hear, he was ashamed. Not of his feelings; they were right and defensible. But he should have kept himself under control. If there was anything the military had taught him—as well as years of living with his father—it was that. He wished to apologize.

"Sir Hugh," the butler greeted him. "It's good to see you. I'll tell Mrs. Grey you're here."

"Thank you, Flynn. Is my mother at home?"

"No, Sir Hugh. She is out making calls."

He felt a guilty sense of relief. "Shall I go up to the drawing room?"

"Certainly, sir. You know the way."

Hugh waited only a few moments until Cass joined him. "Hugh! I'm so glad to see you." If she were angry about the outburst he'd subjected everyone to on his earlier visit, she'd chosen to overlook it. "We're delighted you accepted our invitation for the dinner party." She pointed to the sofa. "Please, be seated. I've ordered tea."

Hugh sat, and when she was settled, he said, "Cass, you have my heartfelt apologies for my ill temper when I was last here. I-I don't know what came over me. It was unpardonably rude."

"Oh, rubbish. You were upset. You didn't wake Kit, so no harm was done. That's all we mothers care about, you know."

Hugh smiled. "You are very gracious, Cass. I don't deserve it."

"Perhaps there is a way you can get back in my good graces."

Hugh stiffened and hoped she hadn't noticed. He knew what was coming. "And that is?"

"Give your brother, and most especially Deborah, a chance. Let them back into your life, even just a little."

Irritated, Hugh was determined not to show it. "I can't do that. Not now. Maybe never." Even as he spoke the words, regret welled. For the loss of the family he might have been close to, if things were different.

"Why not?" Fortunately, the tea tray arrived, giving him a few moments to compose a response. He needed to choose his words carefully. Cass fixed a plate of sandwiches and cakes for him, neither of which he wanted. He doubted he could swallow anything other than a liquid, and brandy would be a hell of a lot better than tea. Cass surveyed him expectantly over the rim of her cup.

"There's a history between me and my brother and mother. Whatever Adam has told you about it is from his perspective. Not mine."

"Will you explain your perspective, then, so I might understand?"

He gulped down some tea and got to his feet. "Forgive me, but it's not something I care to rehash. Can it not suffice for me to say I wish things were different? But I fear it is too late for that."

Cass gazed up at him, and he saw, to his consternation, pity in her eyes. And just when he thought his facade of cool indifference might crack, the door opened, and Eleanor Broxton stepped through. She must have recognized the tension that hung heavily between him and Cass, because she said, "I am so sorry for interrupting. I didn't know you were here, Sir Hugh." She turned to exit, but Hugh stopped her.

"Miss Broxton, please don't leave. Join us."

She looked at Cass, who obligingly said, "By all means, Eleanor, do sit down and drink tea with us. How nice to have you both here." She looked so pleased with herself, Hugh almost laughed.

He resumed his seat, keeping his eyes on Eleanor. She was lovely. Strands of her hair, piled loosely on top of her head, had broken free and brushed her face and neck. Although she wore a more modest dress, with a chemisette covering her chest, he could still envision the way her breasts had practically burst from the gown she was wearing the last time he'd seen her. And that perfect mouth he'd love to ravish with his own.

"Hugh?" Cass said. "Eleanor asked you a question." Her voice held a hint of amusement. Devil take it, he'd been staring.

"My pardon. What did you say, Miss Broxton?"

She chuckled. "Nothing of any import. What brings you to Town?" She gazed at him over the rim of her teacup.

"The dinner party."

"I see." She shot Cass a suspicious look. This was beginning to be fun.

"And you?" Hugh asked.

"To see my London clients and visit the shops. Cass and your brother were kind enough to invite me and my parents to the dinner party, also."

Hugh looked from one to the other. Impulsively, he said, "Would you ladies be interested in a ride around Hyde Park? We should take advantage of the beautiful weather."

"An inspired idea! Don't you agree, Eleanor? Give us a minute to get our bonnets."

As if on cue, a maid entered and spoke to Cass. "Kit has woken up from his nap, so I'm afraid I won't be able to join you. Pray go without me."

"Oh, I couldn't," Eleanor said. "I'd need a chaperone."

"Nonsense. You'll be in full view of half the *ton*."

Hugh had the distinct impression that Eleanor would have preferred to decline, but now she was trapped. He was on the verge of saying, "Some other time," when she excused herself to retrieve her bonnet and said she would meet him in the entryway.

• • •

Hugh was waiting for Eleanor at the front door. When he offered his arm, his smile was so disarming her reluctance to be alone with him evaporated, and she tucked her hand into the crook of his elbow. The curricle waited out front. "We couldn't all three have fit into your curricle, Sir Hugh." But she wasn't angry, or even annoyed. It was too lovely a day, and she had never ridden around Hyde Park with a gentleman before. For a little while, at least, she would try to forget her vow to keep him at arm's length and simply enjoy herself.

"You have me there," he said, smiling. "I'm certain Cass would have offered their carriage if she'd been able to join us."

While the groom held the horses, he lifted her by the waist onto the seat as though she were weightless, then climbed up beside her. She watched him, which might have been a mistake. Before he sat, his thighs were at eye level, and his form-fitting breeches left nothing to the imagination, especially since she'd recently seen him naked. *Oh God*. Even thinking about that day caused her cheeks to warm, and she quickly looked away. When he was finally seated and they were under way, his leg pressed against hers and sent jolts of pleasure through her. It wasn't desire. *Of course it is desire*.

Hugh was threading his way through late afternoon traffic. It would help get her mind off his physical presence if they could talk, but she didn't want to distract him at present. Finally, the traffic eased, and it seemed safe to speak.

"I haven't thanked you for the basket of food you left for me. I'd had a particularly…difficult day and hadn't eaten a bite since breakfast, so it was most welcome."

"I offended you. It was a small offering to make it up to you. I shouldn't have been so presumptuous." He kept his eyes on the road ahead. Eleanor made no response to that, because his assessment was largely correct. "Has your trip been a successful one, Eleanor?"

"That depends on what you mean by successful."

He smiled, and she noticed the little wrinkles at the corners of his eyes. From laughing? Most likely from too much sun. "By your definition of the word…"

Why was she being difficult? *Just answer the man.* "I've seen three clients thus far. Lady Sheffield was put out with me because I neither design nor sew lingerie or stays. In her opinion, any milliner worth her salt makes every bit of apparel in a lady's wardrobe."

Hugh laughed out loud. "My pardon, but I was picturing Lady Sheffield. There is, er, an ample amount there to contain. She could keep a corset maker in business."

Eleanor smiled, wanted to laugh. "You're right about that."

"So you're at a stand?"

"I think it's sorted out. I recommended several seamstresses to her who make stays. Even though she will be 'vastly inconvenienced' by having to visit one of them, she likes my designs and will keep on buying my gowns."

"Excellent. And the other two ladies?"

"One is very enthusiastic. She wants me to design ball gowns for two of her daughters. The elder is making her come-out this year. The third lady hasn't paid me for numerous items I made over the past several months, so I was forced to tell her I could no longer afford to dress her."

"*Hmm.* I could call her husband out, if you'd like."

Eleanor laughed, dragging her eyes away from his mouth. "She's a widow, and I don't think she had much of a jointure. I am sorry for her, but I can't continue to do the work without receiving any money."

They entered the park, and Hugh turned his attention back to the ribbons. When she stole a glance at his face, he was frowning in concentration, busy jockeying for position. As they proceeded around the perimeter, he nodded at people now and then, and more than one fashionable belle of the *ton* stared at him. Ladies strolled arm in arm, showing off their finery. Eleanor couldn't help casting a critical eye on their walking dresses. Slightly too long. Color too subdued or too garish. Too much bosom showing for afternoon wear. Grudgingly, she admitted to herself that there were, however, many beautifully designed dresses on display.

When they reached the Serpentine, Hugh pulled the curricle over. "I'm going to see if I can find a lad to hold the horses while we stroll a bit."

He was back in a few minutes with a young boy who seemed eager to do the job. Hugh handed him the reins, and the boy said, "Thanks, guv'nor," a huge smile breaking over his face.

After Hugh helped her down, they set out on the path. His hands were clasped behind his back, pulling his coat tight across his broad chest. Out of the blue, he said, "Why do you work so hard, Eleanor?"

She hadn't anticipated that question from him, although she'd answered it before. Locals asked her frequently, including her own friends and those of her parents. He was watching her intently, waiting for a response. "I wish to have a life apart from my mother and father."

"And couldn't you achieve that by marrying, as other ladies do?"

Resolutely, she turned her gaze forward. If she looked at him straight on, he'd know she was lying. Or leaving something out. A disquieting way to think about adorable, sweet Lili. A "something."

"Shouldn't one have a purpose in life other than marriage? Men do, after all."

"Many women would disagree with you. They would say marriage and children are their purpose."

"Aren't there an equal number of women who, if they truly

had a choice, would choose not to wed? Marriage is often an escape from one dire situation and a leap into another every bit as grim."

"You have a poor opinion of matrimony."

She shrugged, unwilling to go that far.

"If you so desired, you would not lack suitors, Eleanor." When she didn't comment, he said, "Did you ever have a come-out?"

"No. No, I did not. Tucked away in Surrey, why would I?"

"Many girls who live in the country come up to Town to make their bow. It's an opportunity to meet eligible men. I'm surprised your parents wouldn't have wanted that for you."

Why in blazes was he so concerned about her social life? "My mother thought I was too young, and then I...I lost interest."

"Why?"

Because I was carrying your child.

This was beginning to feel like the Inquisition. And what was it leading to? "What difference does it make? Perhaps I felt it wasn't worth the effort."

"But—"

"Could we talk of something else? Tell me about the wilds of British North America. What was it like there? Did you encounter any natives?"

"Everybody asks that. Why, I wonder?"

"Something strange and new to us. Exotic."

"Yes, I'm sure you're right. Natives of the Mohawk tribe, and by English reckoning, they were exotic, I suppose. Paint. Feathers. Scary hair." He chuckled at her expression. "I didn't have much reason to consort with them, except on one occasion. My work was mostly with British officers, French Canadians, and Scottish immigrants."

They walked on, taking their time. "What did you do there?"

"I acted as liaison between the Governor-General of Canada, Sir George Prevost, and Whitehall."

She cocked her head and gave him an astonished look. "That sounds so…important, for lack of a better word."

"Not really. It was nine parts frustration and one part actually accomplishing something meaningful."

"And what was that one occasion you mentioned, when you did consort with the natives?" Eleanor's gaze was on Hugh when a couple of young bucks on horseback appeared out of nowhere, riding neck-or-nothing toward them. They were racing, oblivious to anyone who might be in their path. Frozen with fear, she stood rooted to the spot, quite unable to move.

"Eleanor!" Hugh called, just before shoving her off the path. She slammed into the ground, the breath whooshing out of her. Hugh shouted, "Ho, there, you idiots! Slow your horses!"

The next thing she knew he was hunkered down beside her. She'd broken her fall with the palms of her hands, her left side absorbing most of the blow. "Are you all right?" His large hands encircled her waist, lifting her into a sitting position. He lowered himself to the ground next to her, and then his arm circled around her shoulder. Still short of breath, she did not respond immediately. Her bonnet had been knocked askew, and she pulled it off.

"Eleanor?" He sounded worried.

"Yes, yes. It's just that I can't…breathe…quite yet." And then she felt the seductive touch of his fingers moving in circles on her upper back. His thumb scraped across the bare skin of her neck, sending stabs of pleasure pulsing through her. She squeezed her eyes shut. *Don't stop. Don't stop.* Shamelessly, she said, "My shoulder. I think I've injured it." She was hoping, praying really, that he would stroke across her shoulder and down her bare arm. Instead, he rose, walked around to her other side, and squatted down.

"May I?"

She nodded, fully aware she'd let him do almost anything he chose right now. He grasped her arm and gently moved it forward and back. She kept her eyes fastened on him, and then, "Yeow!" Had she truly howled like a cat?

"Forgive me for hurting you. I'd better get you home. Your shoulder bore the brunt of your fall, though it doesn't seem to be dislocated."

While Hugh retrieved the curricle, she gradually emerged from her cocoon of pleasure. An injured shoulder would not bode well for sewing. On his return, Hugh helped her rise, then gathered her in his arms and set her gently on the seat. As though she were something precious. How different their lives might have been if Hugh hadn't gone to Canada. When she had learned she was with child, Hugh would have offered her marriage; she did not doubt that. They would be raising Lili together.

While Eleanor was woolgathering, they exited Hyde Park. She didn't even notice, until Hugh's deep voice broke into her thoughts. "Feeling all right?"

She smiled at the concern on his face. "It's kind of you to worry, but I'll be fine."

They made desultory conversation the remainder of the trip. Eleanor allowed herself a feeling of peace and contentment she rarely experienced.

Chapter Six

The next evening

When Hugh entered the upstairs drawing room at his brother's townhouse, the first person he saw was Eleanor. She simply stole his breath. Her gown was a pale green sheer confection, with a bodice that dipped into a *V*, and she'd woven tiny flowers through her hair. He could only gape. She glanced at him and smiled, then quickly looked away.

The second person he noticed was his mother. Deborah. Of course, he'd known she would be present, but he hadn't allowed himself to think about it. Adam had broken loose from the group he'd been talking to and come over to greet him.

"Brother," he said, extending his hand. Hugh grasped it.

"Adam."

Cass joined them, kissing Hugh's cheek. He knew he should get it over with, the greeting of Deborah. He couldn't very well ignore her. "Take me to my mother?" He looked at Cass and hoped she didn't see the unease in his expression.

She glanced at her husband, who nodded. "Of course. And then Adam will introduce you round to the others."

Cass steered him through the room. As he drew near to the group his mother was a part of, she glanced up and stepped to the side, so that she waited for him alone. She held out her hands, and what could he do but grasp them? "Hello, Deborah," he said.

She smiled, but he sensed her wariness. "It's so good to see you, Hugh, back safe and sound. And 'Sir Hugh' now."

"Yes." He let go of her hands, shocked that she still wore the same scent after so many years. Lemon verbena. She was as lovely as ever, even with graying hair and a web of fine wrinkles around her eyes.

"Adam tells me you are rebuilding your father's home."

"Yes. The actual building hasn't begun yet, but it shouldn't be long now. You are well?"

"I am, aside from the usual complaints of one who is growing older." When he made no response to that, she said, "Freddie and I have been traveling. More grandchildren, you know."

"Adam told me. And you've one of your own, right here."

Her face lit with joy. "You've met Kit? He's delightful—reminds me so of Adam at the same age." At that, her jaw clenched, as if she wished those words unsaid.

Devil take it, did Deborah and Adam feel they must tread on eggshells around him? Hugh didn't want that.

And then Freddie interrupted, pumping Hugh's hand, saying, "How are you, my boy? Nice to have you back," as if they were old friends, when in fact he'd met the man just once before. Fortunately, Adam intervened.

"I'd like to appropriate Hugh, if you don't mind. There are people who wish to meet him."

Freddie said, with false joviality, "Of course, of course, old man. Go right ahead." Deborah's mouth drooped. Hugh was relieved that the first meeting with his mother had gone better than he'd expected. He and his brother spent the next several minutes talking to Adam's allies in Commons, many of whom clapped Hugh on the back and congratulated him on the knighthood. Without being too obvious, he glanced Eleanor's way whenever possible. The din of voices was beginning to wear on him. At length, Cass interrupted.

"Darling, Jack and Jenny are waiting to greet your brother. And so are the Broxtons."

Jack, Lord Egerton, was Cass's brother, and Jenny, his wife. Hugh shook hands with both. They'd barely gotten a few words out before Cass whisked him away again, escorting him toward the Broxtons. There was only one Broxton he gave a damn about seeing, but it appeared he would be required to meet Sir William and his wife as well. The people from whom Eleanor was so eager to remove herself.

• • •

At various times since Hugh's arrival, Eleanor had felt his gaze on her. For the sake of her sanity, she did not reciprocate. But it was hell pretending to be interested in the various conversations going on around her and forcing herself to keep her eyes fixed on the speaker. She so desperately wanted to look at Hugh, talk to Hugh, be with Hugh.

Good God, Eleanor, you're mooning over him like a besotted fool.

She had to stay away from the man. If she let him get close, he would find out about Lili, and her tenuous control of the situation would collapse.

But she did, at last, glance around the room, and spotted Cass coming her way with Hugh in tow. He wore black-and-white evening clothes, a cream waistcoat with small sapphire buttons his only nod to fashion. *Good heavens, were those* actual *sapphires?* His elegance was the kind she admired— understated and unaware. Perhaps Benjamin Grey had not been so penniless as everyone had believed, including her own father. Although she never understood why he would have any knowledge of the elder Grey's finances.

Hugh bowed to her mother. "Lady Broxton."

"Mr. Grey," she responded, either forgetting that Hugh had come home with an honorific before his name or choosing to pretend she did not know. It was a slight, in any case, and Eleanor felt ashamed for her mother.

He turned to her and bowed, "Miss Broxton. You are lovely this evening."

Eleanor curtsied and said, "Thank you, Sir Hugh," emphasizing the "Sir."

"Sir William," Hugh said, extending his hand to her father. She had a moment of panic, worried about how he would receive Hugh. But he welcomed him warmly, perhaps to make up for her mother's faux pas. Or maybe he'd changed his mind about Hugh?

Dinner was announced, and Hugh offered Eleanor his arm. "May I have the honor, Miss Broxton?"

Had Cass orchestrated this? She certainly seemed to be pushing them toward each other. No matter. Eleanor was more than happy to walk downstairs to the dining room with the handsomest man in the room. Though other ladies present may argue the point, she was perfectly sure they would be wrong.

She set her hand on his sleeve and they slowly made their way to the stairs. "How is your shoulder today? Did you see the physician?"

"Yes, Cass's doctor attended me, although I didn't feel it was truly necessary. He pronounced my shoulder merely 'bruised,' and I believe he was correct. It's a bit sore, but no lasting damage was done." She waited a moment, then said,

"Which is a miracle of sorts, since you shoved me unforgivably hard. One might think you wished to do me serious harm, Sir Hugh."

He laughed softly. "No. Never that." His eyes moved downward, surveying her. "Is your gown your own design?"

"It is." Then, lowering her voice, she said, "But let it be our secret. It wouldn't do at all to have people believe I was too poor to use a dressmaker."

He looked puzzled. "I thought everybody knew dressmaking was your profession."

She shook her head. "Not in Town. Only my clients know my identity. My label simply says 'EB Creations.'"

"I understand. Your secret is safe with me."

When they reached the dining room, Eleanor was more than a little disappointed to find they hadn't been seated near each other. She was surrounded by political men and their wives, while Hugh was at the opposite end of the table near Lord Egerton and his wife. Deborah Grey sat across from her, but a large epergne in the middle of the table prevented any conversation between them. Earlier, Eleanor had watched Hugh greet his mother. Sadly—for shouldn't a man who had been on another continent for more than two years be happy to see his mother?—she noted the lack of warmth between them and wondered why that should be the case.

The food distracted her. Starting with a richly seasoned curry soup and proceeding on to a fish course of turbot in an herbed sauce, then to a ragout of veal with vegetables and a savory potato pudding. She ate, sipped her wine, and chatted amiably with the MP to her right about Napoleon's return to Paris and what action the British army, under Wellington, was preparing to take. Between courses, they moved on to domestic matters. Unemployment among returned soldiers and sailors was high, which Eleanor was aware of, from talks with her father.

"It must be difficult to arrive home after years of military service and find that no work awaits you, especially for those who have families," she said.

Occasionally, if she leaned far enough back in her seat, she could see Hugh, watch him nod his dark head. Once when he caught her looking, she felt heat rush to her face, but she held his gaze. He smiled, his eyes warm, and she turned her attention to the lady on her other side. They talked of current fashions, something she didn't have any difficulty commenting on while she thought of other…things.

After dinner, it was back to the drawing room for the ladies while the men indulged in their age-old ritual of imbibing port and smoking cheroots. And talking of manly concerns, whatever those might be. Eleanor always wondered why women couldn't do likewise, although she'd no desire to smoke. But port wouldn't go amiss. The berry-saturated tang was a gift on her tongue, and a gown made of silk the exact color of port would be exquisite. Drinking tea in the evening kept her awake. Her mother thought that was nonsense, but Eleanor had tested her theory often enough to be convinced of it.

Cass had been commandeered by two rather strident political wives, and Eleanor didn't care to interrupt. Her mother and Deborah Grey were seated near the pianoforte looking at sheet music and attempting to coax one of the younger wives to play. Mrs. Grey employed a dressmaker who knew how to dress a lady of a certain age. Her gown featured a slightly lower waist and a neckline, modest without crossing over to prudish.

Restless, Eleanor quietly left the room. A breath of night air would be refreshing. After returning to the first floor, she proceeded through the entryway toward the rear of the house, passing the dining room just as the men were emerging. Several were still talking and laughing, some of them sounding foxed. Hastily, she slid into the shadows and kept moving toward the doors. Once outside, she breathed easier. Flambeaux lit the shadowed terrace, casting light upon the lime trees bordering the stone balustrade. Eleanor loved their sweet aroma, but it was too early yet for the blooms. It would be another month at least, so she would have to conjure the scent from memory. She set her gloved hands on the cool stone railing and breathed in the night air.

"Eleanor."

She gasped and spun around. "Hugh, I didn't hear you." He stepped closer. His dark eyes reflected the light in two perfect pinpoints.

"My pardon if I startled you. What are you doing out here all by yourself?"

"Probably the same thing as you. Seeking fresh air and solitude."

"The gossips getting to you?"

"No. Not really. Cass was occupied and, to say the truth, I didn't feel up to the task of acquainting myself with one more person with whom I have absolutely nothing in common." She laughed. "There. Now you know my true nature. Impatient and rude."

"I would never use those words to describe you," he said, his voice low. "I find, since I've been back, I often need to get away from the crush of people, wherever I may be."

"In your case, understandable and even expected. But I'm afraid I have no acceptable excuse." Their arms brushed against each other. Just the merest touch, like a breeze fluttering over her skin, and yet so intimate. If she possessed an ounce of good sense, she would move away, but the tingling in her arm and the trembling in her belly wouldn't allow it.

She started a little when Hugh lightly grasped her arms and turned her to face him. "Eleanor, you are so damned beautiful, you make me lose my reason. I shouldn't be alone with you on this terrace, and certainly I shouldn't kiss you, but I'm going to."

She didn't have a chance to protest. His arms came around her waist and pulled her hard against him, and then he lowered his mouth to hers. His lips were soft and tenderly probing. He slid his hands up her arms and down her back, where a complicated arrangement of bands crisscrossed, exposing much of her skin. He pulled away long enough to say, "Have I told you how much I love this gown?"

A giggle bubbled up from her chest, and then his mouth came back down on hers, harder and more demanding this time. Her hands roamed up to his shoulders, while he explored every inch of flesh on her back. Unlike her, he wore no gloves. When her need to be closer to him became so acute it was painful, he caught her in an embrace that said *I never want to let you go,* and her heart surged.

His tongue, tasting like port, slipped into her mouth and found hers, silk against silk. He drew her closer, until her breasts were thrust against his hard chest. Molding herself against him, she felt the evidence of his desire for her. Had he suggested it, Eleanor would have been willing and ready to be dragged out into the darkest reaches of the garden and… *Good God, what am I doing?*

Wasn't this what happened before? She had allowed her body's desperate need to upend her, to reign over common sense and her own best interests. And look what had happened. She could never regret her actions of that night when she'd gotten Lili as a result, but she could not risk the chance of another pregnancy. It had taken exactly one time for her to fall pregnant, and it could happen again. And inevitably, Hugh would find out the truth.

She wrenched herself away from him. "No, Hugh. Stop."

He let her go immediately. "What is it?"

She shook her head. "We can't do this."

He took a step back, and she could see by the hard set of his jaw that she'd angered him. "You want this as much as I do, so would you mind telling me why not?"

"You are mistaken. I-I do not want it, that is, to do this again."

"And the reason for that is…?"

"I have a business to run. It takes all my time, and dallying with you would disrupt that."

"You mean being intimate with me? Once was all you required?"

"We had sexual congress. That was all." So hard to pretend it had meant nothing to her, when it had meant everything.

He raked a hand through his thick hair. "Sexual congress. That's like carnal knowledge. Coitus. Copulation." He barked a sardonic laugh. "Interesting, they all begin with *C*."

"Call it whatever you like."

"Very well, then. Here's what I call it. I had you on a hay bale, Eleanor, after you seduced me. How does that suit?"

The harshness of his words was like a punch to the stomach. That frightening moment when breath wouldn't come. Had she seduced him? She'd never felt shame about that night, but perhaps she ought to. Hugh apparently thought so, judging from what he'd just said. Her mind went dark, and she couldn't speak. What was left to say, in any case? A voice jarred her out of the place she'd retreated to.

"Pardon me for interrupting." It was Adam. Thank God he hadn't appeared a few minutes earlier. Even if he'd seen nothing, what had he heard?

"Not at all," Hugh said, his gaze still riveted on her. At last he looked away, and she could breathe again. "What is it, Adam?" Hugh's words were clipped, his voice brittle.

"Deborah wants to speak to you before you leave. Can you spare her a moment?"

"Where is she?"

"In my study. I'll tell her you're on your way."

"Not necessary, I'll go to her now." Turning, he nodded curtly in Eleanor's direction. "Miss Broxton."

He strode off, leaving his brother slack-jawed with surprise. Eleanor tried to put a good face on it, or at least to make it somewhat less embarrassing for them both. "I don't think he's feeling quite the thing," she said stupidly.

"*Hmm.* It would appear so. Not a good time for him to speak to Deborah." He offered his arm and she accepted. "Too late to worry about that now," he said.

Chapter Seven

Hugh made his way toward Adam's study in a haze of anger he couldn't dispel. He should have asked his brother to make his excuses to Deborah. Anything would have sufficed.

Had Eleanor's regard for him truly been so trivial? Everything about her manner with him—from her clandestine spying at the pond to the kiss they'd just shared—said the opposite. They had found pleasure in each other's company before. Their dealings since Hugh had been home had been strained, it was true, and he could neither explain nor disregard it. But tonight, she had seemed happy to see him. They'd conversed easily on their way in to dinner, and she'd thrown him flirtatious looks throughout the meal.

So what had happened? Damned if he knew, and now he must meet his mother alone, a situation he'd dreaded, avoided, since he'd been back in England. He had nothing to say to her that wouldn't cause more pain to both of them.

The door was closed, and he knocked lightly before entering. She was standing before the hearth, which was nothing more than ash at this point. "Deborah. Adam said you wanted to see me."

"Yes." Her expression was guarded. Something in his voice must have warned her of his mood.

He should walk over to her, but his feet felt like they had in Canada when he'd sunk into an eight-foot snowdrift. Moving forward was not a possibility. Instead, he stood on the threshold and waited for her to speak.

"Won't you sit down, Hugh?" she asked.

"I prefer to stand." He moved into the room, keeping his distance.

"You won't mind if I sit? I find that I'm exhausted by these parties that require me to be charming, yet on my guard, for an entire evening."

Hugh waited while she rearranged her skirts. At length, growing impatient with womanly tricks and prevarications, Hugh said, "Why am I here, Deborah?"

She looked up at that. "Oh, Hugh, can you not guess?" She tilted her head and fixed her still-bright blue eyes on him. "I want to know if you will come back to us. To Adam and me. Now that your father is gone—"

"You think I am desperate for a family since the old man died? Have I judged it accurately?" *I should leave. Now. Before things get out of hand.* But the pain inside drove him on. "I've had nobody for a long time, Deborah. I don't need you or Adam in my life. Over the years, I learned to get along without you."

Finally, he walked toward her, close enough to see the tears streaming down the oval of her face. "You walked out with my brother and never visited, never even so much as wrote to me."

"But I—"

Hugh held up a restraining hand. "Don't. Please."

His mother seemed to wilt, and sobs burst from her in quiet little gasps. And in an instant, his anger dissolved, and he felt like a cad. He should not have gone to Deborah immediately after Eleanor had rebuffed him.

What sort of man makes his own mother cry? But he had reason, by God. He had reason. He spun around and made for the door, but the pathetic sound of her weeping stopped him. Turning back, Hugh said, "I wish it could be different, Deborah. God knows, I wish it could be different." Then he exited the room, walking swiftly through the entry hall and, nodding to Flynn, out the front door.

The air had cooled. A brisk walk to his lodgings would do him good. Sounds of the city at night surrounded him— hackneys rattling over the cobblestones, the distant cry of the watchman, the shouts of young men on their way to their nighttime carousing. After a few blocks, he stopped. He'd nearly been running, as though an entire regiment of American soldiers were chasing him. He bent at the waist, hands on his thighs, and sucked in deep breaths. When he straightened at last, he'd regained some equilibrium.

Coming to Town had been a mistake. After his cruelty to Deborah, he wouldn't be invited back. What had possessed him to behave in such an ungentlemanly manner toward her? Could he never shake off his past? Christ, he was over thirty years old. Right then and there, he vowed to let go of the perceived hurts inflicted on him by his mother. It was time to move on.

But he could not change overnight. Keeping himself isolated in the country should be no problem and would allow him the time he needed. And he could avoid Eleanor without too much trouble. She'd made her feelings plain, and he wasn't a man to importune a woman who didn't want his attentions.

Because he had arranged appointments with his man of business and his banker, he would remain in London through the morning. And then it was off to Surrey, where he could concentrate on the huge task of the rebuilding in earnest.

...

Surrey, two days later

Eleanor had relived the dinner party and what had happened between her and Hugh over and over since arriving home yesterday. She groaned out loud every time she thought about how things had ended between them. That soul-piercing kiss, and then her resolve to push him away. The ugly things they'd said to each other. *Sexual congress?* Where had she ever even heard that phrase? What must he think of her?

She was seated on the garden bench at the cottage sipping tea, Bobby dancing around her feet as usual. Although she'd slept at her parents' last night, she had slipped away before dawn. With a full day's work ahead of her, she required some time to herself before her two talkative assistants shattered her peace. It was early yet. The sun had just tipped the horizon, bathing the world in a warm glow. It had rained during the night, tapping on the roof and waking her, and the newly scythed grass surrounding her cottage sent up an earthy, fresh scent. Walking here had dampened her slippers, but the sun would soon dry them.

She let out a sigh. If she actually *could* relive the evening, not merely in her memory, would she change anything? She'd certainly leave out the "sexual congress" part. But never the kiss. She wouldn't change that. And the rest of it, even though it pained her, was necessary to keep her secret. She couldn't let Hugh in. He was too smart, too perceptive. It would weigh on her, this secret, if he were a fixture in her life. He would soon guess she was hiding something and would—even if gently and kindly—coax the truth from her.

At odd times, Eleanor was tormented by the knowledge that she was separating Hugh from his child, over whom he had as much of a claim as she. In the past, he'd treated Eleanor with gentleness and patience, and she sensed he'd be that way with children as well. But weighed against the all-consuming fear that churned inside her whenever she contemplated the possible consequences of telling him, she could bear the shame and guilt of keeping Hugh from Lili. At least for now.

Time to get to work. She had plenty to do before her assistants arrived. She rose from the bench and hastened inside to her duties, spending the next hour laying out the gowns and dresses they were working on and the supplies they needed.

• • •

A week after the dinner party

Hugh had immersed himself in work since he'd been back at Longmere. He was quickly finding out that hiring Ned Martin had been the smartest decision he'd made since returning from Canada. The man was a workhorse. Not only did he do everything Hugh asked of him, he took on extra jobs, especially the ones everybody else hated—like digging and hauling away massive amounts of earth. Hugh had quit trying to limit Ned to working with the tenants; if the man saw something that needed doing, he seemed pathologically unable to walk away from it. The one place Ned seemed truly relaxed was at his parents' tavern. He and Hugh had raised a tankard or two there and had even enjoyed a meal together.

John Ridley's crew had arrived at last, and the building had commenced. Ridley himself was there one day and nowhere to be seen the next. Hugh never knew when to expect him. The contractor was residing in Haslemere, however, and according to Ridley, he was the best in the business. Hugh took him at his word and hoped he wouldn't regret it.

He had not crossed paths with Eleanor since the night of the dinner party, and while he hadn't gone out of his way to avoid her, neither had he made any special attempt to see her. During the past week his thoughts had strayed to that meeting between them on the terrace, to the strangeness of it. How she'd kissed him, clung to him, and then abruptly put a stop to the heat blazing through them both. But he'd been mistaken, and it was only he who'd been on fire.

And yet...

He could recognize the difference between a woman who wanted him and one who emphatically did not. And with Eleanor, all the signs had been there. The ones signaling her interest, both the day before, when they had driven to the park, and at the dinner party. What, then, was wrong? One minute she had given in to her urge to kiss and hold him; the next, she had pushed him away. She couldn't "dally" with him because of her work. He'd like to send her dressmaking business to the devil. And he'd like to know why in the hell she needed money.

Devil take it, he'd pressed too far, too fast. He gave his head a shake. He'd no time for analyzing female brains, especially that of one female. If Eleanor wanted him, she would need to make the next move.

Since everything at the site seemed to be well in hand, Hugh and Ned were riding out to visit tenants. After packing up their food and drink, they mounted and set out. Hugh wanted nothing more than to get his mind off Eleanor, and the beauty of the morning seemed suited for that. Rain during the night had freshened the air. Droplets of moisture still clung to trees and bushes. Grouse and cock rustled through the underbrush, and the cooing of wood pigeons helped soothe his wounded spirits.

Ned pointed out various changes along the way. Of special interest were the newly enclosed arable fields for planting and those for grazing. After a few hours spent conferring with various farmers about crops—primarily oats and barley—outbuildings, and fields, they gladly put in some time helping dig a drainage trench for one of the tenants, Peter Allen. Afterward, they drank a tankard of ale with him. Hugh begged off taking a meal with his family, as he wanted to speak privately with Ned about other concerns. The latter suggested a spot by a stream where they could partake of the victuals in the hamper they'd brought, and they rode off in that direction.

After laying out the food on an old coverlet, they quickly tucked in, both so hungry they didn't speak for several minutes. Simple sustenance, but to Hugh, after the morning's labors, it seemed like a king's banquet. Cold roast chicken, bread, a fine, hard cheese, and fresh berries. And more ale, of course. Just when Hugh was set, between bites, to raise some issues about the building of Longmere, Ned spoke.

"Your brother is a fine man, Sir Hugh. He's not like other MPs. He visits here often and talks to the citizens. He cares about us, like you do about your tenants."

None of this surprised Hugh. But he didn't particularly like hearing someone speak of his brother as though he were a glorified guardian angel. Didn't like being compared to him, either. But it wouldn't be politic to reveal that to his steward. "Glad to hear it. He's doing the job well, then. All that Sir William expects of him." He couldn't quite keep the sarcasm from his voice, however, and Ned hurriedly changed the subject.

"Have you thought about a leg shackle, sir? You'll have a fine house to raise a family in."

The man seemed to have a knack for raising topics Hugh would prefer to avoid. In all the time they spent together, they'd never discussed anything personal, which was, perhaps, rather odd. Hugh snorted and tried to make a joke of it. "Not yet. I haven't been back long, and I've much to accomplish before I think about taking anyone to wife." The best tactic would be to throw this back at Ned, and so he did. "What about you? Are you courting?"

Ned looked pensive. "The woman I loved married somebody else. Can you imagine that? I thought it was me she wanted, and she turned around and..." His voice tapered off. "It's water under the bridge now."

"And that's why you haven't been able to let it go?" Hugh asked softly.

Ned smirked. "You've got me there."

"You're a fine fellow, Ned. There are plenty of women who would welcome your suit."

The other man chuckled. "Oh, I know that, but finding the right one is a different matter altogether."

Hugh poured them each more ale. "Anything new to report on the building?"

"I've hired five local men—two carpenters, one iron worker, and a couple of stone masons. And just so you know, one of the men is my youngest brother and another is a brother-in-law. They're good men, all."

"And what about the bricks?"

"The bricks will be made on site from local clay. The color should be what you wanted, a pale gray."

Hugh nodded. "Excellent. I don't know how I'd manage without you on this, Ned. It may not be what you intended, but you've made yourself indispensable to me."

Ned had started clearing up, but paused long enough to say, "No, Sir Hugh. Nobody's indispensable. But I'm not afraid of hard work, I'll grant you that."

On the ride back to Longmere, they discussed security on the building site. "I think you should hire a nighttime watchman," Ned said.

"Is that really necessary?"

The other man shrugged. "Probably not. But glass, stone, wood, bricks, tools...better to take precautions."

"Several men are sleeping above the stables. That's not good enough?" Hugh guided his horse around some brambles, then said, "It would be awfully hard for thieves in the night to haul away such heavy, unwieldy materials. But if you think it best, I'll find someone."

"I have someone in mind. He's a cousin of mine…"

"Oh, for Christ's sake, am I supporting the entire Martin family?" Hugh asked. But he laughed good-naturedly.

• • •

Eleanor was livid. She'd gone to see Lili directly after a light meal, reasoning that she could spare the time for a short visit. Earlier, they'd finished one gown for a come-out ball and had completed all but the flounce on another. She'd told Jane and Minnie to go home for a few hours. As soon as they were gone, Eleanor had walked up to the house and asked a groom to ready the gig.

But when she'd arrived at the Abbots', Lili wasn't there. The detestable Jacob Abbot told her with a scowl on his face that Edith had gone to see her mother and taken the child with her. Abbot left her standing at the front door while they talked.

"Mr. Abbot, I'm sure you are aware this was one of the agreed-upon times of day for Lili to be at home. It's one of the few times I'm able to get away."

He stood there with his arms crossed over his chest, smirking. "Didn't you ever think maybe it wasn't such a convenient time for us?"

Her temper was near to exploding. Because he was goading her, she kept it in check. With great effort. "I shall have my father pay you a visit. Perhaps he needs to review the agreement with you. The one you signed."

He unfolded his arms and made as though to shut the

door.

Eleanor shouldn't argue with the man, but today she couldn't help it. "It's not as though you're not here most of the day, now is it?"

A nervous tick pulsed on one of his cheeks. "You tell your father to come by. We need more money from the deal. We do a lot for that little girl, for all the thanks we get." He slammed the door in her face, and she stomped off toward the gig.

When she was out of sight of the house, she reined in the horse and unleashed a slew of curses. Then she dropped her head in her hands and moaned. Why, why, had she ever let her mother and father convince her that this was the right decision for Lili? Eleanor made up her mind to dine with her parents that evening and discuss the matter. She didn't want her mother involved, though. If Eleanor arrived early enough, she could catch her father alone, before dinner.

What worried her most was the fact that Jacob Abbot's recalcitrance regarding the child seemed deliberate. If that was true, what did he stand to gain? And what had changed? Lili had stayed with the Abbots for nearly two years without any problems of this nature. With a baby coming, perhaps they simply needed more money. But something told her there was more to it than that.

The afternoon dragged on endlessly. Jane continued her work on two rows of embroidery trailing up the center front of a pelisse. She seemed to have endless patience for it. Such close work made Eleanor want to rip her hair out. She herself set in the satin lining of a mantle. She hated working with satin because it was so slippery, and every so often, a curse slipped out, causing Jane to giggle.

When the light grew too dim to continue working, Eleanor dismissed her assistant. As soon as she'd put everything away, she gathered her things and made her way to her family home.

Chapter Eight

Eleanor took extra care with her toilette. She chose a pale rose muslin gown she knew her father admired. After she was dressed and her maid had arranged her hair, she sought out Sir William in his study. The door was open, so she stepped into the room without knocking. "Good evening, Papa."

"Norrie! What a nice surprise. How well you look in that gown. What brings you here so early?" He was not yet dressed for dinner.

"I wished to speak to you privately."

Sir William's expression turned wary. He rose and closed the door. "I think I'll have a brandy. Would you like a sherry, my dear?"

Eleanor accepted, and when her father was seated, she began. "I am extremely concerned about the current arrangements for Lili. Jacob Abbot seems to be doing everything in his power to make visiting her difficult for me. It's time you paid him a call, Papa."

Her father cradled the brandy snifter in his palms, warming the amber liquid. "Perhaps you'd better tell me exactly what has happened to upset you."

Eleanor described her earlier visit, relating Abbot's attempt to keep her out and his sarcasm and outright meanness toward her. "Worst of all, Edith had a large bruise on her face, which she claimed was due to a fall. I could see she was lying, but I didn't press her because Abbot was outside the door listening."

"What makes you so certain she was lying?"

"She wouldn't look at me at first, and her explanation sounded as though she'd invented it on the spot. And I'm sure she knew her husband was nearby. He walked through the door as we were talking."

After a swallow of brandy, Sir William said, "I think because you wish for a different situation for Lili, you are perhaps reading things into this without any real proof. Edith's explanation seems plausible to me. You've never had any indication that Abbot has hurt Lili, have you?"

At some point, Eleanor had set her glass down and grasped her skirts, twisting the fabric in her fists. "No, but that doesn't mean he won't. I'm frightened for her, Papa. Are we to wait until that actually happens?"

"You forget how thoroughly I delved into their business, Norrie. Everybody I spoke to said they were decent people. And in all the months Lili has stayed with them, we've never had reason to believe they were mistreating her."

"Today Abbot claimed his wife had gone to see her mother and taken Lili with her. If that's true, I'm grateful Edith knows better than to leave Lili alone with her husband. But I believe he may have been lying." Pausing, Eleanor let go of her skirts and leaned toward her father. "I have the distinct impression he's deliberately keeping me from her, Papa, for some devious purpose of his own."

Sir William seemed dubious. "What possible reason would he have for doing so?"

Eleanor, frustrated, slapped her palms on the desk. "I know it doesn't make any sense, but why tell me Lili is sleeping when I could clearly hear her voice? Why allow his wife to take her away during one of the designated times for my visits? Doesn't it seem suspicious?"

"Suspicious is going too far, my dear, but it does seem odd, I admit. If he's the kind of man you think he is, he probably enjoys getting under your skin." But wariness flickered once again in her father's eyes. What was he afraid of? Abbot? Her father had never been afraid of anyone. Or perhaps that had been her girlish view of him.

"He wants more money, Papa. That was the last thing he threw at me before I left."

"Impossible. We've increased the amount two times already."

"If he threatens to reveal what he knows, we may not have a choice. I can afford to give you more money. Enough to appease him," Eleanor said. Although doing so would reduce the amount in her savings and postpone her plans for herself and Lili. Plans that were taking on a greater urgency.

She pushed back her chair, rose, and walked to the windows. The sun was just setting, a brilliant disk of orange. At last she turned and faced her father. "This is not acceptable, Papa. The Abbots signed an agreement with us, and he should not be allowed to violate it."

"I don't dispute that."

"So you'll call on him?" Eleanor waited by the windows, hardly breathing. If her father was the kind of man she'd always believed him to be, he would agree.

"Very well. I'm not sure what good it will do, but no harm can come of it."

"We're paying him, Papa!" She walked toward him and said, "And I'm frightened. I don't like this. Any of it. Lili is living with a man who hurts his own wife."

Now Sir William stood and came to her. Patting her shoulder, he said, "I'll see the man, Norrie. We'll get this straightened out. No more worrying, now."

Eleanor looked him in the eye, holding his gaze momentarily. Something was not right, but she couldn't put her finger on it. Finally, she nodded, and her father excused himself to dress for dinner.

After the meal with her parents, Eleanor changed back into a day dress and, despite her mother's disapproval, left for the cottage. Preoccupied throughout the evening with the earlier conversation with her father, she'd paid scant attention to Kitty Broxton's prattling about parties and receptions. At some point she'd even mentioned the Jensens' son, but Eleanor had completely ignored that. Despite her own wishes, she'd agreed to attend the Carringtons' garden party the following afternoon. She could ill afford the time away from her work, but sometimes she acquiesced to her mother's demands simply to silence her.

Bobby pranced along ahead of her, dashing into the woods whenever he scented something he thought worth chasing. What a scamp he was. Eleanor jolted to a stop when she heard someone else on the path. Someone who was whistling. Surely a person intent on mischief would not be whistling. Nevertheless, she moved off the trail. Unfortunately, there wasn't a convenient tree to hide behind.

Whoever it was soon encountered Bobby. "Ho, there, rascal," the voice said. "Are you on your way to my building site again?"

Hugh.

Eleanor knew, of course, she couldn't avoid him forever, but to meet like this, in the dark…how awkward. She must make herself known before he discovered her cowering in the night. "Hugh? I'm here."

"Eleanor? Out so late by yourself?" He was wearing only

his shirt and britches, and his broad chest was mere inches from her gaze.

"I dined with my parents and stayed rather late, I suppose." He was carrying something under his arm, but she couldn't make out what it was. Although she had a good idea it might be a drying cloth with a cake of soap wrapped inside.

"I'll accompany you to the cottage."

"Truly, that's not necessary. I'm fine on my own. I do this frequently."

She could just make out his handsome features, the hard line of his stubbled jaw, his straight nose and wide-set eyes. "You should not. I've several men sleeping in my stables, not all of whom I can personally vouch for." He grasped her elbow and reluctantly, she let him guide her. He let go after he'd made certain her footing was sure, and then, in the next minute, he halted abruptly.

"Hugh? Is something wrong?"

He cocked his head at her. "Will you come with me to the mere? There's something I'd like to show you."

Warmth spread from her chest down to the juncture of her thighs when she recalled how splendid Hugh had looked emerging from the water. If he wanted to kiss her, or do more, Eleanor wasn't sure she would be strong enough to resist. "I don't know if that's a good idea."

"I swear I have nothing devious in mind, Eleanor." When she still hesitated, he said, "Trust me."

Of course, she trusted him. He was the father of her child, wasn't he? He winged his elbow, and she grasped it. The little dog scampering ahead of them, they reached their destination in just a few minutes.

"We must walk around to the other side to get the full effect," Hugh said mysteriously. "There's a bench we can sit on." And then, when they rounded the far end, Eleanor knew what he wanted her to see. The full moon was reflecting gloriously, spectacularly, in the center of the mere. A silvery pillar with a ball of light on top. She gasped with the beauty of it, then heard Hugh's voice.

"The moon shines bright. In such a night as this, when the sweet wind did gently kiss the trees…"

They had reached the bench, and after Hugh ran his drying cloth over it, he motioned her to sit. "Shakespeare?" Eleanor asked.

He lowered himself beside her. "Lorenzo, *The Merchant of Venice*."

She nodded. "It's one of the plays I don't know well."

"You'll recognize this one: "Arise, fair sun, and kill the envious moon, Who is already sick and pale with grief, That thou, her maid, art far more fair than she." Eleanor caught the scent of brandy on his breath, with a hint of orange.

His voice was mesmerizing, low and resonant, and she had to give her head a shake before responding. "Yes. Romeo telling Juliet that the moon is envious of her beauty." The bench they sat upon was small, and their shoulders and arms brushed lightly against each other. She wanted to press herself into him; even the slight touch of their bodies made her skin feel alive, made her quiver inside. Instead, she offered a quote of her own. "But what of this one? O, swear not by the moon, th'inconstant moon, That monthly changes in her circle orb, Lest that thy love prove likewise variable."

"Juliet fears his love will not last. But not all men are so capricious."

Was he referring to himself? No, she was reading too much into his words.

They were quiet a moment, simply taking in the splendor. And then Hugh spoke. "Adam and I used to come here as boys. We would sneak out in the middle of the night, sometimes just to lie back and listen to night sounds. Other times we brought along a spear and caught frogs."

As if on cue, a bullfrog gave a throaty croak, and they both laughed. "You have no siblings, Eleanor?"

"No. My mother had two stillbirths after I was born. I believe it was a great sorrow to both my parents. They never mention it."

"I'm sorry to hear it."

"I was too young—I don't remember at all. What I do remember is my childhood being somewhat lonely and isolated. I longed for a sister or brother."

"Deborah lost a child, too. I was quite grown up when it happened, and I recall to this day how sad and bewildered I felt. It was a girl."

Hugh's voice had caught on his last words. After all these years, he still mourned the loss of a sister who never lived or drew breath. Eleanor wanted to hold him, comfort him, because he seemed so full of sadness, but she didn't dare. A pang of guilt—and regret—stabbed at her. He had lost a sister, and now she was keeping him from his daughter.

Hugh got to his feet. "I'd better get you home."

Reluctantly, she rose. He reached for her hand, clasping it in his much larger one. Its warmth shot spirals of pleasure through her body. She should protest, tell him she'd be perfectly safe by herself, but she wouldn't withdraw her hand even if God himself commanded it.

Eleanor called for Bobby, and Hugh said, "Would you mind if I carried him? I'm afraid I might trip over him, or worse yet, step on him."

She couldn't help laughing. "Be my guest. But I warn you, he wiggles."

Hugh squatted gracefully, scooped up the naughty dog, and rose. "You forget, I carried him all the way from Longmere to your cottage. I know what he's like."

Eleanor couldn't fathom why Hugh was being so considerate of her. She didn't deserve his kindness after what had happened between them at the dinner party. They walked along in silence for a time, and Eleanor noticed that Bobby, clutched firmly against Hugh's chest, held perfectly still, the little traitor.

"You must be working day and night, now that the end of the Season is fast approaching," Hugh said, breaking the silence. Eleanor could feel his eyes on her. She liked the feeling.

"We are. I count it a good day, though, if the light is sufficient to sew into the afternoon. We dare not bring the candles too close."

"Have you tried gas lanterns?"

"Too smoky. Combined with the fireplace, the smell is not only terrible to breathe, it begins to permeate the fabrics. The room already smells of smoke, as you pointed out." She sighed. "I'm afraid there's no acceptable solution."

"I'll ponder it," Hugh said. "I've got an architect working for me, after all. I'd be surprised if he hadn't encountered the problem before."

"Thank you. That would be a great help."

"And I happen to have hired the best steward in Surrey. He's clever and loves tackling seemingly impossible problems."

"How is the building coming?" she asked.

They'd reached the cottage. Before answering, Hugh unlatched the gate, and they both stepped into the garden. "Slowly," he said. "I'll show you around the site sometime, if you're interested." He reached out and handed Bobby to her.

"I'd like that. Can you stay for a moment?" She hadn't meant to ask. After all, they'd just been sitting together by the lake.

"I'd better not. I was on my way to bathe when I encountered you. I prefer to do so at night, under cover of darkness. I wouldn't want to be caught naked. Again." He grinned, the rogue, and before she could come back with a clever riposte, he said, "I would see you safely inside, Eleanor. I'll wait here while you light a candle and lock the door."

She laughed. "I rarely lock it."

"But you will do so regularly, now that I've explained about—"

"Yes, I know, the strange men wandering about who may have designs on me."

"Good night, Eleanor. Pleasant dreams."

"Good night, Hugh. And…and thank you for showing me the mere in the moonlight."

He nodded. "I hope we might do it again."

Before she could answer, he'd moved away. He was leaning against the gate, waiting. Quickly, she opened the door and turned the key. He would hear the bolt click into place. Then she lit a candle, walked to the window with it, and waved. Silly, because he probably couldn't see her.

. . .

It had taken a supreme effort of will to walk away from Eleanor when everything in him wanted to reach for her, pull her into his arms, and kiss those sweet lips until she begged for more. His cockstand was so hard, walking was uncomfortable. As soon as he reached the pond, he stripped and dived in. After a minute, the cold water eased his discomfort.

While he soaped and rinsed himself, he thought about his encounter with Eleanor. Determined not to importune her again, he'd kept his distance as much as possible. For whatever reason, she'd pushed him away the evening of the dinner party, and he must respect that. He would content himself with friendship for now. Befriending her, tamping down his physical desire for her, perhaps was the way to her heart. If he wanted her heart. Did he? Make no mistake, he certainly wanted her body.

Tomorrow he'd talk to Ridley, if he was on the site, about lighting. And he'd see if Ned had any ideas. It remained a mystery to Hugh exactly why Eleanor worked so hard. She was consumed by it. Her parents were well-off and perfectly able to care for her, so why did she not live with them, as other young, unmarried ladies of her age did? They must have had a falling-out. One so agonizing that it had driven Eleanor away.

He wished he were on better terms with Adam. He might know. But Hugh wouldn't dare ask for any favors from his brother. He might take that as a sign Hugh wanted an association, when nothing could be further from the truth.

The next day

When John Ridley showed up at Longmere in the morning, Hugh queried him about lighting. Ridley said poor light made drawing up his architectural plans difficult. Since the actual building was done primarily in the daylight and out of doors, he'd not encountered so many problems there. "In my office, I use an Argand lamp. Are you familiar with them?"

"I've seen them, yes." Hugh recalled his brother having one in his library at the townhouse. "Never used one myself, though."

Ridley rubbed his jowls. "They use whale oil. Cleaner. There's little flickering and less smoke."

"Thanks. I'll check into it. Do you think I could find one in Haslemere?"

"Probably need to order one from London," Ridley said.

Later when he and Ned were hauling planks of wood closer to the house, he put the question to his steward. "I've a friend who's in desperate need of better lighting for her work. She's a dressmaker. Any ideas?"

They dropped the lumber they'd been carrying. Ned pulled out a handkerchief and mopped his forehead. "*Hmm.* Mirrors reflect whatever the light source is and can serve to illuminate an area. Are there windows?"

Hugh frowned, trying to picture the interior of the cottage. "The work area is beneath the casements, but they face north. Candles are too risky—they could drip wax on the fabrics, or worse, ignite them if one were knocked over."

"What about a standing candleholder? I used to work at the ironworks, and we made them. She could position one or two fairly close without worrying about anything catching fire."

Hugh clapped his friend on the shoulder. "Good suggestions, all. My thanks, man."

Ned cleared his throat. "Who is this, ah, friend?"

Hugh was afraid that was coming, so he was prepared. "Just that. A friend, and that's all you need to know."

Ned showed the palms of his hands. "Far be it from me to nose around in another man's business. Especially if it involves a woman." His lips quivered.

"Christ in a cradle. The cheek I put up with around here." Hugh turned and stomped off. When his back was to the steward, he smiled. He was feeling so good, he did not even mind dressing for the garden party he was attending this afternoon. He'd turned down other such invitations, but knew if he continued to do so, his status as Benjamin Grey's dissolute son would take on new life. He believed his standing in Haslemere was on the rise, and he wanted it to continue its ascent. If you employed the citizens and treated them well, it got around. Hugh didn't want to risk his reputation by never making an appearance in Society. And besides, Eleanor might be there. That was the true reason he wanted to attend.

• • •

After Eleanor, Minnie, and Jane had shared a light collation, they resumed their work, taking advantage of the bright daylight. Eleanor had propped open the door, which also helped.

The two girls, as was their habit, were gossiping about various goings-on in the town. Eleanor was half listening, until she heard Hugh's name mentioned.

Minnie was chortling. "Did she really say that?"

Jane nodded, sending them into whoops of laughter. Now Eleanor was curious. "Who said what?"

Minnie's face reddened. "Gracie Allanson said she'd like to do you-know-what with Sir Hugh! But she didn't say it in a ladylike way, if you take my meaning."

Eleanor's mouth quirked up. "Is there a ladylike way to say it?" More giggling. "Really, girls, it's one thing to admire a man from afar, but an entirely different one to announce it in public. I hope neither of you would do such a thing." Good Lord, she sounded missish.

Her lecture fell on deaf ears. "Oh, Gracie's not the only one who's saying it. He's that handsome, miss."

"I'm well aware of his handsomeness," Eleanor said. *Is handsomeness a word?* She wasn't sure.

"So you think so, too, miss?"

"I can't deny that he has a certain male, um, presence about him."

Minnie seemed genuinely puzzled by this comment. "What do you mean by that, miss?"

Since both girls looked fit to burst with laughter, she thought she'd been deliberately caught, and now they were reeling her in. She raised an eyebrow. "You both know perfectly well what I mean."

"Yes, miss," Jane agreed. And then the dam burst, and both girls indulged in unbridled fits of laughter.

"All right, that's enough," Eleanor said, but she was

smiling. Best to change the subject. "Heavens! I nearly forgot, I'm attending the Carrington's garden party this afternoon. You two will need to carry on without me."

Jane poked Minnie in the ribs before saying, "Maybe Sir Hugh will be there!"

Eleanor laughed, despite her determination not to. It was innocent fun, after all. She hadn't thought about Hugh being at the party, but now that the possibility had arisen, she didn't resent going so much. "I must dash. I'll see you in the morning."

Chapter Nine

The Carringtons lived in a classical-style brick house set above the Town. The carriage pulled into a driveway lined with plane trees, and John Coachman dropped them off at the front. Evenly spaced, linteled casements lined up on every story, with wrought iron balconies featured on the second. The doorway was arched, with a pediment. Mr. Carrington had made his money in ironworks, and his home left no one in doubt as to the level of his competence.

In the entryway, a receiving line awaited them. Eleanor had hoped for less formality, but it was too late to back out now and too early to make her escape. Mrs. Carrington, her long nose and narrow face lending her an air of superiority, shook her hand. "We don't see enough of you, my dear. I have some friends I would like you to meet later." She smiled, and Eleanor was sure the matron winked at her mother. *Oh, no.* That meant *male* friends. Coming here had been a terrible mistake if Mama and Mrs. Carrington were conspiring to introduce her to eligible men.

Eleanor distanced herself from her parents and

meandered through the crowd toward the terrace. *Ah.* She could breathe again. Despite her distaste for the party, she had to admit the gardens were lovely. She walked along a path with lavender borders toward the roses, where she spied some of her girlhood friends gathered in a group.

"Eleanor!" Her dearest friend, past and present, Alice Porter, greeted her first.

They embraced and kissed each other's cheeks. Alice was with child, and her growing middle made it difficult to get very close to her. "How I've missed you, Allie," Eleanor said. "Pregnancy suits you. You are glowing." In Eleanor's opinion, Alice always looked like a true English rose, with her ash blond hair and flawless skin.

"Ha! I feel rather like a sow at present. Did you make your dress, Eleanor?"

She nodded. It was a sprigged muslin, a primrose color, and Eleanor loved it. She'd spent hours embroidering the tiny flowers and leaves. She, who hated embroidery.

Eleanor greeted the others, sorry to discover a woman whom she roundly disliked was part of the group. Naturally, she was the one who spoke first. Eleanor was expecting a snide comment, and Marianne Haines did not disappoint.

"So good to see you, dear. How is the dressmaking business faring?" Smirking, she glanced at her friends to gauge their reaction.

Maud Hensley and Roberta Fairchild, the other women in the group, snickered. Alice said, "You are making quite a name for yourself, Eleanor. Everyone wants one of your creations."

"You exaggerate, Alice," Eleanor said, smiling. "If that were the case, I wouldn't have been able to come today."

"Such a pity you haven't married," Marianne said. "Then you would not need to, to…have employment."

Eleanor sucked in a breath. *Lord, give me strength.* "I enjoy my work, Marianne. As you well know, it's not a necessity. I do it by choice." She paused briefly, then said, "What is it you do all day, Marianne?"

Maud and Roberta chortled, but ceased when Marianne glared at them. Eleanor was surprised when Marianne answered, as the question had been rhetorical.

"I see to the day's menus, play with the children, make calls. Spend time with my husband. If you accepted the proper duties of a lady in Society, you would be doing likewise."

Eleanor spied Marianne's boorish husband holding forth in a cluster of his cronies and shuddered. "Thank heaven, then, that you are the one called upon for such duties and not me."

Alice had pressed her lips together so hard they'd turned white. "So nice to see you all," Eleanor said, "pray excuse me." Then sotto voce to Alice, "Let's talk later."

As Eleanor slipped away from the group, Marianne shouted, "And I attend monthly meetings of the Haslemere Ladies Benevolent Society for Aid to the Poor and the Needy." One of Kitty Broxton's favorite charities. People standing nearby were staring, including Marianne's unpleasant spouse, with a disapproving look on his puffy face.

Alongside her, a voice said, "Tormenting your friends, Eleanor? And at a social event, too. For shame."

"Listening to my conversations, Sir Hugh?" He'd suddenly appeared beside her, and she was so rattled, she hadn't even noticed. But now, because he was dressed in a cobalt blue swallowtail coat that hugged his shoulders and chest, she couldn't help but do so. She didn't dare let her gaze roam downward.

"Your voices carried, especially Marianne's. What was it—The Ladies Benevolent…what?"

"The Haslemere Ladies Benevolent Society to Aid the Poor and the Needy. One of my mother's most passionate causes, provided she isn't required to be anywhere near said needy and poor. Or poor and needy."

"My, my. The cat has claws."

She had been moving fast, the better to put distance between herself and her so-called friends, and now they'd arrived at the banks of one of the lily ponds. Eleanor lurched to a halt, turned to Hugh, and said, "I beg your pardon. That was not well done of me. To say that about my mother."

He shrugged. "Mothers can be difficult."

She wanted to ask him about his mother. Would it offend him? Perhaps if she went about it indirectly. "Did your mother belong? To the Haslemere Society?"

There was a bench, and Hugh gestured to it. After they were seated, he said, "Not that I recall. She didn't socialize much."

"I don't remember seeing you and your family around Town. Perhaps I was too young."

"Probably. I was what, already nine or ten when you came into the world?"

He wasn't making this easy. Eleanor was about to conclude that a conversation about his mother was simply off-limits when he said, "She left when I was fifteen. Took Adam with her and moved to London." His eyes held a world of hurt, and she was shocked to her core. Never had she seen him so vulnerable.

"I'm sorry. That must have been terribly difficult for you." How she longed to hold his hand or take him into her arms, but both were out of the question.

And then it was gone, the brief flash of pain that had been there, and the Hugh she was more accustomed to returned. "Don't be sorry. Deborah made her choice. My father and I managed."

Not well. According to the little Eleanor knew, Benjamin Grey hadn't been much of a father to the son who had remained behind. It had been more the other way around.

"Do you get on with your mother now, Hugh?"

From the look of him, she'd gone too far. She'd hoped after last night, after what they'd each shared regarding their families, he might be willing to speak to her about the difficulties with his mother, but she'd been wrong. His body stiffened, and his face signaled a storm approaching. She did not expect him to answer and was grasping for something to say when he spoke.

"Deborah would like me to forgive and forget, but I can't."

• • •

How in the hell had he let this conversation go so far? He should have nipped it in its cankerous bud. Now he had Eleanor looking at him with pity in her eyes. The one thing he could not abide.

"I don't want your pity, Eleanor, so you can stop staring at me with those mournful eyes." The words were harsh, a contradiction to this beautiful woman before him, but so be it.

"What makes you think I pity you?" Damn her, she was edging closer to him, pressing her thigh against his. "I empathize with you, Hugh, one human to another."

He gave a bitter laugh. "Empathy, sympathy, pity—they all amount to the same thing, and I don't want it, from you or anybody."

She went on as if he hadn't spoken. "Do you feel the same about Adam?"

"Not that it's any of your business, but yes, I do. Let them be a family. Mother, son, grandson. I neither need nor want them in my life." His words were cold and unforgiving, but he couldn't seem to control his trembling hands or the hard clenching of his jaw.

Her voice was soft and gentle. "Are you certain of that?

Your brother is a decent man, Hugh. And your nephew…"

His temper flared. Adam again. Was he doomed to be compared to his younger brother—and come out looking like the lesser man every time? And her manner implied, no matter how steadfastly she denied it, that she was sorry for him. "What do you truly know about any of this, Eleanor?" He sprang to his feet, needing to loom over her and assert his power. "We were intimate once, but that doesn't give you the right to question me and judge my decisions regarding Adam and my mother."

"N-no, of course not. I beg your pardon if I offended you." Her eyes were cast down, but he could see tears threatening to spill out.

Well, he'd gone and done it now. Making women cry seemed to be his forte. He needed to escape. Now, before he did any further damage. He nodded in her direction. "Good day, Eleanor." And then he left her sitting there on the bench by herself, a rude and unfeeling act that made him ashamed.

• • •

A weight pressed on Eleanor's chest. Tears streamed down her cheeks, and she could only be grateful Hugh had stormed off. Although she resented him for it, too. Leaving her there alone was unforgivable. There was something more profound than she'd imagined in Hugh's feelings toward his family. A hurt that ran so deep, he was drowning in it.

He'd mentioned their liaison so carelessly, as though it had been an everyday occurrence for him. She could hardly blame him, when she'd referred to it as "sexual congress." Perhaps making love with her had been nothing extraordinary. Maybe it was so to her because of Lili. Lili, who could bring Hugh so much joy. She must tell him. She would tell him, no matter what the cost to herself. He needed Lili to make his own family.

No. Don't be a fool, Eleanor.

She was fishing in her reticule for a handkerchief when Alice Porter slid onto the bench beside her. "Here," she said, handing Eleanor the very item she'd been looking for. She blotted her tears and tried to compose herself.

"Did you tell him?"

Alice knew about Lili. In a moment of weakness, when Eleanor had been feeling alone and isolated after Lili's birth, she'd confessed all to her friend, including the father's identity. Alice, true and loyal, had never betrayed her confidence, not even to her husband. Sniffling, Eleanor shook her head. "No."

"My dear—"

"Do not say it. I know I must. It has all become so complicated."

"Maybe you should bring me up to date."

Perhaps it would be beneficial to confide in Alice. Doing so might relieve some of Eleanor's guilt and worry. With a sigh, she began to speak. "Telling him he has a child would spell disaster. For Hugh, it could mean scandal, and for Lili and me—well, that's unknown, isn't it?"

"Scandal if he acknowledges he has a child out of wedlock. Is that what you're referring to?"

"Exactly. My mother reminded me that while such a thing would not be shocking in Town, here in Haslemere, attitudes are different." Eleanor twisted the handkerchief into knots as she spoke. "More provincial. And Hugh has just begun to rebuild his reputation and his standing in the community. He arrived home with a knighthood, for pity's sake! He is a good man, Alice. I don't want to be the instrument of his ruin."

"It would be your ruin, too, Eleanor. But are you sure you're not exaggerating the risk?"

"That is not the only issue. There is also the matter of Hugh's tangled relationship with his mother. I've just learned he bears a deep resentment toward her for leaving him with his father. I fear his judgment of me will be no less harsh."

"Because Lili is with foster parents? Your choices were so limited, dear. You're doing the best you can."

"I am afraid he will not see it that way. He may believe I gave up Lili to protect my own reputation, and in a way, that's true, even if my parents demanded it of me."

Alice patted Eleanor's hand. "He has a right to know about his own child. Give him a chance. If he is a good man, as you say, he will understand in time."

Eleanor looked up and saw Alice's handsome husband, George, strolling toward them. The two beamed at each other, and Eleanor couldn't help smiling. Rising, she said, "George, I apologize for monopolizing your wife."

"Hello, Eleanor. Lovely to see you. Alice has been looking forward to learning all your news." He turned to his wife. "Are you ready, darling?" Extending a hand, he helped her to her feet.

The two women embraced, and Alice whispered, "Be brave, dearest. You can do it."

Eleanor nodded. "You will let us know when the baby arrives?"

"Of course," George said.

After they left, Eleanor resumed her seat on the bench. How she envied Alice's happy life with her husband, something that seemed vastly out of reach for her. Despite feeling hurt by Hugh's curt dismissal of her, she recognized that it was for the best. The mutual attraction they felt could never be acknowledged. She wasn't prepared to reveal her most closely guarded secret to him, and he refused to expose his deepest self to her.

Eleanor glanced up and saw her mother waving at her. Oh, how she wished she could hide behind one of the hedges. Wasn't there a maze somewhere? No doubt she was now to be subjected to a series of tedious introductions, although she did not believe there were that many eligible men about. As she walked toward her mother, she noticed that Hugh had been waylaid by a few matrons with virginal-looking daughters by their sides. Hugh courting one of them would be ideal in terms of getting him out of her life for good.

She allowed her mother and Mrs. Carrington to introduce her to several gentlemen, not one of whom she was remotely interested in. Every so often, she glanced about to see where Hugh was.

The thought of him kissing another woman, holding her, touching her, etched a wound onto Eleanor's soul.

Chapter Ten

The next morning

Hugh stood, arms akimbo, surveying the building site. The masonry workers had arrived and brickmaking was under way. Some of the internal walls and the entirety of the rear wall would be brick, but the facade would be of stone. Ridley had frowned on the extravagance, but it was what Hugh wanted.

Ned had been helping with the bricks, but now strode over and stood beside Hugh. "What are you thinking?" he asked.

"That we've made more progress than I could have hoped for in such a short time. I'll be sleeping in an actual bedchamber in my own home before too long."

Ned laughed. "You will. Have you thought about furniture for this dwelling, Sir Hugh? Maybe a trip to Town is in order."

"You're right. I ordered a few pieces from a local furniture maker, but I'll need to get the rest in London. I want to check into Argand lamps, too. For my friend."

"Ah, yes, your seamstress friend. The one without a name." Ned wiggled his eyebrows, earning a scowl from Hugh.

Hugh turned and began to walk toward his cottage. "I've some correspondence to take care of." Ned followed, but Hugh barely noticed. When they reached the door, he seemed surprised Ned was still with him.

"You're thinking about the lady, then?" Ned asked.

"What lady?" And then he laughed. Hugh was sick of subterfuge. Perhaps Ned was someone he could confide in. The man would be discreet, Hugh had no doubt.

"I said, you're —"

"I heard you. Come in. You might as well make yourself useful. Sit." After Hugh had poured them each a cup of tea, he said, "I'm afraid I've upset her. Something I said to her yesterday at the garden party. Any ideas for a gift that might assuage hurt feelings?"

Ned scratched his head. "It can't be too personal."

"I know that much. I took her a basket of food a while back for a similar reason, so that's out."

Ned chuckled. "So you've made a habit of offending this lady, have you?"

"You might say that, although never intentionally."

"Flowers?"

Hugh shook his head. "No. She has a profusion of them in her garden."

Ned tipped his cup and swallowed the remainder of his tea. "One of the barn cats has a new litter of kittens. Would she like one?"

"That's a thought, although she's got a puppy. Are the kittens old enough to be separated from their mother?"

"They're getting underfoot quite regularly, so I'd say so. Probably about six or seven weeks old."

"That's it, then. A kitten. Although I suppose she could refuse it."

"She could, especially if her dog takes it in dislike. May I assume the lady is Miss Broxton?"

Hugh laughed. "I trust you to keep my confidence."

Ned got to his feet. "Certainly. I'll leave you to your correspondence and get back to work."

Before Ned left, Hugh said, "How are the new hires?"

"Good workers. There's one who's got a bit of a chip on his shoulder. It may be his way of adjusting to a new job and his fellow workers, but we should keep an eye on him."

"Possibly, but we don't want a troublemaker about. Let me know if we need to speak to him."

Ned nodded and left.

Hugh remained, gazing out the window and musing. A kitten. Would the gift of a kitten make up for what he'd said to Eleanor at the garden party? She'd gently urged him toward reconciling with Deborah and Adam, and that had set him off. A mere week after he'd vowed to let go of the past and the pain it had caused him. He was a damned fool.

Perhaps, instead of vowing to renounce the past, he should take some actual steps toward doing so.

• • •

Eleanor was working on a gathered bodice when her father knocked at the cottage door. "Papa!" she said, genuinely happy to see him. She'd been making little progress with her sewing, since with every poke of her needle she pictured Hugh Grey's face. Both his vulnerable look and the furious one that had replaced it.

Sir William bowed. "Good morning, Norrie. Jane." Her father had an old-fashioned courtesy about him that Eleanor found endearing.

She rose from her work and kissed his cheek. "What brings you here?"

"May we sit outside, my dear?" he said, tilting his head toward the door. "You will pardon us, Jane."

When they were settled on the bench, he spoke. "If you can spare the time, I thought we could ride out to the Abbots' together. We can see Lili, and I will talk to Abbot and set him straight on a few things. What do you think?"

Eleanor could hardly spare the time, but she would never turn down a chance to see Lili. And it was especially important for her father to speak to Jacob Abbot. "Give me a half hour. I'll finish up and meet you at the stables." A thought occurred to her. "Is Mama joining us?"

Sir William's face drooped, indicating to his daughter that there had been a row about it. "No."

Of course not. What had she been thinking? A short time later, Eleanor set out on the path leading to her family home. Her two assistants didn't know about Lili, and Eleanor never explained her occasional absences. As their employer, she was not obliged to do so. Nor did they have the right to question her—and they never had. They were good girls, Jane and Minnie. Eleanor considered herself lucky to have such talented seamstresses, and worthy friends, working for her.

They rode in the carriage, a venerable old conveyance that had seen more elegant days. The squabs were cracked, the seat covers worn, and it could no longer be described as well-sprung. But Eleanor's father had an attachment to it and insisted he would use it as long as the wheels continued turning. It got them to the Abbots' in good time, which was all Eleanor cared about. She'd brought Bobby along, since Lili loved to play with him.

The footman set down the steps, and Sir William alighted first. As he was helping Eleanor down, Abbot strode up, emerging from somewhere near the stables.

"Sir William. Miss Broxton. I reckon you're here to see the little girl."

"Good morning, Abbot. You assume correctly. Can you take us inside, please?"

Eleanor noted Abbot's lack of combativeness with Sir William. The man would never have admitted her without an argument. They found Lili in the parlor with Abbot's wife, who was pacing back and forth, jiggling the child against her chest. Lili sounded fretful, emitting little jagged cries.

"She's got a fever," Mrs. Abbot said. "She was up and down during the night."

Lili lifted her head and looked at Eleanor. A tiny smile flickered, and she reached out for her mother. Eleanor gathered her up and sat down on the sofa. When she placed her cheek on Lili's forehead, heat radiated against her skin. "She's very warm. Is she coughing?"

"Not so far. She's just been restless and cranky."

Sir William rested his hand atop Lili's head. "Poor little one." Then, turning to Abbot, he said, "I'd like a word. Is there somewhere private we can speak?"

"Outside all right?"

"That will be fine."

After the two men left, Lili wanted down to pet Bobby, and Eleanor thought it would do no harm to allow it. Relieved to see that the other woman sported no new bruises, Eleanor said, "How are you, Edith?"

"I'm all right. A little tired, because of the pregnancy. I'm trying to rest when Lili does."

"Good. Getting up with her during the night can't be easy."

"No, but it doesn't happen most nights."

"While Sir William and your father are talking, why don't you lie down? I'll look after Lili."

Edith hesitated. "I don't know. Jacob doesn't like me lying about during the day."

Because he's a brute.

"I promise to alert you when I hear their voices. At least you can get off your feet for a few minutes."

After Edith left the room, Eleanor lowered herself to the floor and played with Lili and Bobby until the child began to fuss. She had been rubbing at her ear, and Eleanor wondered if she might have an earache. She'd been prone to them herself as a girl. After a moment, she picked Lili up and settled onto the rocking chair. After a time, rubbing the child's back and whispering soothing words sent her off to sleep. If Lili's earaches were at all like those she'd suffered as a child, the worst was yet to come. There would be hours more of pain, followed by nausea and sometimes vomiting. Eleanor resented the fact that she wouldn't be able to nurse Lili through this. A mother should not be separated from her child because of the dictates of Society.

Before leaving, she would check with Edith to make certain Lili's foster mother knew the remedies for earaches. Eleanor was beginning to feel sleepy herself when she heard her father's voice and Jacob Abbot's much louder one. Hastily, she rose and went to rouse Edith. No sooner had she shaken the woman awake than her husband was calling for her. Bellowing was a more apt description.

"Be right there," Edith said groggily.

Eleanor grasped her arm to keep her from hurrying off. "Edith, do you know what to do for an earache?"

"What? Why…?"

"Because I think that's what is wrong with Lili. Warm compresses help the pain. And have you any willow bark, or another herb to lower her fever?"

"Willow bark, I think."

"Good. Steep it in some tea and try to get her to drink it. It won't be easy. Put some honey in it, and give it to her in spoonfuls. It should lower her fever and ease the ache, and she'll probably fall asleep." Edith nodded, and Eleanor, still carrying Lili, followed her out to the hallway.

The two men were waiting, her father's manner ill at ease, and Abbot glaring, looking like a volcano about to erupt. Eleanor ignored him and said, "Papa, I think Lili has an earache. Do you remember when I had them as a girl?"

"No, love, but it's mothers who recall these things. Are you ready to go?"

So much for any sympathy from that quarter. Eleanor sighed and passed Lili into Edith's waiting arms. "Call for a physician if she's not better tomorrow. We will, of course, assume the cost."

Abbot snorted. "We never have a physician for any of our ailments. They pass eventually."

Eleanor struggled to remain composed. "That may be, Mr. Abbot, but Lili is a child, a baby still, and illnesses are harder on them and can lead to complications. Pray do as I ask."

Abbot nodded, his jaw clamped shut.

On the drive home, Sir William told Eleanor about his conversation with the man. "He did not like being called to account, but he swore he'd be more cooperative in the future. I reminded him that we're paying them well to look after Lili." His mouth twisted into a wry smile. "And Abbot reminded me that they've kept the secret by pretending Lili was their orphaned niece. We must be grateful for that."

"He did not demand more money?"

"He must have reconsidered. Wise of him."

"*Hmm.*" Eleanor despaired over the whole arrangement. Some days it made her sick inside, and this was one of them. "I resent feeling beholden to him for anything. What are the chances he'll keep his word?"

"I believe he needs the money, although he told me he's lately found work as a carpenter on a building project. If you visit in the mornings, there's an excellent chance he'll be gone." He hesitated a moment before saying, "On the whole, Norrie, I believe your fears about him are largely unfounded."

She didn't argue the point. Clearly, her father felt she was overwrought and too emotional regarding Lili. Eleanor didn't have much experience with hate. But on the remainder of the drive home, she thought that was exactly what she felt for Jacob Abbot.

Chapter Eleven

At twilight, Hugh headed off to pay his call on Eleanor. Since he knew she often dined with her parents, he was afraid she might not be home after the dinner hour commenced. He set off carrying a basket in one hand, with the kitten he'd chosen tucked into the crook of his other arm.

Candlelight shone from the windows of the cottage. His spirits leaped, even though he'd no idea how she would receive him. Ah well, nothing ventured, nothing gained. He opened the gate, marched up to the door, and rapped lightly. Eleanor opened it, and for a moment, he thought she was going to slam it in his face.

He spoke before she had the chance. "Good evening, Eleanor. I wouldn't blame you if you barred the door against me, but I was hoping you might allow me to apologize." When she said nothing, he went further. "And explain."

Hugh could see she was thinking it over, even though there wasn't a hint of forgiveness in her hazel eyes, and her pretty lips didn't curve even minutely. He didn't blame her. He'd been an ass, after all. Finally, she relented. "I'll come out.

There's really no room inside for us both to sit down."

They claimed their usual spots on the bench. "And what's that you're holding, Sir Hugh?"

"That, Eleanor, is a fine specimen of female tabby cat fresh from weaning."

"And you brought her here for what purpose, if I may ask?"

Hugh gently set the kitten in her lap. "Peace offering? Olive branch? You must admit, she's a fair lady. Look at those green eyes."

Eleanor picked her up and held her at a distance, looking her over. "She's a beauty, I'll grant you that, but I don't need a cat, Hugh. I've already got one bothersome pet, in case you've forgotten."

"I haven't. But they could be great friends."

Eleanor plunked the kitten onto Hugh's lap. "Enemies, more likely. I don't think so."

"But—"

"I was preparing to walk up to the house when you arrived. What did you come here to say, Hugh?"

Having hoped she would be more receptive, her abruptness of manner rather crushed him. Time to come to the point. "Look, Eleanor, I humbly ask your forgiveness for my behavior yesterday. It was unpardonably rude."

"Then why should I forgive you?"

For a moment, Hugh was at a complete loss for words. And then he said what seemed like the truth to him. "I think you need a friend."

Eleanor sighed. Deeply, obviously, so he couldn't miss it. "And that would be you. The man who said, only yesterday, that I knew nothing about him and had no right to question him about…well, anything."

"That is not precisely what I said. I was referring to my family. To Adam and Deborah." The kitten had crawled over to Eleanor's lap and was batting at the fringes on her shawl. While Hugh watched, the green-eyed little minx crawled up Eleanor's bosom and made herself right at home. He hid a smile, thinking how he'd love to do the same.

"I see." She attempted to lift the kitten from her person, but its claws were embedded in the bodice of her dress. No sooner did Eleanor pry one paw away than the other one stuck fast. She was flustered, and even in the dim light, he could discern a flush on her cheeks. When she glanced at him in befuddlement, his laugh barked out. She tried to look annoyed, but her eyes were laughing. "It's not funny. My dress will be ruined."

Still laughing, he said, "I beg your pardon. May I help?"

Eleanor narrowed her eyes at him, but said, "Please do."

Hugh moved closer, turning so that he faced her. She held quite still, her hands at her sides. He would need to go slowly. Taking advantage of the situation would not serve, except to put him squarely in the category of overeager swain stealing liberties. Wrapping one hand around the kitten's body, he began to pry her claws away with the other. He tried, but it was damned near impossible not to brush her breasts with the back of his hand.

He glanced at Eleanor. She was trembling. He could feel her breath on his face, and blood rushed to his cock. *Sweet Jesus, this was torture.* God, he'd love to kiss her…

"This is taking a long time, Hugh," she said, though she giggled, breaking the spell.

"Apologies. Almost done." He freed the kitten and set her on the ground. "My pardon for intruding on your evening, Eleanor. I apologize for my…" *Try again, man.* "My sincere pardon for what I said to you. I have a blind spot where my mother and Adam are concerned. When someone challenges me on it, I become somewhat irrational."

The gloaming was fading to darkness, and it was hard

to make out her features. But he sensed a softening of her demeanor. "Ah, at last we're making progress. I won't press you on it, Hugh, but you just admitted your attitude toward them is unreasonable."

"From your perspective, I'm sure it's difficult to comprehend. Permit me to say I'm working toward adjusting my attitude."

Her eyes warmed. He could easily lose himself in those eyes. There wasn't much he would not do to earn the sweet softness of that look.

"What is in the basket?"

It was such an abrupt change of subject, he wasn't sure at first what she was talking about. "Ah. The basket." He set it down. "Open it."

She did, smiling when she saw the contents, which she removed one by one. A jug of milk. A saucer. A ball of catnip. "You were very sure I would accept your gift, Sir Hugh." The kitten pounced on the ball, then rubbed against it.

"Will you?"

"She'll wreak havoc inside, with the fabrics, trims, spools of thread, and the rest. I suppose I could keep her in the back room. And out here in the garden."

"Good lord, I didn't think of that. Perhaps this wasn't such a good idea after all."

She smiled wryly. "It's all right. I accept your gift. Lili will love her."

"Who is Lili?"

Her smile disappeared. "Minnie. I said Minnie, my assistant. She loves cats, and so does Jane."

Hugh was quite sure she'd said Lili, but since he knew of no one by that name, he let it drop. "I'll walk with you to your parents' house if you're ready."

He thought she would protest, but instead she asked, "What about the kitten?"

Hugh opened the jug of milk and poured some into the saucer. "Leave her here in the garden. I'll check on her on my way back to Longmere. She'll be fine."

"Are you sure? She might be cold."

"It's a warm evening, and she's a hardy little thing."

"Wait one minute." Eleanor hurried into the cottage and returned with a worn coverlet, which she placed on the bench. "There. She can curl up on that."

"Ready?" Hugh asked.

Eleanor nodded and grasped the arm he held out for her.

• • •

Oh, damn and blast! What had she done? She'd gone and mentioned Lili by name, for pity's sake. She hadn't fooled him for a minute with her pathetic cover-up, but for whatever reason, he'd chosen not to inquire who Lili might be. Never had she let down her guard to such an extent. Not before Jane and Minnie or Cassandra Grey. It was second nature for her to never mention her daughter, but somehow Hugh had managed to disarm her so thoroughly with his kitten, she had forgotten herself.

Too late to worry about it now.

The evening was lovely, with a light breeze grazing their skin and muted animal sounds in the distance. Birds settling for the night, weasels prowling, raccoons scurrying through the grass. "The night is so alive, isn't it?" she said. "I usually don't have time to notice."

"It is. Let's hope we don't scare up a skunk." Just then, something scurried across their path. Eleanor let out a little shriek and grasped Hugh's arm more firmly. "Only a bunny," he said. "I was joking about the skunk. In all the years I've prowled these woods, I've never come across one."

Somehow, she'd moved closer to Hugh, so that the length

of her body on one side moved against his with every step they took. Eleanor knew it would serve her best to put more distance between them, but she didn't want to. Touching him felt so good. Her body tingled with awareness and longing.

When he spoke, she was forced to emerge from her fog of desire. "Thank you for letting the topic of my family lie for now. It's something I never discuss, and I'm not sure that will ever change."

Eleanor was taken aback by this. Thanking her was almost as good as if he'd confided all. So she should respond in kind. "You were right about me, Hugh. I do need a friend. But even though friends confide in each other, they never make demands. They sense when the other person is ready to reveal things held close."

They were approaching the stables and the rear of the house. Hugh stopped and, grasping her arms, spun her to face him. "You are a remarkable woman, Eleanor Broxton." He leaned toward her, and she knew he was going to kiss her. And this time she would not stop him.

He pulled her close and slowly lowered his head. She felt as if she'd been waiting years for this, even though it had been just a few weeks since their kiss on the terrace. When his lips brushed hers at last, her knees begin to give. She slid her arms up and around his neck and pressed as close to him as she could. This was not wise, but clearly her heart had, for the time being, overruled her brain.

Now his kiss became more heated, more insistent. He stroked her lips with his tongue until she opened her mouth and allowed him in. Their tongues clashed, tasting, stroking, inviting. Jolts of desire shot through her, demanding and insistent. When Hugh gripped her bottom and drew her against him, the hard swell of his arousal pressed against her.

Abruptly, he pulled back, breathing hard. "Eleanor, if you don't want this, walk away now, because I don't think I can stop."

"I'm not going anywhere, Hugh."

He took her hand and led her off the path toward a giant old oak. In one move, he pushed her against it and claimed her mouth again. His hands were at her waist, then slid upward until they cupped her breasts. When she arched, he found the tips and gently rubbed them between his fingers.

He paused long enough to say, "This would only be improved if I could see you."

Eleanor laughed. "Yes." Her voice was raspy. In the next moment, Hugh had gathered her skirt in one hand and was pushing it up. Higher and higher, above her garter. His fingers moved toward her most intimate place, and that was exactly where she wanted them.

And then she heard voices. Worse yet, lanterns were bobbing along toward the path. "Hugh. Someone's coming."

"Christ almighty," he said. "Your father must have been worried about you." He picked up her shawl, which had fallen to the ground, and wrapped it around her shoulders. Lightly kissing her cheek, he whispered, "Good night, Eleanor. Go now." His warm breath caressed her ear.

She hurried out onto the path, not daring to turn around and glance at Hugh, even though she sorely wanted to.

Eleanor lay wide awake in her small bed at the cottage. Her mother had wanted her to stay the night, practically demanded it, but Eleanor said she had to get back to feed Bobby and see to her new kitten. She'd been evasive about how she'd come into possession of a kitten.

During the meal, she'd conversed with her parents in a desultory fashion, because all she could think about was Hugh. His kiss, his hands caressing her body. How alive she'd felt. And that they'd forged a bond. She'd told him she needed a friend, and it was true. So deep in thought had she been, she nearly missed it when her mother said, "You spent quite a long time with Hugh Grey at the garden party, Eleanor. What was that about?"

She hadn't anticipated the question, but she should have. A friend had offered to take Eleanor home from the party, because Kitty Broxton had not been ready to leave. Sick at heart over her squabble with Hugh, Eleanor had desperately wanted to escape, and so she'd accepted the offer. She hadn't seen her mother yet today, so she should have known this was coming.

Between bites of pudding, she said "He is a friend. I've run into him several times since he's been back, including the dinner party in Town."

Her mother had given a slight frown. Eleanor had long ago coined a name for that expression. The fake puzzlement look. It was mean to mask disapproval, but failed on every level. "What, Mama? Is there a problem?"

"Like father, like son. That is the problem." Her mother took a tiny sip of wine and dabbed at her lips with her napkin.

Remain calm, Eleanor. "An entirely unjust assessment, in my opinion. He is every bit the gentleman."

"And he's been knighted, don't forget," her father put in.

Her mother continued as though her husband hadn't spoken. "Even Deborah Grey's conduct is lacking. Leaving her home to live the life of a Society belle in London." She clucked her tongue. "Very poor taste."

"Enough, Kitty!" Sir William said. "You know perfectly well the woman had few alternatives."

Eleanor glanced from one parent to the other. They were looking daggers at each other. What on earth…?

"Was it of no consequence to you, Eleanor, when he left you sitting alone on that bench by the lily pond? He seemed riled by something you said, dear."

Aware that her mother was simply fishing for information, Eleanor was determined to reveal nothing. What occurred between herself and Hugh, past and present, was no one else's business. "No. He needed to speak with someone."

"I see. The various matrons and their offspring, I collect."

Ignoring the sarcasm, Eleanor had changed the subject. "Did Papa tell you that Lili is sick? I'm worried about her. She has an earache."

Surprisingly, that took her mother's mind off Hugh. "You suffered terribly from them when you were a child."

"You nursed me through them all. I remember sitting in your lap for hours in the nursery, and you rocking me and singing. I would give anything if I could do the same for Lili."

Her mother had made no comment.

And now, in her lonely bed, Eleanor felt guilty that she'd been ruminating about Hugh all evening, hardly sparing a thought for her beloved child. She hoped Edith Abbot would have the sense to call a physician, if necessary, and contact her if Lili's condition worsened. And that Jacob Abbot would stay out of it.

Sir William had escorted Eleanor back to the cottage. After he'd gone, she opened the door and glanced around the yard. It was ridiculous, but she'd been hoping Hugh would be there waiting for her. Her brain was growing addled, no doubt about it. She curled up on her side, said her prayers, and finally drifted off.

Chapter Twelve

The following week

Hugh had ordered an Argand lamp from London, and it finally arrived. He wished using it were a bit less complicated, but after he figured it out himself, he would teach Eleanor. The industrious Ned had purchased two wrought iron candlestands for him, and Hugh had experimented with mirrors as reflectors. The problem was, in the small cottage, there wasn't enough space for a large enough mirror. Perhaps he could find a piece of hardware to accommodate one. In the meantime, he could present Eleanor with the candlestands and lamp.

All this took his mind off the missive he'd received this morning from the clerk of the parish. The citizens of Haslemere wished to honor him with a ball. Of all the crackbrained ideas, this one claimed the prize. He'd dreaded having to appear at Court to receive his knighthood, and now to be subjected to a ball was too much. But how could he refuse without seeming churlish? The organizers were already forging ahead, even sending him a guest list for his approval. His mother and brother, of course, were on the list.

A light tap on the door, and Ned entered. "Are you ready to go?"

Throwing the letter down, Hugh sighed. "Yes. Should we take a cart?"

"I think so. Though it's not far to Miss Broxton's cottage, the wrought iron is heavy, as is the lamp. And the tin of oil."

Hugh nodded. "Let's see to it, then."

• • •

Eleanor was attaching a flounce to the hem of a ball gown while the light held. The end-of-season demands were killing them. Jane and Minnie arrived by eight o'clock and worked until four or five, with barely a pause for a bite at midday.

Though she had not had time to visit Lili again, Edith Abbot had sent Eleanor a short note telling her the child had recovered from her earache. It had not been necessary to summon the physician.

Thank God.

As for Hugh, Eleanor hadn't seen him since he'd escorted her to her parents' and kissed her in the woods. She spent half her waking hours dreaming of it, reliving the kiss. It simply would not do. She couldn't keep changing her mind about him, one minute putting him off, the next assuring herself they could simply be friends. Friends didn't kiss like that. Or touch each other with such abandon. Her rational mind told her that where Hugh was concerned, a friendship would not be possible. And if they became intimate, she wouldn't be able to keep Lili a secret from him.

Concentrate on your work, Eleanor. One stitch. Another. She was weary of it, and lately, especially at night when exhaustion set in, she didn't know how much longer she could keep up the long workdays. But she must be able to provide for Lili before she could bring the child to live with her.

And therein lay another predicament. She hadn't the slightest idea of how she would explain Lili to friends, neighbors…Hugh. Lately she'd been thinking the best solution would be to move to another part of England. Her mother would probably approve, since any revelation of Lili would disgrace the family. There were Broxton cousins in Devon. Her parents had sent her to them once her pregnancy had become obvious, and Eleanor had given birth there. They were kind, and they already knew about Lili.

A knock at the door interrupted her train of thought. *Drat.* Who could that be? They'd no time for visitors. While Eleanor remained hunched over her work, Jane rose and went to see who it was.

When she heard Hugh's voice, she looked up. For pity's sake, she was a mess. Her hair was falling from its knot, and her face was pinched in concentration; the dress she'd donned this morning was one of her oldest and most worn frocks. A work dress. *Ugh.* A less than inspiring sight. She got to her feet, only then noticing another man had entered behind Hugh. Ned Martin, whom she had known for years.

"Don't let the kitten in!" Eleanor shouted, too late. The energetic little ball of fluff hurtled past them before anybody could stop her. Eleanor, used to this by now, ran her to ground rather quickly. "Beatrice, you minx. You know you're not allowed in here."

"Beatrice?" Hugh said.

"When you gave her to me, you said she was a fair lady. So I named her Beatrice."

Hugh grinned. "*Much Ado About Nothing.*"

She nodded, glancing toward the others. "Sir Hugh. You have met Jane and Minnie, I believe."

"Of course. Ladies." He nodded in their direction,

producing blushes and giggles from the girls. "Miss Broxton, do you know Mr. Martin?"

"Of course." Eleanor stepped forward and shook his hand. "Hello, Ned. I hope you and your family are well."

"Very well, Miss Broxton. I am Sir Hugh's steward now."

"And general factotum," Hugh said, laughing. "The man can do anything. And does."

Hugh's face, even at this hour, was shadowed with dark stubble, which served to enhance his rugged attractiveness. While her dowdiness was on display for all to see, Hugh looked every bit the handsome country gentleman, in buff britches, bright linen shirt, ivory waistcoat, and the green coat she'd seen him in before. He wore it so well.

Stop it, Eleanor. She was staring, for pity's sake. And standing there like a helpless ninny.

When nobody spoke, Hugh said, "We've come to assist with the lighting."

"You have?" Eleanor replied stupidly.

Hugh laughed. "I told you I'd ponder it, didn't I? I'm a man of my word."

"We've tried various solutions before. Nothing really works."

"But I—that is, Ned and I—have never tackled the problem. And we have a few ideas."

Eleanor's face must have shown her skepticism, because Hugh said, "I have the smartest architect in England working for me. As well as the cleverest steward in the county."

Why not let them get on with it? Then they'd leave and she and the girls could get back to work. "Very well. Perhaps you'll have more luck than we did." Why was she being so obstinate? They only wanted to help, after all. But Eleanor knew it was because she had just, for the umpteenth time, dismissed the idea of Hugh. Of herself and Hugh. And now he was complicating things again. Encroaching on her life.

The two men disappeared out the door and returned with two large wrought iron candlestands. Eleanor had seen them in private homes occasionally, but had never thought of using them here. While Ned was inserting the beeswax candles they had brought into the holders, Hugh slipped outside, coming back in with a lamp of a kind she'd never seen before.

"It's an Argand lamp," he said. "It burns whale oil, and doesn't smoke or smell bad."

"But the wick…"

"Only needs to be trimmed a few times a day. And the flame is brighter than you'll have seen before." He took her arm and led her to the table. "Allow me to show you how it works." They all watched while Hugh demonstrated how to fill the reservoir, trim the wick, and clean the mechanisms.

As if they'd worked it out ahead of time, Ned began to light all the candles while Hugh poured oil into the reservoir and got the lamp going. Ned asked the three women where they thought the candlestands would be most effective, and eventually, they all stepped back and surveyed the newly lighted work area.

"By all the saints," Jane said, "we can see! Look, miss, what an improvement it is!" Minnie clapped her hands in excitement.

But Eleanor said nothing. *God said, let there be light. And there was light.* She felt tears gathering in her eyes. "I'd like a word in private with Sir Hugh, if you would pardon us for a moment." Her voice sounded as if it was coming from a long way off. Before she knew it, they were gone, and she and Hugh were alone, facing each other.

"This was so kind of you, Hugh. I don't know what to say." She brushed a tear off her cheek.

He edged closer. "Don't cry, Eleanor."

She reached out a hand and flattened it against his chest. "But how could I fail to? Nobody has done anything like this for me in such a long time. I don't know when, or even if, I can repay you."

Now he was smoothing her tears away with his thumb. "This is a gift. I don't want you to repay me."

"A lady cannot accept gifts of such great expense from a man. You know that."

"They're hardly personal. And nobody needs to know."

"The girls will talk. It will be all over Haslemere by tomorrow."

"Ask them not to. Or tell them you're paying me for everything. I don't care what you say, just don't let it be no." He grabbed her shoulders and spun her toward the light. "Look, Eleanor. Have you ever seen the like?"

She laughed through her tears. "No, indeed, I have not."

She turned toward him. "I see what you're doing, Hugh Grey. You're trying to worm your way into my life. You think if you make my work easier, I shall tell you everything about myself, because, well, how could I not? I'll owe you so much and be so grateful. So bloody grateful, you'll own me. Isn't that what this is really about? Isn't that why you want to help me?" She ended her rant on a gasping sob.

Hugh looked stunned. "You've got it wrong, Eleanor. Most of it, anyway. I don't care about your secrets. I don't want to own you. Yes, I do wish to make your life, your work, easier, because frankly, sometimes it hurts like hell to see you so tired all the time. And sad. In case you haven't already guessed, I'm exceedingly fond of you, and it vexes me no end."

Eleanor felt a little blip in her heart. She grabbed him by the lapels and kissed his lips, his face, every surface she could reach. And he let her, his breath coming in short bursts, until finally he gently pushed her away and called the others back inside.

· · ·

Two weeks later

The final weeks of May were hectic. Hugh had reluctantly accepted the offer of a ball in his honor, to be held at the assembly rooms in Haslemere on June 16, and after adding a few names, approved the guest list. While he could not pretend he was looking forward to the event, he'd made peace with his decision to allow the plans to proceed.

Work on his house had progressed rapidly, thanks to a long spell of fine weather. The roof was on, and plastering of the interior walls was under way. With the builder's approval, Hugh had been moving his personal belongings into his new bedchamber. He had ordered a bed, due to be delivered any day, from a specialty furniture maker in London.

Hugh wondered if he would ever get Eleanor into that bed.

Just thinking of it set up a pulsating throb of pleasure that went straight to his groin. When he considered it might never happen, his chest felt hollow.

Since the day of the lighting scheme at the cottage, Hugh had been ruminating about Eleanor and the way she'd lashed out at him. And, almost simultaneously, had thanked him over and over and smothered him with her sweet kisses. Something was amiss with her. Whatever it was pushed her to work herself half to death and put that sadness in her eyes. He'd told the truth, perhaps unwisely, when he'd said he couldn't stand seeing her that way, and most of the time she appeared far worse than he'd described.

Since the morning he'd first seen Eleanor, after his return from Canada, he'd sensed something different about her. When he had met her at the house party three years ago, she had been young and immature. He'd been fascinated by her naiveté, her girlish charm. So completely opposite from him. And then, later the same year, their liaison. She'd been like a different person, no longer a girl, but a mature woman, confident in what she wanted. Full of sensuality. Neither time had she seemed burdened by some unnamed sorrow as she did now.

What had driven her to move from her family home and work impossible hours? The one time he'd questioned her about it, the day they'd gone driving in Hyde Park, she had claimed she wanted her independence and a life separate from her parents. He'd countered by saying most ladies achieved that by marriage. As he recalled, she had a poor opinion of the matrimonial state. She had said she wanted her life to have purpose.

All well and good, but did she need to cut herself off from the joys of young womanhood and let her "purpose" consume her? There was more to it, he was sure. Heartbreak, or a misfortune she was concealing. Why else would she drive herself so unmercifully?

Several times during these last few weeks, he'd wanted to call on her. He had gotten halfway to her cottage two or three times, only to turn around. How would she receive him, after she'd scolded him about intruding on her privacy? But he wished to banish his doubts. If she didn't want him near her, she could say so. She required someone to turn to, and who else was there? What if he weren't there when she needed him?

Ned walked in, interrupting his reverie, and Hugh threw the dregs of his tea on the hearth. "How are you fixed for ball dress, my friend?"

Ned looked baffled. Hugh, laughing, clapped him on the shoulder, and they headed for the building site together.

• • •

Later, when the sun was in the first stages of its descent,

Eleanor made her way toward Longmere. If Hugh, stubborn man, wouldn't come to her, she would go to him. She was tired of waiting on him to call. She had sent the girls home early and gone up to the house to bathe and change. There'd been no need to explain herself to anybody, since her father was out and her mother was resting.

Now here she was, approaching the site, wearing her best walking dress, one she'd made herself. A soft blue cambric, with a square décolletage, the very one she'd had on that day at the mere when she'd watched Hugh bathing. An involuntary sigh escaped. Best not to dwell on that. Because she wanted her hands to be occupied, she'd begged some apple tarts from the cook and tucked them, along with the empty milk jug, into the basket Hugh had left her the night he'd brought her the kitten.

Although Hugh couldn't have heard her, he glanced up from his work as if he'd grown a pair of antennae and sensed her approach. He and Ned Martin were at either end of a two-man saw. Hugh's sleeves were rolled up, and thick cords of muscle bulged as he wielded the saw. Before his look turned sheepish, she detected an appreciative gleam in his eye. After saying a word to Ned, he walked toward her.

"Eleanor. Welcome. Will you excuse me for a moment?" Before she could respond, he dashed into the house. Probably to change, but she rather wished he wouldn't. Seeing him wearing nothing but formfitting britches and an unbuttoned shirt pulling loose at the waist had its attractions. Not to mention the mussed hair and sweating brow.

He was back, adjusting his coat sleeves as he approached her, before she'd even finished her wicked fantasies about him. "What is in the basket?" he asked, relieving her of it.

"Some apple tarts, made by our cook, and the milk jug you brought over with Beatrice. Empty. I decided to accept your offer of showing me the progress you're making."

"Ah. My thanks. For the tarts. Would you like to see the house? It's perfectly safe inside if we dodge the laborers going about their work."

"Please. I want to see everything." She paused a moment, gazing up at the newly built structure. "I can hardly take it in, Hugh, the old place gone. Somehow I didn't expect that."

"You did not realize I'd had the house razed?" Hugh winged his arm, and she grasped it. "That was not my original plan, but after inspecting it, the architect deemed it unsafe." Gesturing to an expanse of ground, he said, "This will be the front gardens. Whatever was once here is long gone." When they entered the house, they were greeted by a cacophony of hammering, sawing, sanding. Hugh dropped the basket onto a table.

"It's a bit difficult to envision everything, but I'll try to explain." He glanced up. "We are standing in the entry hall. As you can see, it has a high ceiling. I haven't made up my mind how to decorate it, but nothing too grand."

He went on. "To your left is the dining room, with kitchens and larder to the rear."

"Kitchens on the ground floor?" Eleanor said. "That's unique."

Hugh laughed. "I prefer my food hot. Transporting it upstairs from the basement doesn't allow that, and it amounts to more work for the servants who must carry it up."

He touched her shoulder, gently turning her toward the opposite side. "Over here is a parlor or morning room, whatever you prefer to call it."

"Lovely," Eleanor said. "It will get plenty of light." It was hard to concentrate when he kept touching her.

"Let's walk toward the back. We're in the central hall now. On your right is a billiard or card room." They had arrived at the rear of the house. "French doors here, leading to the terrace and gardens. Not constructed yet, of course."

"And what's this on the right? It looks like a large space."

"This, I have the feeling, will be my favorite part of the house. The library and study."

"Oh, Hugh, this will be a wonderful room. The windows face your back gardens. So very cozy on cold winter days."

He eyed her speculatively, a sparkle in his eye, and she thought he might have kissed her if they'd been alone. Instead, he said in a low voice, "Cozy, yes." His breath was featherlight against her ear, and she felt her face flood with warmth. Hugh smiled. "Let's go upstairs."

They had to walk back to the front to get to the stairs, and he grasped her arm again. "Mind your step. The floor is littered with building debris." He didn't let go of her until they'd reached the first floor. "As you can see, this is a gallery of sorts." Again, he glanced around, as if he couldn't quite believe this belonged to him. "Not for portraits; the Grey family hasn't any."

The space looked down over the entry hall. "I love it," Eleanor said. "And maybe you will have portraits someday."

His smile was wry. "Perhaps. At the back, through these doors, is a drawing room. This space, taken in its entirety, could be opened up for entertainments, if the occasion arises."

Now he took her hand and guided her down a hallway off the gallery. He stopped at the first room, and Eleanor peeked inside. "Oh!" This was obviously Hugh's bedchamber, which was partially furnished. Embarrassed, she spun around, but not before she'd caught a glimpse of the rumpled shirt and worn britches he'd been wearing when she arrived. They lay in a heap on the bed, which was an impressive piece of furniture. Made from a dark wood, mahogany most likely, and massive. It made quite a statement. *The bed of the lord of the manor.* Could she help it if her heart beat a little faster?

"My personal domain," Hugh said, lifting an eyebrow at her.

"I gathered as much," she said, ducking her head. There was no one about up here, and the noise of the workmen would drown out any sounds. If they... *Oh, Lord, pull yourself together, Eleanor.*

Hugh was gazing at her as though he was thinking the same thing she was. "That's a fetching dress you're wearing, Eleanor. One I believe I've seen before."

Oh, dear God, he remembered. Blood rushed to warm her cheeks.

"I wish you weren't wearing this bit, here. What's it called? A fish-something?" He glided a finger along the inner edges of her bodice.

She sucked in a breath. "It's a fichu."

"Yes, that's it." He stepped closer. "I quite like it. The dress, I mean. Minus the fichu." He gave her a devilish smile, then said, "We should go back downstairs."

"Yes, of course," Eleanor managed to stammer, doubting her ability to walk on her trembling legs.

Once they were outside, he pointed out the various materials yet to be incorporated into the house. "The glaziers haven't started yet, but soon. The first floor windows are not yet hung."

He pointed out the brickmakers, and then took her over to some long tables where carpenters were hard at work constructing cupboards, shelves, moldings, and doors. Just then, Ned called to Hugh.

"Pardon me for a moment, Eleanor," he said, striding off.

While she watched, one of the carpenters glanced up, and Eleanor found herself looking into the malicious eyes of Jacob Abbot.

She nearly shrieked.

Chapter Thirteen

"Well, if it isn't Miss Broxton," Abbot said. He'd been sanding a door, but set it aside and came around the table toward her. She took a step back. "Didn't know you were a friend of Mr. Grey's."

Nonsensically, she said, "Sir Hugh. Call him Sir Hugh."

His laugh was sharp. He lowered his head close to hers, and in that act Eleanor saw a drowning of all her hopes for the future. Abbot was about to expose her, to tell Hugh her secret, and her life with Lili would be swept away like so much flotsam and jetsam. Abbot had a discolored incisor, and how odd she'd never noticed it before. It rather sickened her to look at it.

"Does Mr…Sir Hugh know about the little one? Know you're the mother of a bastard?" he whispered.

Eleanor came to her senses. No matter what havoc Abbot was about to wreak, she couldn't be seen like this with him. She spun and blindly moved away from him. And bumped into Hugh's solid chest.

"Are you all right, Miss Broxton?" He glanced over her

shoulder. "Get back to work, Mr. Abbot." Hugh offered his arm, and she grabbed it and held on tight. They walked toward the path.

"I must go," Eleanor said, trying not to sound as flustered as she felt.

"I'm not blind, Eleanor. Something happened. Did he hurt you? Insult you?"

"No, nothing like that. I'm fine."

"Will you be home tonight? At the cottage, I mean?"

She was trembling all over and had to get away before he noticed. "Probably. I don't know. Good-bye, Hugh. Thank you for the tour."

• • •

Hugh remained standing where the path disappeared into the woods, hands on hips, staring at nothing. What had happened? To his gratification, Eleanor had appeared to love the house as much as he did. While he was guiding her through the rooms, he couldn't help but envision her in each one. The two of them breaking their fast in the dining room while they looked over their correspondence and the newspapers; curled up together in the library, reading; greeting guests in the gallery. And Eleanor in his bed, naked, splendid, letting him worship her with his eyes and then his body.

And then he'd stepped away for a moment, and it had all gone to hell. Hugh had no idea what had occurred with Abbot. Whatever it was had rattled her so badly, she could barely speak sensibly and had insisted on leaving immediately.

Tonight he would call on her and get to the bottom of this. If Abbot had hurt her in some way, Hugh would let the man go instantly.

• • •

Eleanor could not remember how she arrived back at the cottage. But the next time she had a coherent thought, she was standing inside the main room. Out of habit, she stirred the fire back to life and placed the teakettle on the hangar. A warm drink would restore her senses.

While the water was heating, she moved about the cottage straightening, sorting, and putting away. She moved the mannequin to the back room, out of sight, and pushed the cutting table under the shelves near the door. Then she ran her hands over each garment they were currently working on—a gown of a fine, white muslin, a striped satin petticoat, and the pelisse Jane was still embroidering, although she was nearly done now. She held them against her face and inhaled the clean scent of them. When the water had boiled, she brewed the tea in her china teapot, served herself, and sat down. After a few swallows, her brain began functioning again.

What to do about Abbot? It was only a matter of time until he demanded something from her. Money, probably. With a shudder, she imagined what else it could be. But Abbot had never made any advances toward her, had never behaved in a lewd or suggestive manner, merely a menacing one. Whatever his demands, she would be forced to a decision. Pay him off. Or refuse, and wait for him to inform Hugh of Lili's existence. Or tell Hugh herself. In her deepest self, she knew that was the most rational and unselfish choice.

If she called Abbot's bluff and refused to meet his demands, was he truly prepared to reveal her secret? By doing so, he and his wife would lose the extra income she and her father provided for Lili's care. And he would also sacrifice his employment at Longmere. Surely, he couldn't afford to lose both sources of income.

Hugh, meanwhile, was sure to quiz her about Abbot. She had to invent a plausible explanation, or he would become suspicious. That was his nature, especially where she was concerned.

Eleanor had loved seeing Hugh's house, had even imagined herself as its mistress, and Lili running about from room to room. She needed to rid her mind of such fantasies. They were dreams. Impossible dreams. Because when Hugh learned about his daughter, he may want nothing more to do with Eleanor. If he acknowledged his child, the scandal would be most unwelcome. Given how he felt about his own mother, heaven only knew what he'd think about Eleanor's decisions regarding Lili.

Someone knocked on the door, and she had a wild notion it would be Abbot. But it was much more likely to be Hugh. He'd as much as said he was coming. With a hesitant voice, she asked, "Who is it?"

"It's Hugh, Eleanor. May I come in?" He stood a moment in the doorway, a halo of fading daylight framing his big body. He was holding something, the basket she'd brought him earlier. "I'm glad to see you are being more cautious about visitors," he said. "Do you realize you're sitting in the dark?"

"Oh." No, she had not. It had still been daylight when she'd arrived back at the cottage. Night must have settled in as she lingered at the worktable, musing. She got to her feet and said, "I'll light some candles."

"Let me." Holding up the basket, he said, "I brought the apple tarts. Thought we might need something for breakfast." And as though he hadn't said anything to turn her world topsy-turvy, he set about igniting the spills for the candlelighting.

Should she argue? Ask him to leave? She could do neither. The thought of spending the night with him raised gooseflesh, made her breath catch, sent prickles to every nerve ending. "Would you like tea? I was just having some."

"No. I don't want anything. I came to see you were well. Will you tell me what Jacob Abbot said that upset you?" He paused and looked at her.

She loved his voice. In the darkness, it was a violin, vibrating with a spellbinding resonance. But that was not what she should be paying attention to at the moment. "It was nothing. He mistook me for another acquaintance and said something…inappropriate. It startled me."

Hugh walked toward her. "He shouldn't speak in such a way to a lady. I'll have him sacked tomorrow."

"No. Please don't do that. He didn't know—"

"Abbot knew well enough he was addressing a lady and that you were my guest."

"He may need this job to support his family. He's an uneducated man, unrefined, and no doubt accustomed to such talk. Give him another chance."

"You defend him most heartily, Eleanor. Do you have a previous acquaintance with him?"

"No, of course not. I simply believe you shouldn't judge him so harshly."

He studied her face, her eyes, and she wasn't sure what he would discover there. Fear? Deception? After a long moment, he gave a decisive nod. "Very well. But you will tell me if anything else untoward happens with him. Promise me that much."

Relief flooded her. "Of course."

He caught her hand, raised it, and lightly kissed her fingers. His touch was electric. When he drew her close, she did not resist, although the thinking part of her reckoned that would be the wiser course of action.

"Eleanor, if you don't want me here, tell me at once." His voice was both a plea and a demand.

"Don't leave, Hugh. I couldn't bear it if you left."

He crushed her to him with one arm, his other hand gripping the back of her head, smoothing her hair and sliding down to her neck. Before she could reply, his lips had covered hers.

And then it was too late to refuse him, because she wanted him so very much. Had been wanting him for two long years. When their tongues collided, he drew back and then quickly renewed his sensual invasion, turning his head, kissing her harder and more fiercely than the first time. It was fearsome and exquisite all at once. She nipped at his bottom lip, then sucked it into her mouth. When their teeth clashed, they both laughed.

Eleanor unbuttoned his coat and tugged his shirt free of his britches, sliding her hands beneath it. She skimmed her fingers over the dark hair on his chest, caressing each sculpted sinew. Hard and soft at the same time. Like stone and satin. With a gasp, Hugh picked her up and carried her to the back room. She'd forgotten her bed was covered with journals, her sketch pad, swatches of fabric, patterns. Hugh set her down and with one hand swept it all to the floor.

Ordinarily, this would have driven her mad, but another kind of madness was overtaking her. "Turn around," Hugh commanded. He began to unfasten her dress, dropping kisses on her nape while his fingers fumbled with the hooks. "Can't you design something that doesn't require so much work to get in and out of?"

Eleanor laughed, then reached back and ran a hand over his thigh, until finally, brazenly, she found his erection and caressed it.

"If you continue with that, this will be over before it starts." At last he finished and shoved her dress down until it lay in a puddle of cambric at her feet. "Now the damnable stays. You women and your excess apparel. I grow weary of it." Eleanor couldn't help giggling.

When he'd finished unlacing her, she was left in nothing but her stockings and gauzy chemise. Hugh moved the candle holder so that more light reflected on her. He glided his hands up her calves, up her thighs, until he found her garter, which he untied in one yank. And then he slid her stocking down, lifted her foot, and pulled it off. He repeated the process with the other leg, but this time while doing so, he leaned his head into her and did wicked things with his mouth, things that made her moan with pleasure. Who would have guessed a tongue could feel that good through fabric?

"Hugh, you're torturing me," she said, half serious.

"*Mmm.* Am I?"

"I want your clothes off, Sir Hugh. Now."

He smiled, tried to hide it, but then laughed. "If that is what you want, far be it from me to gainsay you." He rose, tugged his shirt off, then his boots. When that was done, he pulled off his britches. Eleanor thought it was probably gauche to stare, but she couldn't help it. Since that day at the pond, when he'd risen from the water, she'd known, if given the chance, that's exactly what she would do.

Hugh's shaft rose from its nest of black hair, his bollocks taut beneath. "What should I do now, my goddess? Athena, are you?"

"Lie on the bed. I want to see you." Her throat was so dry, it was difficult to speak.

He did as she asked, stretching out with his head propped in one hand. "What would you like to do to me, Eleanor?" His dark gaze seared her.

"Touch you all over. With my hands. With my mouth."

He lay back and opened his arms. "Have at it, my beautiful warrior."

She climbed onto the bed and straddled him, lifting her chemise out of the way. Hugh motioned her toward him. "Let's remove this, shall we?" He pulled it off in one swift motion. Now he was sitting up, his shaft rising between them. He wrapped her in his arms, and they were so close, as close as two people could be outside of the ultimate joining. His arousal pushed into her abdomen. And then he kissed her, running his hands down her back to her bottom.

He smelled of sawdust. And the woods, and summer. Fresh and strong and male.

"I know this was your time to explore, but will you give me just a moment?"

Blushing, she nodded. How could she refuse him?

"Don't be embarrassed, sweetheart. Your breasts are perfection. I couldn't see them properly in the stable that night." He held one in the palm of each hand, massaging, gazing at her face and then back at her breasts. He lightly caressed their tips until she gasped his name. Heat pooled between her legs, along with a torturous pressure begging to be relieved.

He chuckled softly and lay down. Eleanor began by kissing and licking his chest, then grazing his nipples with her teeth. Judging from his intake of breath, Hugh enjoyed that, as she suspected he might. She nuzzled her face into his neck and peppered it with kisses. Then she worked her way down, kissing, nipping, dipping her tongue into his navel. And there was his maleness, waiting for her attention.

She knew, she'd heard, that men liked women to…to kiss their male parts, but she didn't quite have the courage to do it. Instead she wrapped her fingers around his member and, gently twisting and rotating her hand, moved up toward the crown at the tip. He moaned and moved his hips until they found a rhythm together.

"Oh, God, Eleanor, I must have you now." He pulled himself up and rolled her onto her back. She opened her legs for him, and his fingers played, teased, until she was reduced to moaning and begging.

"Stop. No, don't you dare stop. Oh God, Hugh."

He trailed a finger downward and slid it inside her. A slow smile spread over his face. "You're ready, my Athena."

All at once he was there, pressing into her, burying

himself inside her. As he stroked in and out, a pulsating need gripped her. Hugh propped himself on one arm, using his other hand to find her sensitive bud. With every thrust, he lightly massaged it, until she came with a piercing, burning sweetness. She clung to Hugh, repeating his name over and over while the exquisite pleasure peaked and slowly began to ease.

And then he drove into her again, this time with a greater urgency, and she felt him deep inside. Eleanor ran her hands up his arms and over his chest, squeezing his nipples between her fingers. Before she realized what he was doing, he'd withdrawn from her, just as he cried out his pleasure and spilled onto the sheet. He lowered himself onto her, wrapping his arms around her and holding her so close she could barely catch her breath.

When he finally lifted off her, he said, "I'm sorry, love. To prevent a child, you see."

Yes, she did see. Clearly, he was more concerned with the consequences than he'd been the first time they had made love. She was glad he'd had the presence of mind to withdraw. Hugh got out of bed and fished a handkerchief from a pocket inside his coat. He cleaned the mattress and threw the cloth to the floor. Eleanor watched him, knowing what he was looking for.

"In the basket by the door. Fabric scraps." He grabbed one and handed it to her, discreetly looking away while she tidied herself.

He climbed into the bed and spooned himself around her, kissing her nape, running his big hands over her. Had anything ever felt this good? This perfect? They fell asleep like that, with his arms holding her close against him.

• • •

When Hugh awoke, the gossamer light of dawn was filtering through the window. Eleanor lay on her side, facing away from him, a wash of her dark blond hair flowing over the pillow. Leaning down, he dropped a kiss on her bare shoulder. She did not stir.

They had company on the bed. Eleanor's little dog, Bobby, had slept there with them at least part of the night. Now he was fidgeting, and Hugh thought he'd better let him out before he woke Eleanor. Not wishing to disturb her, he climbed carefully out of bed and pulled on his britches and shirt.

After he let the dog out, he prodded the fire to life, added kindling and charcoal, and put the kettle on. He wondered momentarily where the kitten was. She hadn't been around since he'd arrived last night. He'd ask Eleanor later.

It felt exceedingly odd to be in this room without her, so clearly a ladies' domain, so he stepped out into the garden and leaned against the fence. His thoughts turned instantly to Eleanor and what had passed between them last night. She had given herself to him, joyfully and with abandon. He loved her passionate nature, her fearless lovemaking. He hoped to hell she wouldn't hold him at arm's length, and there was every possibility she would choose to do so once again. It was part of her secretiveness, her melancholy, and she might not be able to let it go.

There was more to the Jacob Abbot story than she'd admitted. She wasn't the missish type who would be embarrassed to tell him what the man had said. He was of a mind to fire Abbot, despite Eleanor's urging him not to. What could Abbot have said to upset her so? Hugh had the feeling it was related to the part of her she withheld from him. If only he could break down that barrier she'd built around herself. For her own protection, he assumed. But protection from what? The urge to know, to discover her secrets, was strong, but if he pressed her, she would retreat. And hadn't he told her he didn't want to know her secrets? He would need to tread lightly or run the risk of scaring her off. In his mind, they had reached a turning point. There was no going back now, not for him.

The door opened. Hugh turned and glimpsed her standing in the doorway, looking uncertain. She wore her chemise and a shawl draped about her shoulders. Smiling, he ambled over to greet her. "Good morning, Eleanor." Grasping her shoulders, he pressed a kiss to her forehead. She surprised him by gripping his arms, rising on her toes, and kissing him on the mouth. The kiss tasted of the sweet softness of morning, and yet it bespoke desire and longing. And it was incredibly arousing. Gathering her up in his arms, he drew her close and said, "You didn't think you could kiss me like that without any consequences, did you?"

"So you think I am seducing you? Again?" She laughed softly while he kissed his way down toward her breasts.

"Oh, hell. Let's do this the right way." He picked her up and carried her inside to the bed. The very small bed. "The next time you seduce me, we'll be in my bed, which was actually made to accommodate two people."

If last night's lovemaking had been about the culmination of desire, the frenzied coming together of two people who had barely been keeping their attraction for each other under control, this morning's was slow and sweet and achingly tender, and Hugh loved every minute of it. She smelled of rumpled sheets and languor. And the musk of a woman's sex. He explored each of her perfect breasts, sucking lightly on the tips, delighted when she moaned her pleasure. Eleanor stroked his chest, and then ran her hands down his back and over his arse. *Oh holy God.* Her touch was going to send him to oblivion. He flipped her to her side, pulling her against him, stroking her thighs until she opened her legs for him. Dipping his fingers into her folds, he sought her wet center and her sweet bud. She was ready for him.

When she reached back and wrapped her hand around his cock, he nearly leaped off the bed. Lips at her ear, he said, "Now. Please, now." He entered her from the rear, and she gasped. Hugh went still. "Did I hurt you, darling?" he croaked out.

"It feels…very full. But good. I like it."

He moved slowly, allowing her time to adjust. When she was ready, he found the core of her and stroked, and her whimpers whet his desire even more. "That's it, love. Let go. Let go." And she did, with a breath that burst out of her with such force it shocked them both.

He couldn't wait any longer. With his hands clutching her hips, he drove deep into her. Eleanor was perfect for him. She fit him like a kidskin glove. At the end, he thought the angels had come for him, his spasms coming long and hard and endlessly.

They remained exactly as they were. Hugh dozed off and Eleanor must have as well. When, at length, she moved away from him, taking her warmth with her, he protested. "No. Don't."

"Hugh, it's late. I must dress, and you must leave."

"Oh hell. Truly?"

"Yes. The girls will be here in no time."

"Couldn't we at least have tea and the apple tarts?"

"Just like a man, always thinking about food." Hugh heard the smile in her voice. She was scurrying about, looking for her clothing. "Help me lace my stays," she said, after pulling her chemise over her head.

"My pleasure." He climbed off the bed and donned britches and shirt, then laced her stays and did up the fastenings on her dress, a different one than she'd worn yesterday. "Not wearing the blue today. I'm exceedingly fond of that one."

Eleanor rushed him out the door, handing him an apple tart to eat on his way back to Longmere. He kissed her quickly, then remembered about the kitten. "Where is Beatrice? What have you done with her? You're not one of those cruel people who drowns kitties, are you?"

She laughed. "She is spending some time at the Broxton stables. I simply couldn't have her here. But I'll bring her back when she's grown."

"One more thing. You and your parents should have received an invitation to a ball being held in my honor."

"Oh? When is it?"

"Next week." He cocked his head at her. "Please say you'll come." He stepped close and slid his hand through the hair at her temple, cupping her face with his palm. And then he whispered, "I would be sorely disappointed if you did not."

"Of course," she said, smiling. "I'll be there."

Chapter Fourteen

After surveying the cottage interior and getting rid of all traces of Hugh, Eleanor brewed herself a cup of tea and settled on the garden bench with an apple tart. Euphoria prevailed. Was this what heaven was like?

Sadly, Eleanor discovered euphoria was fleeting. She must face reality. She had a child with Hugh, and she'd kept that child from him. Lili's foster father was primed to blackmail her, if her deductions were accurate. The man was already denying her access to Lili on occasion, or, at the very least, making her visits difficult and worrying. And she suspected one or both of her parents might be in collusion with Abbot.

Things were spinning out of control, and she'd no bloody idea how to fix them.

Her chest grew tight with gnawing dread. *Drink your tea. Eat.* She forced herself to swallow some of the strong brew and take a few bites of the tart, then she rose and paced around the garden. There had to be a way.

By the time Jane and Minnie had arrived, Eleanor had a plan. Was she brave enough to carry it out? Telling Hugh about Lili seemed the best course of action, despite the consequences for all of them. Hugh was the best of men. He might be angry at first, but when she explained her reasons for withholding the truth, perhaps he would forgive her.

Once Hugh knew the truth, Eleanor didn't know what would come next. He may not wish to acknowledge a child born outside of marriage. He may be too angry to forgive her deception. She must steel herself to accept his decision, no matter what.

Perhaps he would insist on marrying her, after he'd had sufficient time to absorb everything. She'd thought she didn't want to marry him, but now…well, now things were different. She liked him. Maybe even loved him. They were compatible physically, and they had always enjoyed each other's company. They would be good parents to Lili.

What was the point of dwelling upon a serendipitous outcome? Certain as she was that Hugh cared for her, his feelings could be upended by her revealing Lili. Speaking of Lili, it was time for a visit. Eleanor hadn't been back since her daughter's illness, and given all she'd learned about Abbot, she was worried about Lili's well-being. If she completed the vandyking and rouleau trim on the muslin dress before noon, she would borrow the gig and head for the Abbots'. She hoped Jacob Abbot would be at Longmere and not at his home.

A few hours later, Eleanor approached the Abbot home with fear knotting her stomach. How ironic, to experience such unpleasant feelings during what should be a happy occasion, both for herself and Lili. The door crashed open before she'd even stepped down from the gig, and Jacob Abbot strode toward her with a look meant to intimidate.

He stopped, standing so close to her she could see the tiny red blood vessels in the whites of his eyes. Eleanor stood her ground. "Step back, Mr. Abbot."

He didn't move. "What did you tell Grey about me?"

"I won't answer until you step back."

Grudgingly, he moved a few feet away from her. "Go on, then. Out with it."

"He asked me what you'd said to upset me. He wanted to sack you immediately, but I told him to give you another chance."

"I don't believe you. If that's true, why did the steward tell me to take the day off today?"

"I have no way of knowing what passes between you and your employers, Mr. Abbot." When he didn't respond, she said, "Now, if you'll excuse me, I'm here to see Lili."

When she tried to sidestep around him and walk toward the house, he said, "Not so fast. The little girl's not available."

Eleanor wanted to scream her frustration, but she knew that would make matters worse. She kept walking until Abbot grabbed her arm and jerked her to a stop.

"Let go of me! You cannot stop me from seeing Lili."

"You and me have matters to talk over."

So here it was. Though she'd feared his intentions, she'd been able—temporarily—to consign her worries to the back of her mind. "What can we possibly have to talk over?"

"Looks like you and Sir Hugh are good friends. I'd wager he might like to know he's got a little girl."

The words hit her like a blow. Reeling with shock, Eleanor grappled for words. This could be no more than a wild guess. "That is a ridiculous statement, as you well know. Now, get out of my way."

But he blocked her once again. "A friend of mine saw you sneak into the stables with Hugh Grey one night a few years back. And lo and behold, nine months later, you've got yourself a child. That's no coincidence."

Could her heart be thumping any louder? Had Abbot known this for years, saving it up to use in some perverse way? And just who was this other person? "Your friend needs spectacles, Mr. Abbot."

He shrugged. "Maybe. Me and my wife have a lot of expenses, what with a baby coming soon. Seeing as you make a lot of blunt with that fancy dress business of yours, I thought you might want to help us out. What do you say?"

"I say that smacks of blackmail. My father and I pay you generously, more than generously, to care for Lili. And you have employment with Sir Hugh. So, no, I'm afraid there's no more money from me in the offing."

A sheen of sweat had broken out on his forehead. "You'll be sorry about that decision when I tell Grey the truth."

Would Abbot sense the underlying fear in her words? "You don't know the truth, Mr. Abbot. Speculation and lies have nothing to do with fact. Your threats are meaningless. And don't forget, one word from me to Sir Hugh and you'll be dismissed. He won't hesitate for an instant."

Arms flailing, he said, "Get out of here. Now."

Any further arguing with him would not get her anywhere. Eleanor spun around and climbed onto the gig.

All the way home, she thought of nothing besides telling Hugh about Lili. How she would do it, and when. She couldn't put it off it any longer. Eleanor could no longer risk letting her child stay with the Abbots.

• • •

The following week

Hugh hadn't been in the Haslemere assembly rooms since the night of his unforgettable liaison with Eleanor more than two years ago. Tonight's ball, in his honor, was a private one, by invitation only. Hugh arrived in his carriage, ahead of the guests. He'd been given a schedule of sorts. People would be presenting themselves at nine o'clock, and he must be ready to greet them.

He strolled into the main room and surveyed the splendor. The scene couldn't have been more different from his last visit. The organizers had gone out of their way to beautify the main room. The two enormous chandeliers were lit, and a fire blazed in the massive hearth. The musicians had already taken their places in the gallery at the far end. Violins, violas, horns, flutes. Garlands of greenery festooned the gallery up and down the room, and large urns of fresh flowers stood on high stands in niches, flanked by candelabra on either side. Perhaps the good citizens of Haslemere were finally prepared to acknowledge that he was his own man, not a copy of his father. Maybe some of them even liked him. He derived some satisfaction in that.

Mr. Beckwith, the magistrate, bustled over to him. "Sir Hugh, welcome. Very festive in here, eh?"

"My thanks for all you've done, Mr. Beckwith. I've never seen these rooms looking so grand."

Apparently, he'd said the right thing, because the other man beamed at him. "I'm glad you approve." His gaze flickered away from Hugh. "Ah, here are the first guests. I believe it is your family, Sir Hugh."

Hugh's back was to them. Unease pressed inside his chest, but he was determined to be every bit the gentleman tonight. To make up for the last time he'd seen his mother and brother. He turned slowly, and there they were, looking a bit guarded. Not that he could blame them. And, would miracles never cease, Hugh was damned glad to see them. He hastened to greet them.

"Deborah." Leaning in, he kissed her cheek. "You're looking lovely tonight." And here was his mother's beau, Freddie Cochran. "Mr. Cochran, welcome."

His brother and Cass stood by, waiting. "Cass, you are a vision, as usual. You're a lucky devil, brother." That broke the ice. They all laughed, and Hugh shook hands with Adam.

"How are you, Hugh?" he asked, looking his brother in the eye. "How does the home building progress?"

"I'm well enough. The reconstruction is coming along nicely. Why don't you see for yourself before you leave Town?" Then, looking from one to the other, Hugh said, "Won't you join me in the receiving line?"

He'd shocked them. Obviously, they hadn't expected the courtesy. But in his heart, Hugh knew it was the proper course of action. The kindest one. And truth be told, he wanted them there. He'd rather not do this alone.

Soon after they took their places, the guests began arriving. Hugh was first in the line, with his mother standing next to him. Adam might have been of more help in identifying people, but it would have seemed ill-mannered to place him before Deborah. Hugh shook so many hands, he lost count. But he was gratified to realize that he remembered many of the friends of his youth, as well as their siblings and parents. The women congratulated him on his honor; the men clapped him on the shoulder.

Ned Martin stepped up, tugging at his neck cloth and appearing altogether self-conscious in his ball attire. Hugh had to hold back a smile. "Ned, welcome. You look grand, my friend. May I introduce you to my mother?"

Eleanor was the one person Hugh gave a damn about greeting, and she hadn't come through the line yet. Since they'd made love, she'd been in his thoughts every moment. He was beginning to worry that the Broxtons had prevented Eleanor from attending, when at last he looked up and glimpsed them a little back in the line. Her parents were blocking his view of her.

Sir William, wearing a powdered wig, approached him and shook his hand warmly. "Well done, my boy. Sir Hugh now, eh? One day you must tell me what you did to earn the honor."

Hugh smiled and thanked him for coming. He was shocked—and gratified—that the older man was so cordial to him. Maybe it was due to Adam. Or maybe Sir William had finally concluded that Hugh was all right. His wife, however, was less sure. Having Eleanor so close, while forced to keep his eyes fixed on her mother, was painful. "Lady Broxton, welcome. Thank you for coming. I'm honored."

"Sir Hugh," she managed to choke out.

Deborah seemed to sense the awkwardness and took charge. "Lady Broxton! How lovely to see you again. The house party, wasn't it, when we last met?"

And then Hugh quit paying any attention, because Eleanor stood before him. Oh God, she was so lovely. Her hair was swept up, but loose strands lay curling at her cheeks and brushed her nape. She wore a lemon colored gown with quite a daring décolletage, making it difficult not to stare at her breasts. If he had his way, he would rush her out to his carriage and back to Longmere. He would have her over and over in the massive bed he'd bought with her in mind.

"Hugh?"

Holy God, he had been staring—and daydreaming. He reached for her hand and squeezed it gently. "Eleanor. I'm overwhelmed. You are so beautiful."

Her smile melted him, sent heat straight to parts that didn't need it right now. Her eyes were lit by the branches of candles in the entrance hall, and he fancied they gleamed with warmth. For him. He didn't want to let her go. "Hugh," she said. "I'm so happy to be here, but I should move on."

He laughed, like a schoolboy in the throes of first love. "Yes, but not before you've promised me the opening set."

"Of course." And then she was gone, shaking hands with all his family, and finally disappearing into the main room. What if he couldn't find her again? Ridiculous thought. He turned to the next guest. The musicians were already playing, and before too much longer, the formalities were at an end.

After they'd greeted all the stragglers, Hugh said, "My thanks to all of you. I must find my partner, as we're to lead the dance."

His family were all gazing at him with peculiar expressions. Adam was scrunching his face up painfully, as though to beat back a grin, while Cass beamed openly. His mother smiled. "She's lovely, Hugh."

Good God, is it that obvious? He supposed it was, so he took it in stride and smiled. "Enjoy yourselves." And then he went in search of Eleanor.

He found her near the entry, speaking to friends. Conversation came to a halt when he approached. He crooked an arm at her. "Miss Broxton? My dance, I believe."

• • •

Eleanor had been debating with herself whether she should tell Hugh about Lili tonight, or wait until they were completely alone. Of late, her sleep had been restless rather than restful, and she was shocked when Hugh had said she looked beautiful. Obviously, he hadn't looked closely enough. When she'd glanced in the Cheval glass before leaving her chamber, a gaunt face with dark circles under the eyes stared back at her. She felt as if she'd been sucked into a bog, unable to claw her way out.

They took their places at the top of the line, nearest the musicians. Someone gave the signal, and the dance began. It was one she knew well. She could dance her way through the steps and patterns without paying too much attention. When she glanced at Hugh, though, he was staring at her with worried eyes.

She mustered a smile and kept it in place. It wasn't hard. Hugh was magnificently, starkly handsome. His body was made for evening dress. A black coat fit snug across his shoulders—with his Knight Grand Cross badge pinned to it. Pale gray waistcoat with gold thread embroidery, and a perfectly arranged neckcloth. His pantaloons clung to his thighs like a second skin. To her amusement—or perhaps chagrin—she noticed more than a few young ladies who had their eyes on him. She had one thing to say to them.

He's mine, ladies. Hugh Grey is mine.

She corrected her posture, arranged her arms in an elegant curve, and smiled at Hugh whenever the steps brought them in physical contact. When at last they were back at the top of the line, and the dance had ended, Hugh offered his arm. "Would you care for some lemonade, Eleanor? I'm parched. All that talking in the receiving line."

She nodded, and he led her toward the refreshment table. Instead of ending up there, however, Hugh changed course, veering toward a corner partially concealed by two large potted palms. He snatched a glass of lemonade from a tray held by a footman. Grabbing her hand, he pulled her into the corner.

"Hugh," Eleanor protested. "Someone might see us."

"I very much doubt it. Look how dark it is. And nobody's paying us any mind." He gulped the lemonade until it was almost gone, then handed the glass to Eleanor. "My apologies. I should have offered it to you first."

She swallowed the rest and set the glass down. Hugh immediately caught her up in his arms and kissed her, a sweet, tender offering. He ended the kiss, and she cradled his face in her hands. "Congratulations, Sir Hugh. This has turned out to be quite a crush. You must be pleased."

He turned his head and planted a kiss on her palm before letting her go. "It appears I am not so disliked as I feared. I'm finally more than just Benjamin Grey's son."

And then Eleanor could have kicked herself. How could

she have contemplated for one moment giving him the news on this night? *His night?* The secret she was guarding was impairing her ability to think straight.

"Your family is here," she said.

"Their names were on the guest list I was sent. I couldn't very well ask that they be removed."

"They helped receive the guests right alongside you. You must have invited them to do so."

To her surprise, he said, "I've made up my mind to try for a reconciliation. The last time I saw my mother, at the dinner Adam hosted in London, I said some things I regretted. I made her cry, in fact. Afterward, I felt ashamed and disgusted with myself. And shortly thereafter, I did the same thing to you at the garden party."

She smiled. "And I forgave you."

"Yes. Thank you for that. With my family, it will be one step at a time. Perhaps tonight represents the first step."

She leaned in and kissed his cheek. "I'm so happy for you, Hugh. Now, hadn't we better get back to the festivities?"

· · ·

Hugh danced with several different partners, some amusing, some witty, some smart. And several who boasted a conventional sort of beauty. The sort that did not particularly appeal to him. Eleanor's beauty was unique. Fragile, complex, rare. Not easily defined. Even the sadness he often perceived in her eyes added to her mystique and the allure she held for him.

He glimpsed her off and on, dancing with Adam, Ned, and other young men in attendance. She was probably acquainted with many of them. And once he caught her standing alone, looking out at the dancers, a lost look on her face. Why hadn't somebody engaged her for this dance? Men were such asses.

He had the mad urge to beg the pardon of his current partner and hasten to Eleanor's rescue. After this dance, he would seek her out and ask her to stand up with him again.

To his disappointment, another gentleman, curse him, claimed Eleanor for the next set before Hugh could even make his way toward her. He snatched a glass of wine from a footman and retreated to the sidelines. In a moment, Adam strolled over and stood next to him.

"The evening seems a great success," he said.

Hugh snorted. "So far. One never knows with these occasions."

"I'm glad, Hugh, very glad you allowed this. They asked me about it first, you know. If I thought you would agree. I wasn't sure you would."

"You know me too well. But I decided it would seem crass not to." He glanced around the room. "These people seem to like me, Adam. Of course, it may be that they enjoy balls and socializing more."

"Of course they do. And there's nothing the good citizens love more than a war hero." He looked askance at Hugh. "Someday I hope you'll tell me something of your exploits in North America."

"And I've never heard exactly what happened to you at Walcheren. If I were a betting man, I'd wager it's you who deserves the knighthood, not me."

"Every chap who's suffered the horrors of this never-ending war with Bonaparte probably deserves one, but that's as may be."

"You know, Adam, I'd grown tired of being thought of as nothing more than Benjamin Grey's son. The one who is just like him."

Adam seemed shocked. "Do you think that's how people view you?"

Hugh shrugged. "Broxton certainly did. He glared at me

every time I so much as glanced at Eleanor. And her mother still barely tolerates me. But overall, I believe most people hold me in higher regard than they once did." He watched as Eleanor floated by in the arms of an older man. His hackles rose when he recognized the fellow as a widower from Haslemere. One who needed a mother for his brood. He'd better not be considering Eleanor for the position.

"You have an interest there," Adam said, amusement in his voice.

Hugh looked at him squarely. "Very much so." He paused a moment, considering. "Step outside with me a moment?"

Adam nodded, and the two made their way toward the doors. His brother fished a cheroot from his pocket and lit it from a candle on his way outside. Hugh walked a short distance down the sidewalk before he stopped and said to Adam, "This is strictly between us. Agreed?"

"Of course. Always."

Hugh swallowed the remainder of his wine before speaking and set the glass on a ledge. "Did anything happen to Eleanor while I was in Canada? Something that hurt her, wounded her in some way?"

Adam puffed on the cigar before answering. "We didn't see her for a long time, even though we dined with the Broxtons fairly often after the election. Other times I was there by myself. Eleanor was never present. I recall remarking to Cass once that it seemed odd she never made an appearance. Then, suddenly, we began to see her occasionally, although not at private dinners."

"Did they make excuses for her absence?"

"Let me think. Cass would remember better than I. Once, they said she was ill, or indisposed, or some such. I honestly can't recall beyond that."

Damn. "I see."

"What's this about, Hugh?"

He debated how much to reveal, then decided if he'd gone this far, he might as well tell all. "I'm in love with her, Adam. I want to marry her." Christ, Hugh couldn't believe he'd just said that. Something he hadn't even admitted to himself yet.

"But that's wonderful news, Brother."

"Too soon to celebrate. I haven't asked her yet." He spun around and walked a few paces away. "She's keeping something from me, I know it. Have you ever noticed the sadness in her eyes? Something terribly painful is buried deep inside her, and I don't have a clue as to what it might be or why she's keeping it hidden."

"Have you asked her about it?"

"Not directly. Doesn't it seem odd to you that she works so hard? That she doesn't live in her family home, with her parents?"

"I thought she did."

Hugh raked a hand through his hair. "Nominally. In truth, she spends most of her nights at that cottage where she runs her business. There's a bed in the back room."

Adam cocked his head and lifted a brow at his brother. "And you know about the bed because?"

"None of your damn business. That's beside the point, anyway. Sometimes Eleanor looks so drained, I can't bear it. I've asked her why she drives herself to such an extent. Her justification is that she wants to be independent, wants her life to have a purpose. But she doesn't have to work herself into a state of exhaustion to achieve that."

"I've never paid much attention to the situation, but I'll ask Cass what she knows. With your permission, of course."

"You're sure she can be discreet?"

"Absolutely. I'll let you know if she can shed any light on this. I'm optimistic she may remember something, or have sensed something, I did not. Women are better at these sorts of delicate matters than we are."

"You're right about that," Hugh said ruefully. "We'd better go back in. And thanks for listening."

When they reentered the assembly rooms, the guests were streaming into supper. Adam went off to find Cass. Hugh looked around for Eleanor and glimpsed her with Ned, of all people. Well, better she eat supper with his friend than with the widower.

Chapter Fifteen

Eleanor desperately wished she and Hugh were anywhere but this blasted ball. Someplace they could be alone and she could bare her soul.

Ned had escorted her back to the main room after supper and was currently describing his work with the tenants in excruciating detail. She hoped her "*mms*" and "ohs" and "I sees" were coming at the appropriate places. Hugh, who had taken supper with his family, was leaning against the wall to one side, a glass of wine in hand, staring at her and Ned. He was alone. Earlier, the Grey brothers had been absent from the ball for a while, and Eleanor wanted to believe they were mending their fences.

Eleanor had danced nearly every set. When at last she sat one out, the truth of her situation fell on her like a bag full of gold guineas. Hugh believed his own mother had deserted him, and as soon as he found out about Lili, he would find Eleanor guilty of a similar crime. And in a way, it was true. She wanted to weep when she thought about the necessity of surrendering Lili to the Abbots.

Whatever her guilty thoughts were at present, she had to survive the ball. Later tonight, she would tell Hugh the truth. Losing her patience at last, she interrupted Ned. "My pardon, Ned, but would you escort me to Sir Hugh?"

She'd embarrassed him. He stammered a reply and offered his arm. They headed toward Hugh, who watched her with blatant admiration the whole way. Ned excused himself and moved a short distance away from them.

"I knew if I stared at you long enough, you would come to me," Hugh said, giving her a slow grin.

"I'm afraid I was rude to Ned. I interrupted him in mid-sentence." Eleanor smiled wryly. "He's certainly enthusiastic about his work."

Hugh laughed. "That he is."

Laying a hand on his arm, she said, "Hugh, I must see you about something. It can't wait. Could we meet after the ball?" Glimpsing his smoldering eyes, she said, "No. Not for that."

"Damn." When she didn't smile, he stopped teasing and grasped her hands. "I thought something was amiss. Tell me now, Eleanor."

A voice seeking the attention of the gathering interrupted them. It was Mr. Beckwith, beginning the official part of the celebration. The reason for the ball. Hugh leaned toward her and whispered, "I'm sorry."

She mustered a smile and nodded. Eleanor was relieved they'd been interrupted. She didn't want to tell him until after the ball. Especially since the denizens of Haslemere were honoring him, acknowledging him as a respected member of the community.

"Ladies and gentlemen, we've gathered here tonight to celebrate the knighthood of Sir Hugh Grey, an honor recently bestowed upon him by the Prince Regent." There was a smattering of applause.

"Sir Hugh is one of the first recipients of the Knight

Grand Cross from the Royal Guelphic Order, founded by the Prince of Wales himself. He was awarded this honor for acts of bravery during the Battle of Châteauguay, fought near Montreal in the year 1813.

"Risking his own life, Sir Hugh carried out a rescue mission, saving five members of the Fencibles who had been too gravely wounded to save themselves. Sir George Prevost, Governor General of Canada, put his name in for the knighthood. Very well deserved, Sir Hugh."

Now the room burst into enthusiastic applause.

Eleanor sneaked a glance at Hugh. This must be torture for him. His modesty and reserve did not allow for bragging about his exploits in the service of his country. In fact, that day in Hyde Park, when she'd asked what he'd done in North America, he had never mentioned how he had earned the knighthood, and after she'd nearly been run down, she had forgotten to ask.

Her attention was diverted by a man who suddenly appeared at Ned's side. Someone distinctly not dressed for a ball, but attired in a laborer's clothing. Since Ned didn't seem at all shocked, she assumed he knew the man. The stranger, from what Eleanor could observe, was agitated about something. In a moment, Ned and the other man headed their way.

Hugh spoke briefly with Ned and then turned to her. "A fire has broken out at Longmere," he said, and began making his way to the front of the room before she had time to react. Mr. Beckwith was in mid-sentence when Hugh interrupted him. By now, the crowd had grown restive, speculating about what could be wrong. And then Hugh broke the suspense.

"Peter Allen, one of my tenants, has just brought the news that the Longmere stables are on fire." The murmurs turned into a din in no time. Hugh was forced to shout. "Obviously, there is no time to lose. My thanks to all of you for this wonderful occasion. It meant a great deal to me." He glanced about the room. "We could use all available hands for the bucket brigade." And then Hugh strode out of the room, followed by Ned and Mr. Allen.

Adam, after speaking briefly to Cass, hurried after his brother. Most of the other men also rushed out. Poor Mr. Beckwith looked stricken. He was attempting to get everybody's attention, but to no avail. Throwing his arms up in frustration, he finally conceded defeat.

The evening was ruined. But that was not what disturbed Eleanor. For one thing, she was horribly afraid for Hugh. Fire spread rapidly in a stable, and it could be out of control by now. What if he lost everything? The fire might easily spread to other outbuildings, the woods and orchards. And the house. Hugh's cherished new home. But even that was not the most alarming part of this. No. The most horrifying aspect was the corrosive, clawing fear that Jacob Abbot was responsible for setting the fire, in a twisted attempt to bend her to his will.

"Eleanor?"

She glanced up into the worried eyes of her father. "Come along quickly. I'm taking you and your mother home, and then I'll be off to Longmere."

She did not trust herself to speak, but followed him mutely, wondering what she had wrought with her secrets and lies.

· · ·

Very early the next morning

Hugh, Adam, and Ned Martin sprawled in Hugh's bedchamber in the new house. By the grace of God, it had been spared. It smelled of smoke, but that was the least of his concerns. Everything smelled like smoke. He glanced at the other two men. Their clothes were covered in grime—that is, the parts that weren't torn to shreds. Their faces were almost comically streaked with soot. Hugh had lowered himself to the edge of the bed and now rested his head in his hands. The other two men sat on the floor.

"You warned me, Ned," Hugh said, dejection in his voice. "You advised me to hire a watchman, and I never got around to it."

"But *I* did. I hired my cousin. By God, I'll have his head if he shirked his duty last night."

"Let's not jump to conclusions," Hugh said. "You'll question him, Ned, and inform me."

After a cavernous yawn, Adam said, "What *do* we know?"

"Not much, I'm afraid, except that the fire was started deliberately. The remnants of the torch the bastard used were found. We were damned lucky to have gotten the animals out."

"Nobody gave chase?"

"They considered it, but thought it was more important to bring the horses out. I would have done the same." Hugh had pieced together what happened based on various things he'd been told since last night. The men—the footman, groom, and a few laborers—had been playing cards in the tack room. One of them thought he'd seen a shadow, but nothing raised an alarm until they had smelled the unmistakable odor of burning hay. By the time they'd investigated, the flames were licking at the loft. One of the men hastened to alert the tenants, who'd come running with buckets. Soon, dozens of men from all around Haslemere had arrived to help, including most of those who had been at the ball.

The stable was a complete loss. As were the cupboards, shelves, and moldings the carpenters had completed thus far, which had all been stored outside.

"Do you have any enemies, Hugh?" Adam asked. "Any disgruntled workmen who might bear a grudge for one reason or another?"

Hugh glanced at Ned. "Do we?"

Ned didn't answer immediately, taking some time to gather his thoughts. "There is the one fellow, Abbot, who can be surly at times and doesn't mix with the others. But he seems harmless enough."

"Abbot." Hugh rose and began pacing. "Good God, I forgot about him. He said something that upset Miss Broxton when she was visiting."

"What?" Ned said. Hugh hadn't mentioned the incident to him.

"Eleanor wouldn't tell me, only that it was unfit for a lady's ears. I wanted to sack him, but she asked me not to. She worried his family would suffer if he lost his employment."

Adam had produced a flask of brandy, and after taking a swig, passed it to Hugh. "That doesn't explain why he would be nursing a grudge against you."

"When I noticed that Eleanor was upset, I ordered him back to work. But that was the end of it."

"Do you want to question him?" Ned asked.

"Not yet, but let's keep an eye on him. If he's the perpetrator, he may decide to make more trouble. We might be able to catch him in the act."

Adam slowly rose. "I'm dead on my feet," he said. "Ned, can I give you a ride to Town? Since the Broxtons conveyed Cass and Deborah home, I have the carriage."

"My thanks. I'll return in the morning, Hugh." It was the first time Ned had left off the honorific. Fighting the fire had been a bit like going through a battle together. Rank became insignificant.

"Like hell you will. It's nearly morning now. Take the day off and get some rest. You'll need it in the days ahead."

When they were gone, Hugh stripped and crawled beneath the covers. How he wished Eleanor were there with him. He hadn't had time to spare her a thought since he'd learned of the fire, but now he recalled her troubled countenance. She'd said she needed to see him. Damnation. He would find the time later today to pay her a visit.

Sir William had worked alongside the other men most of the night, taking a position in the bucket brigade. To Hugh's relief, Broxton had even offered to stable the horses. One less thing to worry about.

He didn't want to think about fire or destruction, or the close call with the house. So he pictured Eleanor. How elegant she'd looked at the ball, the way she'd felt in his arms. He wished he'd had that second dance with her.

• • •

The worst of Eleanor's fears had been realized.

After staying the night at her family home, she breakfasted early, before anybody else was up, and walked to her cottage. As soon as she entered, a note resting on the floor caught her eye. Obviously, it had been pushed under the door. Momentarily nonplussed, Eleanor calmed as she bent to pick it up. She'd expected it, after all.

Unsure if her legs would support her, she sat down at the worktable to read the note. It was short and to the point: *Things can get worse for our friend and for you. Fifty pounds would protect your secrets. Don't be a fool about this. JA.*

For the present, she would ignore it. Abbot wasn't likely to take any further action immediately. The man must be desperate to have committed such a heinous crime. Arson was a hanging offense. At the very least, it could mean imprisonment or transportation. And now she held the proof in her hand that he'd also committed blackmail. Abbot was unpredictable, and she must remove Lili from his home. She couldn't risk his striking out at Hugh again, or someone else close to her.

Eleanor considered whether she should speak to her father. She badly needed advice. Unfortunately, that meant telling him that Hugh was Lili's father. Reluctantly, she concluded there was no good alternative, since Hugh would be occupied with cleaning up after the fire. That could take a few days. In the chaos, she doubted he even remembered she'd asked to see him after the ball.

To her shame, she had brought calamity down on Hugh's head. She was so grateful they'd been able to save his home. But according to her father, almost everything else was lost. She wanted to weep and pound her fists into something, but she couldn't lose control. She must figure out what to do.

A line from one of her favorite poems came to her: *Oh what a tangled web we weave/When first we practice to deceive.* By keeping Lili a secret, she'd woven a web of deceit, ensnaring both herself and Hugh. And now she must find a way out. She would. She had no choice. Her father would help her.

Eleanor rose and began to set out the items they'd need for today's sewing. The act of readying things soothed her. After a while, Bobby scratched at the door, and she paused to let him in. Stooping, she picked him up and cuddled him against her chest. He was her true friend, and she needed one right now.

· · ·

Hugh had intended to sleep late, but he jolted awake after a few hours and was too restless to drift off again. He dressed in work clothes and ventured outside to view the damage in the clear light of day. Of course, Ned was already there. He'd brought coffee, pastries, and bacon, bless him. It was a fine thing to have a steward whose family owned the local tavern.

"I recall telling you to take the day off," Hugh said, eyeing Ned sardonically.

"You tell me a lot of things, Sir Hugh."

Hugh laughed, but only briefly. He gulped black coffee as he gazed around the ruins of his stables. "Do you think there's anything salvageable?"

"Doesn't appear to be, but I suppose we should sort through the mess to make sure. We have to get rid of it, anyway."

"Tell the men I'll pay for new work clothes and whatever else they've lost. Shall we get started?"

Using shovels, they worked for a long time, plunging through wet ashes and shards of wood and glass. They dumped most of it into carts to be hauled away. It was a filthy and unproductive effort, yielding little. Now and then, one of them would find an object that miraculously had survived the blaze. A piece of tack. A boot. A hammer. Small bits, such as buttons and buckles. Finally, Hugh called a halt.

Motioning to Ned, he said, "Let's eat the victuals you brought." Earlier, he'd filled a jug with water from the well. After pouring some over his hands to get the soot and ash off, he drank his fill and passed it to Ned. They tucked into the apple puffs and bacon and drank the rest of the coffee.

"What's next?" Ned asked when they'd finished eating.

Hugh wiped his mouth on his sleeve, then laughed at himself for doing it. "Have you checked with your cousin yet? Was he on duty last night?"

"He was, but he neither saw nor heard anything. He left his post once, for a trip to the privy, and that may have provided just the opportunity the perpetrator needed."

"Unfortunately, setting a fire doesn't require a lot of time. Let's set up a rotation for the men, myself included, beginning tonight. Shifts will start as soon as the workmen have left for the day."

"Do you reckon this Abbot fellow could have set the fire?"

Hugh shrugged. "No idea, at this point. What would he gain by it? And if he were caught, he'd lose everything."

"No disrespect meant, sir, but might Abbot have a connection with Miss Broxton?"

Without pausing to think, Hugh said, "No." Quite firmly. Then, "I don't know. I asked her, since she'd advocated for him pretty strongly. She denied it, and I don't think she'd lie to me." He must find the time to see her today. She'd said she wanted to tell him something—could it somehow relate to Abbot?

Ned was trying to stifle a grin, but didn't quite succeed. "You care for the lady, don't you?"

Hugh cracked his own grin. "I do. Very much."

"I know her only in passing, of course. People think a lot of her. Her father's a force to be reckoned with," Ned said, quirking his mouth. "But you're likely in good standing with him because of your brother."

"Since the knighthood, I've risen in his estimation," Hugh said wryly. "Eleanor and I are…close, but she's a private person. I suspect she's keeping something from me. Something significant."

"We all have our secrets, Hugh. A part we hold back from others."

"Yes, you're probably right. But for Eleanor, it's almost like a burden. One she would like to share, but can't, for some reason." Hugh was tempted to ask his friend what he knew about Eleanor during the time Hugh had been in Canada, but then thought better of it. He didn't want Ned thinking Eleanor had done something wrong.

"Do you love the lady, sir?"

Hugh was surprised by the question, but found he didn't mind Ned asking it. The man was his closest confidante right now. "I believe I do." He laughed. "Rather desperately, actually."

"Then you should tell her so. And no matter what her secret is, her burden, it doesn't matter and shouldn't change your feelings."

Hugh felt as though someone had thrown a bucket of cold water on him. "How did you become so wise in matters of love, my friend?"

Ned's face turned crimson. "I have my regrets."

They resumed their work, and the other men joined them eventually. While he was shoveling enormous amounts of ash and rubble, Hugh thought over Ned's advice. It made perfect sense and might represent the only way to win Eleanor's heart. And he couldn't imagine any secret she might be harboring that could possibly change how he felt about her.

Chapter Sixteen

The evening after the ball, Eleanor dined with her parents. Unfortunately, there'd been no opportunity to speak with her father privately. After she refused her mother's repeated requests that she stay at the house, her father insisted on walking her back to the cottage. But the hour was late, and she didn't want to raise a topic that could conceivably take hours to discuss.

After seeing her safely inside and helping light candles, he bid her good night. She felt a sudden burst of affection for him. Despite his deep disappointment in her when she'd confessed her pregnancy, he had stood by her. He could be gruff, too quick to judge, and sometimes provincial in his thinking, but never had she doubted her father's love for her. It still saddened her to recall how he'd grieved for his nephew, Benedict, who had died during the Peninsular campaign.

Eleanor glanced around the workroom, thought about straightening up, but quickly dismissed the idea. Whatever needed to be done could wait until morning. She made her way toward the back room, already tugging at her clothing.

This room would always and forever remind her of Hugh. And with that thought, she sat down hard on the bed.

As quickly as she'd sat, she leaped to her feet. Before she had a chance to rethink her decision, she would go to him. She would tell him he was the father of a delightful little girl named Lili, who resembled him, with her dark hair and eyes. If he never wished to see Eleanor again, so be it. She was tired of carrying this burden of secrecy, of lying to him. He had a right to know he was a father. If he wanted to be a part of Lili's life, he would devise a way to prevent a scandal. Hugh would help to ease her financial worries, and his connection to Lili would protect her. They could raise their daughter together.

Or not.

There could be a much different outcome. Lifting her skirts as she hurried along the path, she made straight for Longmere and would not allow herself to consider what that outcome might be. If she did, she'd lose her courage, and it was past time she showed some. Night sounds surrounded her, but none that didn't belong. She was cognizant of the fact that an arsonist had been prowling about last night, but her newfound resolve wouldn't allow her to dwell on it. As she drew near Longmere, the acrid odor of smoke and burned wood pricked her senses. Where the stables had stood, an empty space now yawned. Rubble was strewn about. Eleanor's guilt ratcheted up a few notches.

What she hadn't anticipated was someone standing guard. He called out to her. "Who's there? Stop!"

Drat! She recognized Ned Martin's voice. Nothing to be done about it. In for a penny, in for a pound. "Ned, it's Eleanor. I need to see Sir Hugh."

To his credit, he didn't appear to be shocked. "Evening, Miss Broxton. I'll get him for you."

She looked him in the eye. "No. If you don't mind, I'd rather find him myself." He stared at her a moment, as if she might be up to no good. Finally, he stood aside and gestured. "Go ahead, then. And mind your step in there, miss."

Thankful that Ned couldn't see her flushed cheeks, Eleanor scurried past him and made her way in the dark toward the staircase. Hugh would be in his bedchamber. When she reached the gallery, she paused, listening. It was still and quiet, until she entered Hugh's chamber. Then she heard the gentle susurrations of a slumbering man.

Softly, Eleanor moved toward the bed until she could discern his sleeping form. He lay on his side, with one arm flung out. His chest was bare, and his thick, dark hair looked like an ink stain on his pillow. She lowered herself to the bed and gazed on him. He was at peace. Didn't Hugh deserve to rest? To have an undisturbed night's sleep after the horrors of the previous night? Her resolve began to slip away.

And then his voice, low and menacing, startled her. "I know someone is there. If you value your life, you won't move." Eleanor nearly cried out in shock, but caught herself in time. "I'm going to slowly sit up, and then, whoever you are, you can explain what you're doing in my bedchamber."

He'd lied. He didn't move slowly at all, but lightning fast, and before she could say anything, Hugh was on her, tackling her. She hit the floor with a thud and an unladylike grunt. "*Oomph!*"

Hugh's big body covered hers. His big, naked body.

Suddenly, he went completely still. "Eleanor? Is that you?"

She couldn't breathe and therefore could not answer. She nodded dumbly, her cheek rubbing against his chest. "Christ almighty! Have I hurt you? Of course I have." He rolled off her, then helped her sit up. "What are you doing here? I thought you were an intruder." He got to his feet. She hoped he intended to pull on his britches.

Eleanor waited a moment before speaking. "I wanted to

see you. About…something."

"Bloody hell," Hugh said. "I completely forgot." She glanced up at him, then looked away, embarrassed. He was aroused. Before she could object, he lifted her into his arms and sat down on the bed, holding her firmly on his lap.

"Good God, Eleanor. I wanted you so badly last night. After the ball, I'd planned to bring you here and make love to you in this bed. But things didn't go according to plan."

"Hugh, I can't stay. Ned let me come in, and he'll suspect something if I'm here too long." His arms cocooning her made her wonder how she'd lived without their strength for so long.

"Ned will understand, and he would never give away our secrets."

Secrets. Hadn't she rushed over here to give up her own? "Hugh, I—"

"*Shh*. Make love to me, darling. Then we'll talk, I promise. But let's christen the new bed first. The new house."

He buried his face in her neck, kissing, nipping, gently sucking. She was weakening. When she lifted her head, he turned her face so that he could kiss her. Gradually, her body relaxed into his, and oh God, nothing had ever been so arousing, yet so infinitely tender as this kiss. Eleanor would willingly give him her deepest self and, in return, take whatever he offered. She wanted him to bring her from darkness to light, if only for these few precious moments. This might be the end. The last time they made love.

And so she kissed him back, as though a kiss could be a panacea. As though their lovemaking could bring the peace and happiness she craved. Dragging her fingers through his silky hair, she murmured his name over and over. *Hugh. Hugh.* His hair smelled like soap and the out-of-doors. Feeling his thickness pressing into her, she shamelessly rubbed against it, making him gasp.

Laughing softly, he whispered, "Minx." He tugged at

her bodice until her chemise was revealed, and then pushed the thin straps off her shoulders. "Ah. What have we here?" Eleanor was wearing short stays. They laced up the front and took no time at all to divest oneself of, or, in this case, for Hugh to do it. He threw the garment to the floor, and now her breasts were fully exposed to him, the cool air raising gooseflesh on her skin. "God, you're so beautiful, Eleanor. As lovely as a Botticelli."

While he caressed her breasts, she threw her arms around him, stroking first his back and then his chest. In the darkness of the bedchamber, she could not see him well, but touching him, learning the shape of him, made up for it. By now, her breath was coming in short bursts. She ran her hands over each curve of sinew, each band of muscle, as though seeking the depth and breadth of him. Her fingers danced down his spine, and she felt him shiver. Sliding her hands around to his chest, she teased his nipples, just as he was doing to her.

Hugh lifted her off his lap and laid her on the bed. "I want to taste you, darling." She raised her knees, and he gently spread her thighs apart, his breath coming hard. Lowering his head, he paused to look at her. She felt no shame, only a desperate hunger for him. He licked and sucked at the sweetness between her legs, and she moaned, writhing. When he slid a finger inside her, she came fast, intense spasms of pleasure seizing her, making her cry out with abandon.

He entered her, and she put her legs around his hips and drew him inside as far as she could. Hugh's gaze was tender and devouring all at once. In this moment of their union, he was everything to her. With each thrust, she learned more of him. Understood the depth of him. And when his release came with a great, shuddering gasp, she found the peace she had been longing for. His lips brushed hers before he separated from her. He reached for a handkerchief and handed it to her, and when they had both cleaned themselves, he pulled her close.

"I love you, Eleanor. Every part of you. Your lustrous hair, your teasing lips, your smile. I love your breasts and hips and thighs. Your belly. Every inch of you."

Her hand against his heart, she said, "Yes. I love you, too. So very much." She felt the rush of tears, tried to hold them back, and failed. "Remember that." Hot tears slid off her face and dripped onto Hugh's hand.

"You're crying, love. What is it? You arrived here tonight determined to tell me something, and I prevented you."

"I'm sorry. It's nothing."

"Of course it's not nothing." Gently, he pushed away from her, rose, and began to dress. Eleanor let the tears flow. She felt them dribbling off the sides of her face, past her ears, into her hair.

Hugh handed her a fresh handkerchief. "Stay right there," he said, and hurried away. While he was gone, she dragged herself upright, blotted her face and neck, and blew her nose. How was she going to explain this? She must tell him everything, for Lili's sake. For his sake. But now that she had the perfect opportunity, she would rather flog herself, like a Christian martyr. It would be less painful, in the end. A future together after she revealed the truth was about as probable as the Prince Regent reconciling with Queen Caroline. Hugh was back before she'd thought up any plausible excuse for weeping. He was carrying a bottle and two wineglasses.

• • •

They had declared their love for each other, and a few moments later, Eleanor was in tears.

Hugh was determined to get to the bottom of this. Whatever it was that caused her sadness and pushed her to the brink of exhaustion. If she loved him, surely she would confide in him. Tell him what was making her so unhappy. When he returned to the bedchamber, she was dressed. With a forced joviality, he said, "Come. Sit with me in the chair and have some wine." When she did not move, he said, "Do you like port? It's all I could find."

"I do like it, but I'll sit on the ottoman."

Hugh lit a few candles and poured wine for them. He could barely believe this was the same woman who had just made such rapturous love to him. "Please, Eleanor, take the chair. It's very plush, molds itself to your form. I insist."

Eleanor obliged him and sank into the chair. Handing her a glass of the port, he lowered himself onto the ottoman. The silence stretched out, and he hoped the wine was relaxing her. Finally, he could wait no longer. "Do you want to tell me why you were crying?"

Her face was shadowed. "The last few months have been very demanding. I feared we'd never finish all our orders. As you well know, there's a flurry of parties and balls before London's elite take themselves off to their country houses after the Season ends, and the girls and I have been working ourselves to death."

"So it's fatigue that has you in such a fragile state?"

She bristled a bit at that.

"If I work hard to achieve a goal, is that the same as fragility? Do you consider yourself fragile when, after a day of lifting, hauling, cleaning up ashes and rubble, you're exhausted?" Her chin wobbled.

Obviously, he'd said the wrong thing. Hugh looked down before she could glimpse the frustration on his face. When he raised his head, he hoped all traces of it were gone. "My apologies. I never think of you in that way, but tonight, you seem altered. And our situations are different, you must see that. I have plenty of help. If I'm worn out, I simply take myself off and have a rest. I wouldn't need to be involved at all if I so chose. But you…you drive yourself, Eleanor. For a long time, I've been wondering why."

She swallowed more wine. "I've explained before."

"You have." He cocked a brow at her. "Your reasoning doesn't make a lot of sense to me. But let's put that aside for now. How do you explain the sorrow and melancholy I see in your eyes? You accused me of wanting to know your secrets. I didn't, then. But things have changed between us." He reached out and caressed her arm gently. "I simply want you to know that you can tell me. Nothing you could say would make the slightest difference in my feelings for you."

Her eyes shone with tears. "Thank you, Hugh. I'm afraid I don't deserve your trust."

"Why not let me be the judge of that?"

She set the wineglass down and covered her face with her hands. Ah. Now they were getting somewhere. At length she raised her head and fixed her eyes on him. "When you were in North America, I gave birth to a child. Our daughter. Her name is Lili, and she'll be two years old in August."

He stood abruptly and stared down at her. "My pardon. I must not have heard you correctly. I thought you said you—we—have a child. That cannot be right. I would have known. In two years, you would have told me."

She said nothing, merely stared up at him with tears trickling down her face.

Never had he suspected such a revelation. She couldn't have shocked him more if she'd said she was the Prince Regent's mistress. He knew his voice sounded judgmental and cold, but the question must be asked. "You are certain the child is mine?"

An ironic laugh burst from Eleanor, and he glimpsed the hurt in her eyes. "Do you mean, did I have another lover after you? No, of course not. Lili is yours."

He gulped the remainder of his wine, poured more, and

began to pace. After a minute, he spun around to face her. "Why, Eleanor? Why keep it from me?"

She leaned forward slightly. "It was wrong of me. Unforgivable. And yet I hope you will forgive me. I am so terribly sorry for not telling you before now."

"I asked you to inform me if there were consequences. A child qualifies, wouldn't you agree? I even recall telling you Adam would know how to reach me. So I ask once again, why?"

"When I discovered I was with child, you were already gone to Canada. Would you have come running back to me? A woman you hardly knew, because I'd fallen pregnant after one reckless night of passion?"

He said nothing. His mind was still trying to take it in.

Eleanor misinterpreted his silence and said, "I thought not."

"Do not turn this around and pretend I wronged you! If I'd known, I would have found a way. Requested leave to return to England so that we could be married. Perhaps we might have been married by proxy."

She raised a hand, let it drop to her lap. "The likelihood of that happening was slim, since you'd only just arrived. Even you can admit that much. And I did not know you well enough to judge the kind of man you were."

He took that as a subtle reference to his father. Hugh couldn't deny that Benjamin Grey's reputation as a libertine might put any young lady on her guard. "And after my return, when I so obviously cared for you? Why not then?"

She sighed audibly. "You said you wished to know if there were consequences, but isn't that simply what gentlemen say under the circumstances? And when you came home, I had no idea what to expect. You'd been awarded a knighthood. You were rebuilding your home *and* your reputation. Proving to society that you were a better man than your father. The last thing I wanted was to drag you into a scandal."

He scrubbed a hand over his face. "Scandal be damned! You knew I cared for you. You didn't trust me enough to tell me. I'm a wealthy man, Eleanor. I was in a position to help you—and our daughter."

Eleanor said nothing, and after a few minutes, during which Hugh watched her between gulps of wine, he said, "Ned will accompany you home. I'll call on you tomorrow."

"Hugh, please—"

He held up a hand. "Enough. No more tonight. We both need sleep." Eleanor nodded, her lips pressed together so hard they were white. If Ned was surprised at Hugh's request to walk her to the cottage, he didn't let on. Hugh bid her a polite, restrained good night, if only to save face before Ned. Taking over guard duty was what Hugh needed. Perhaps the cool air would clear his head. What Adam had told him about Eleanor at the ball made sense at last. Hell, his own observations and reflections had finally become clear.

He paced about the property, pausing every so often to throw something onto the rubble heap. Gradually, shock loosened its grip on him, and clarity gained the upper hand. Eleanor had given birth to a child while he'd been away, and the likelihood that he was the father of that child was great. In fact, the odds of it belonging to anybody else were so small as to be nonexistent. Eleanor was not the sort of woman to keep a gaggle of lovers on a string. He believed her when she said he was the father of their daughter. *Lili.*

Where *was* Lili? Hugh was certain she was not currently at the Broxton home, or Eleanor would not be spending most of her time at the cottage. Unless…unless she didn't wish to raise their child.

Who was caring for the babe? Was Eleanor's obsession with her business more important to her than her child? He could not fathom why, rather than inform him they were to become parents, she would have chosen to give up the child. Because that was precisely what she must have done.

When dawn broke and there was enough daylight to ensure nobody would dare make trouble, Hugh shaved, bathed, and dressed. Although it was Sunday, because of the fire and the dire straits it had left them in, everybody had agreed to be back on site. He hoped to be done here by midmorning, so that he could call on Eleanor.

When he heard sounds of the workers arriving, he hurried downstairs and found Ned passing out scones and sausages. While waiting his turn, Hugh noticed Abbot standing a little removed from the others, drinking coffee and eating. He didn't join in the talk. Definitely a man who kept to himself. Hugh would give his right arm to know what, if any, role he played in Eleanor's life. Now that he knew she'd been lying to him for more than two years, how did he know she wasn't lying about Abbot? Ridley showed up before long, and Ned handed him a mug of coffee. Hugh decided to let the architect walk around and study the damages on his own. After a time, he called Hugh over. "How did you manage to save the house?" he asked.

"We had a separate brigade for it. They had strict orders to douse any flames that came close, and they did their job."

"I don't see any water damage to the house, which is a blessing. We might have had to pull up floors and redo some of the framing."

Hugh nodded. "I told the men to throw water on flames or sparks, but no water inside unless it caught fire. Fortunately, it never did." Hugh glanced around, then at Ridley. "Where should we start?"

"Set your carpenters to work on rebuilding the items we need to complete the interior. The sooner that's done, the sooner we can finish the kitchen, larder, storerooms. And the library. While they're doing that, we'll finish the walls and get all the windows hung."

"I'm going to call the men over in a minute and have you instruct them. What about the stables?"

"Unless it's a significant hardship to do without them, let's leave them for last."

"Agreed. A neighbor is stabling my horses temporarily, and I don't expect him to quibble over a delay. And I would like to make the kitchen a priority. I'm growing weary of bringing in all the food."

Ridley chuckled. "I can't blame you for that."

Hugh took a last swallow of coffee, then threw the dregs on the ground. "I've an appointment and will be gone the remainder of the day. You'll stay?"

Ridley nodded. "I'm planning on it."

"My thanks." Hugh called to the men, who shuffled over and waited to hear what Ridley had to say. Meanwhile, Hugh took Ned aside and asked him to keep an eye on things during his absence.

"Consider it done."

Hugh clapped him on the shoulder. "You're a good fellow, Ned. The best."

Chapter Seventeen

Later that day

At noon, Eleanor sent Jane and Minnie home.

She had waited all morning for Hugh to make an appearance, and her frayed nerves were at the breaking point. Better to sit by herself, considering what she wanted to say to him, than attempt to concentrate on her work. She brewed a pot of tea, poured herself a cup, and sat on the garden bench.

Her deception had gone on too long, and she feared Hugh would never forgive her for it. Just as he'd never forgiven his mother. *The truth will out*. Wasn't that a quote from Shakespeare? How many times had she chided herself for not telling him about Lili? How many times had she tormented herself with the knowledge that she was keeping his own child from him? And yet she hadn't acted.

The irony of the situation was not lost on her. Hugh learning the truth just after their declaration of love for each other. How would she explain? She'd had her reasons, but would she be able to make him understand? Last night, after she'd told him, his voice had been cold and completely devoid of sympathy or understanding. Perhaps, after having time to mull it all over, he'd had a change of heart. Maybe he was reserving judgment until she fully explained her situation.

And then she glanced up and saw him opening the gate. He had the most fearsome look on his face. Like God must have appeared right before he hurled Lucifer into hell. And that's when she knew that her dreams of building a family with Hugh and Lili had been shattered by her own folly.

Rain had been threatening, and now big drops hurtled down. She waved Hugh into the cottage and motioned toward one of the two chairs. "Please, be seated, Hugh. I've made tea. Would you like some?"

He remained standing. "No. Let's get on with this. We are alone?" His eyes cut toward the back room.

"Jane and Minnie have gone home."

"Good." His gaze swung back to her. "Now, tell me what happened from the time you learned you were with child."

So there were to be no pleasantries, no words to ease her fears or to reassure her. Her apology, her stated hope for forgiveness meant nothing, apparently. Very well, then. If this was the way he wished to carry on, she would not argue, aware just how deserving of his censure she was. "Months of isolation in the house, then to cousins in Devon, virtual strangers, for the birth. Afterward, Lili was immediately fostered out. My father made all the arrangements beforehand. I had no say in any of it."

"The child is illegitimate. I don't blame him; I blame you. You could have prevented that. Lili's surname is Broxton, I take it?"

"Yes, of course." His words were damning. An icy stab to her heart. Throat thick with emotion, she said, "How could I have prevented it? I was barely one and twenty, completely dependent on my parents."

Coldly, he said, "You could have prevented it by informing me."

"You may as well have been a million miles away! At the time, informing you seemed impossible. I realize you don't see it that way, but can you not try to understand how it was for me, at least until I formed the plan of starting a dressmaking business? Doing that would give me some independence, enable me to save money so that Lili and I could one day live together. I have no money of my own."

"Do your parents know that I am Lili's father?"

"No. Despite my mother's relentless prodding, I've resisted telling them. They may have guessed by now, but if so, they haven't said."

Finally, Hugh pulled out the other chair and sat. She hoped maybe this signaled a diminishment of his ire and a more empathetic view of the situation. But she was wrong.

"How could you do it? Abandon our daughter to someone else to be raised?"

A loud peal of thunder delayed her answer. "You must see I had no other alternative. I had no resources, no means of raising her on my own, and nowhere else to live." She clasped, and then unclasped, her hands. "I hated giving her up. It was the hardest thing I've ever had to do." Pausing, Eleanor wondered if anything she said would matter. "You are always asking me why I work so hard. Lili is the reason."

Hugh cocked his head. "Some fantastic notion of living together in your own home? You'd be an outcast, and so would Lili. Society never forgives these indiscretions. You know that."

"I was not planning to remain in Haslemere. When I saved enough money, I planned to move somewhere I'm not known. To pretend I'm a widow. I hadn't worked it all out yet." She paused, swallowing over the thickness in her throat. "And please, no matter what you think of the idea, do not make sport of my hard work, my efforts to take care of Lili by myself."

"For God's sake, Eleanor, earning enough money would have taken years." Hugh leaned so close to her, she wanted to draw back. "Where is she? Who has her?"

Oh God, how she'd dreaded this question, but she could not keep it from him. "Jacob Abbot and his wife are caring for her at present."

Hugh stood so fast, his chair tipped over backward, cracking against the floor. "That scoundrel? The man we suspect may have set the fire?" He stepped back, as though afraid he might strike her. "So that is why he spoke to you that day at Longmere!"

Should she admit her own suspicions? It seemed there was nothing left to lose; she may as well confess all. "He is trying to extort money from me. He guessed that you are Lili's father. According to him, a friend of his saw us enter the livery together that night. I believe he set the fire to show me he could hurt the people I care about."

"Christ almighty, Eleanor. Even then you didn't tell me of your suspicions. I might have lost everything in that fire, and he might have returned to do more harm."

"I intended to tell you all of it. About Lili and Abbot both, last night."

If anything, his glare was more hostile than before, and she was struck dumb by his response. "I shall see my solicitor in London tomorrow and find out what actions I must take to declare Lili my daughter. Legally. Then I'll remove her from the Abbots' home and place her with someone I deem fit. At least until my house is ready to be occupied, and I can employ a nursemaid."

When Hugh moved toward the door, as if to leave, Eleanor leaped to her feet. "Remove her from the Abbots, by all means. I've been longing for the day I could do that. But bring her to me. I am her mother."

He turned, staring at her with those cold, judgmental eyes. "You're not fit to raise her. A woman who would give up her own child. You're cut from the same cloth as my mother."

And there it was. What she'd been waiting for. The comparison to his mother. Eleanor was weeping now. "Can you so easily dismiss what we've meant to each other these past weeks? Can you not try to understand?"

"I see now how wrong I was about you. You didn't have the courage to defy your parents, nor did you do the sensible thing and contact me. How can I trust you with her when you were so willing to be cajoled into handing her over to the Abbots, of all people?"

Hugh unlatched the door, poised to leave and set his plan in motion. Eleanor moved toward him, letting him see her tear-streaked face, her misery. "Whatever you think of me, Lili loves me, and I love her. Don't tear her world apart to wreak vengeance on me, I beg you."

He hesitated, and for a moment she thought he might relent. But he said, "You had your chance, and you failed. I am her father, and I'll take responsibility for her now." He exited without a backward look, pulling the door closed behind him.

Hugh's words, spoken only last night, echoed in Eleanor's ears. "Nothing you could say would make the slightest difference in my feelings for you." But it wasn't what she'd said, rather what she'd done, that had ripped them apart.

. . .

After Hugh left, Eleanor wallowed in self-pity for a long time. She understood his feelings of hurt, betrayal, and even a degree of anger. But she'd not anticipated the fury she'd seen in his eyes. Or the complete lack of empathy. At length, she pulled herself together.

A long afternoon stretched out before her. Eleanor hadn't been back to the Abbots' since Jacob Abbot had barred her from entering. She would visit this afternoon and check on her daughter's welfare. Seeing Lili presented the perfect opportunity to take her mind off her own wretched state. Given that she did not know when Hugh would make good on his threat, she'd do well to take advantage of every spare moment she could spend with her daughter. For a long time now, whenever she had a free moment, Eleanor had been sewing a wardrobe for Lili's cloth doll from scraps of the finest silks and satins, and she wanted to teach Lili how to dress it.

She was taking a risk, not knowing if Abbot would be there. But Eleanor suspected he was at Longmere. Since so much had been lost in the fire, Hugh would need every available carpenter to replace what had burned. Not long after she'd made her decision, Eleanor pulled up at the Abbot home. Edith answered her knock, wariness in her eyes. "Miss Broxton. I wasn't expecting you."

Eleanor had to restrain herself from a sarcastic response. Her visits should be a surprise to nobody. They had been prearranged and agreed upon. "I would like to see my daughter, Edith. Your husband wouldn't allow it the last time I drove out."

The woman's jaw tightened, but she didn't respond to Eleanor's statement. "Come in, then."

"How are you feeling?" Edith's belly had swelled and rounded since Eleanor had last seen her.

"Well enough, I suppose. Lili's in the kitchen."

The toddler was sitting on the floor, playing with spoons, bowls, and cups. When she saw Eleanor, her face glowed with excitement. Eleanor dropped down beside her. "What are you making, poppet?" Lili crawled into her mother's lap, and she drew her close, inhaling her scent. "She looks much healthier than the last time I saw her."

Edith had returned to kneading dough. Without looking up, she said, "You mean, when she had the earache. She got over it pretty fast."

Eleanor got to her feet, holding Lili in her arms. "I've brought her something. I left it in the gig, so we'll just go and get it. Do you know where her doll is?"

"In her bed, I think."

That afternoon, mother and daughter spent a long time together dressing the doll in the clothes Eleanor had lovingly sewed. A chemise. A bright yellow cambric dress with pin tucks and a sash. A vivid red ball gown with a flounce. "Here, love. Mama will help you with the dress. Which one?" Lili pointed to the red gown. Her little fingers couldn't quite do what she wanted them to, but in her mother's opinion, for a child of her age, she showed a great deal of patience.

Eleanor studied her, so like Hugh in her coloring. What would he make of her? Her sparkling dark eyes, the joy she found in simple accomplishments, the radiant smile that greeted Eleanor every time she visited. Although she bitterly resented Hugh's plan to take Lili away from her, one part of her was glad for him, that he would meet his daughter at last. And glad for Lili, too. A wave of despair washed over her, so strong she wanted to weep. Her dreams for herself and Lili would never come to pass. And she must also let go of her foolish hope that Hugh might play a part in those dreams.

When Eleanor took her leave, ominous dark clouds were gathering, staining the sky a purplish black. She drove as fast as she dared, eager to arrive ahead of the storm. After dropping off the gig with one of the stable lads, she hurried down the path toward the cottage. But the storm burst before she made it home, soaking her clothes, bonnet, and half boots. It was dark inside, and she lit a few candles before changing her dress. Then she looked for a drying cloth to blot her wet hair.

Suddenly drained, she dropped onto one of the chairs and forced herself to think rationally about her situation. Hugh was planning to cut her off from her daughter completely, and she couldn't stand by and let that happen. She would seek her father's help, but not until tomorrow. She was far too upset to have such an important conversation tonight, while her feelings were still so raw.

Chapter Eighteen

The next day

Hugh had wanted to set out for London immediately upon leaving Eleanor, but the hour was too late, and he was in no frame of mind to travel. Instead, he waited until morning, checking in with Ned and Ridley before departing. The cleanup of the site was proceeding apace, and the carpenters were making good progress on the rebuilding of all that had been lost in the fire. Abbot was present, seemingly hard at work. Hugh sought a private word with Ned.

"I must go up to Town for the day."

"Oh?"

Hugh did not feel like elaborating. He hadn't yet decided how he would explain the sudden introduction of a child into his life. "Needs must. I'll be back in a few days. Have you any idea of where we stand with the kitchen?"

"The carpenters are still working on the cupboards. But we can start bringing in supplies to stock the larder."

"See to it, would you? And while you're at it, ask around

about a cook."

"My mother will probably know of somebody," Ned said.

"Good. The sooner, the better. And maybe your mother could help make a list of the provisions we need."

Ned laughed. "I can most likely do that myself."

Hugh took his carriage to Town. He'd purchased it from an earl and had it refurbished, and right now he was thankful he'd spent the blunt to make it so comfortable. Riding would have been faster, but he needed time to collect his thoughts. To concentrate on what he would tell McBride about his predicament. Leaning back against the squabs, he closed his eyes. Eleanor's countenance was there, as it had looked when he'd left her yesterday. Her face wet with tears, and her horribly anguished eyes.

Hugh knew he'd handled the meeting with Eleanor abominably. Hell, that was an understatement if ever there was one. After weeks of worry about the sadness he always sensed in her, an uncontrollable rage had supplanted the affection that had filled up an empty place in his heart. How could he have been so cruel and judgmental?

But he quickly hardened himself against her. Eleanor had made a series of poor choices, beginning with her decision not to tell him she was with child as soon as she'd found out. She'd chosen to keep their daughter a secret even after he'd arrived back in Surrey and had all but laid his heart at her feet. Despite Abbot's threats and attempt to extort money from her, and her suspicion that he'd set the fire…despite all that, she'd said nothing.

And God above, he was a father. Because of the adversarial nature of his conversation with Eleanor, he hadn't asked anything about Lili, and knew nothing except her age and name. Was she a serious child? Or more happy-go-lucky? Did children her age talk yet? Could she walk? *Dunderhead.* Of course she could walk. Didn't babies start to walk around a year old? He imagined she resembled Eleanor, with light hair and hazel eyes. Yes, a miniature version of Eleanor, most likely.

He asked the coachman to drop him off in Southwark, intending to take a wherry over to the City. After the footman let down the steps and Hugh climbed out, he touched the man's shoulder. "John, I have an errand for you." Hugh handed him a brief missive he'd composed to his brother the night before, stating that he'd be visiting his solicitor this afternoon and would stop by the townhouse later.

When Hugh arrived at Stewart McBride's office, the clerk informed him the man was currently with another client. Hugh said he'd wait. He was no closer to knowing exactly what to say to the solicitor, but overall he felt the best approach was to keep it simple. McBride could ask questions if he needed more information.

"Sir Hugh," McBride said when Hugh was finally ushered in. The solicitor asked the clerk to bring tea before gesturing to a chair.

"How are you, McBride?"

"Well enough. Surprised to see you here today. How can I help you?"

Hugh cleared his throat, suddenly feeling nervous. He wasn't accustomed to sharing his deepest secrets. But this was necessary. "I've recently discovered that I am the father of a two-year-old child. A girl. I want to take full responsibility for her. Remove her from her current situation and raise her myself in my home. How can I bring this about? Legally?"

If McBride were shocked, he gave no sign of it. "What is her current situation?"

"She was fostered out after her birth and has remained with the same family since then."

"Was there an agreement drawn up between the parties involved?"

Hugh shrugged, realizing there was much he did not know. "I didn't ask. I assume so." It was likely Broxton had insisted on some type of formal agreement.

The clerk brought in the tea, giving both men a chance to ponder. After McBride had poured and handed Hugh a cup, he said, "Legally, Sir Hugh, the child doesn't belong to anybody."

"What?"

"I am sorry if this offends, but I'm simply stating the truth. The child is baseborn. Your name is not listed in the baptismal records, I assume?"

"That's correct." Having Lili called "baseborn," even though McBride meant nothing by it, appalled him. It was no better than "bastard."

"Would you consider marrying the mother?"

"No," Hugh said immediately and decisively.

"Is she of low birth? Immoral character?"

This was growing worse and worse, and Hugh had to work at keeping the irritation out of his voice. "No. Not at all. She's a gentlewoman. Her father insisted the child be placed with foster parents."

"Of course. Any father would, to protect his daughter's reputation." McBride selected a biscuit and bit into it. "The mother, of course, would stand a much better chance of making a marriage without the stigma of a child."

Hugh spluttered, choking on his last swallow of tea. Christ, what he needed was strong spirits, not weak tea. Eleanor, married? To somebody else? He'd not contemplated it, but surely that was what her parents had hoped for when they insisted she give Lili into the care of strangers. If it became known she had a child outside of marriage, she'd be an outcast in the eyes of Society.

He looked up to see Mr. McBride gazing at him speculatively. "Are you all right, Sir Hugh?"

"Yes, of course. Go on."

"Would you like my opinion? My unadulterated opinion?"

Growing impatient, Hugh raised a hand and let it drop. "That's why I'm here, man."

"Among all the parties involved—that is, the mother, the foster parents, and yourself—you are in the best position to care for a child. I'm correct in assuming that?"

Hugh nodded.

"Then simply take the child by right of power and money."

"What about the agreement?"

"Most such agreements would surely stipulate that the child could be reclaimed at any time. Unless the mother truly wished to rule out having any part in her life. Is that the case here?"

"It is not the case." Hugh scrubbed a hand across his face. "I simply want to ensure that neither the mother, nor the grandparents, nor the foster parents, can legally take the child away from me."

McBride let out a sigh. "So the mother does want to be involved in her child's life? And you object to that?"

"Yes."

"Might you ever change your mind?"

"No." Hugh felt McBride's eyes studying him.

"Are you certain of that?"

"I am. In any case, that's not actually germane to the fundamental question. Which is: Can I legally remove my daughter from the foster parents? And restrict her mother's access to her?"

"As I said, a baseborn child legally belongs to nobody. By the fact of your wealth, your reputation, your standing in the community, I believe you can." McBride hesitated, again directing his assessing gaze at Hugh. "However, I would weigh carefully the benefits of separating a mother from her child. It could do irreparable harm to them both."

Hugh rose and held out his hand. "I must be the judge of that. Thank you for seeing me today. Your counsel has been very helpful."

McBride shook his hand and walked with him to the door. "I've worked for your family a long time, Sir Hugh, so I hope you'll forgive me if I offer a piece of advice. I would urge you not to act in haste and to consider all the ramifications of your actions. Do nothing until you are in a more calm and rational state of mind."

Hugh nodded curtly. He walked toward the river. His mouth was hard and his jaw set. By God, he was doing what was right, and nothing would throw him off course. McBride could go to hell.

Chapter Nineteen

Later the same day

Eleanor waited for her father to join her in his study. When Sir William entered the room, she was standing at the window. "Norrie, my dear. How good to see you. Will you stay for dinner?"

She'd wanted to be calm and rational when they spoke, but the mere sound of his voice provoked a new bout of crying. "Papa. I need your help." Eleanor ran to him and buried her head against his shoulder. She'd thought her tears would have dried up by now, but she seemed to have an endless reservoir of them. At length, her father gently pushed her away and led her to the sofa set against one wall.

"Sit down, love, and tell me what has happened."

For the next several moments, she poured her heart out. She revealed that Hugh was Lili's father, but she'd never informed him. That Abbot had tried to blackmail her and had most likely set the fire that destroyed much of Hugh's property. And that Hugh was going to take Lili from the

Abbots and not allow her access to her child.

"But why would he do such a thing? In these cases, the fathers usually wish to distance themselves…" His words petered out. Her father was probably ashamed that his own daughter was one of the "cases" to which he referred.

"He believes I willingly abandoned Lili to the Abbots, who, as it turns out, are the worst kind of people." Eleanor wiped her eyes and nose with Sir William's handkerchief. "I was unaware of this until recently, but Hugh was deeply hurt when his mother and Adam moved to Town. He viewed it as desertion, and now accuses me of the same thing."

"Did you tell him that you visit the child often? That your own money helps to pay the Abbots for her care?"

She grabbed her father's sleeve. "Don't you see—it doesn't matter what I say. He won't listen. Will you talk to him, Papa? Persuade him to change his mind?"

Her father rose to pour a glass of sherry for her, a brandy for himself. "Drink up. It will help." He waited until they'd both taken a few swallows before speaking again. "Of course I'll speak to him. Whether I can persuade him of anything is another matter. He is angry, Norrie, and you must see he has good reason to be. Why did you not tell him, love? A man has a right to know he's fathered a child."

"He was already in Canada when I learned I was with child. I believed the likelihood of his returning to wed me were slight. I should have told him when he came home, but I kept putting if off. I didn't want to cause a scandal for him. And I was afraid. I had no idea of how he would react to the news. He might not have wanted Lili or me."

"By all appearances, love, he does want you."

"Not anymore," Eleanor said.

They were both silent. It had started to rain, and the drops were pattering against the study windows. They should be slashing. Thunder should roar and lightning flash. Not this weak display. It didn't come close to matching the turmoil churning inside her.

"Papa, what if we went to the Abbots, right away, tonight, and removed Lili? We could bring her here, just until I find someplace else for us to live. That was always my plan anyway, to move to a town where I'm not known."

"Norrie, you know as well as I, you can't bring her here. Your mother…the servants—"

"We wouldn't stay long. I'd always planned to move somewhere else. I would need to borrow money from you—I haven't saved enough yet to be completely self-sufficient."

Sir William patted her hand. "We need more time to think this through, my dear. Sir Hugh isn't going to do anything immediately. Besides, even if we brought Lili here, what's to stop him from removing her from us?"

"He wouldn't dare! You wouldn't allow it. *I* wouldn't allow it."

"We don't know what he would do. You said he was going up to London to consult with his solicitor? Chances are, he will have found out his rights in the matter. We should not act hastily."

"I don't want Lili with the Abbots anymore, Papa. I fear for her safety there."

"In that case, dear, perhaps you should look upon this as a fortuitous turn of events. Sir Hugh has the means to provide for her *and* keep her safe."

Eleanor blinked. That much was true. But did Hugh providing for her and keeping her safe mean Eleanor must be cut off from her forever?

Her father sighed, head bowed. "Your mother must be told about all this, Norrie."

"Yes." Good God, how she abhorred the idea of that. Her mother would offer no consolation. Most likely she would see this as an opportunity to be rid of her granddaughter for good. Eleanor said, "Thank you, Papa. I'll dress for dinner. We'll tell Mama after we've eaten."

Sir William nodded. By his dour expression, it was obvious he dreaded the confrontation as much as she did.

. . .

Arriving at his brother's townhouse, Hugh was surprised when Wesley, his father's butler for many years, opened the door. With shaky hands, he accepted Hugh's hat, gloves, and walking stick. Despite his ill humor, Hugh smiled. "Wesley, it's good to see you. Are you working for my brother now?"

"Yes, Master Hugh. Pardon, *Sir* Hugh. Takes a bit of getting used to. Mrs. Grey—your mother—took me in after your father died. I fill in for Flynn and polish silver and the like. Afraid I'm not much use anymore."

"Nonsense. I'm sure they're glad to have you. Would you tell my brother I'm here?"

"They're in the upstairs drawing room, sir, expecting you. They will be delighted to see you."

Not likely, but he went up anyway. "Good evening," he said, standing in the doorway. Adam and Cass were seated next to each other, heads bent close together. Both rose at once.

"Hugh. Welcome." His brother shook his hand, and Cass stepped forward. Hugh kissed her cheek.

"From your note, we assumed you had a serious matter to discuss," Adam said.

Hugh nodded. "You assumed correctly."

"Brandy or sherry?"

"Brandy, please."

Cass said, "If this is a matter you wish to discuss privately with Adam, I shall see you at dinner."

"No. Please stay, Cass. I need both of you here."

When they were seated, Hugh drew in a steadying breath and exhaled slowly. "It seems I am a father," he said.

Adam beamed at him, but Cass's reaction was more subdued. "Oh, Hugh. Eleanor—?"

He nodded. "Before I left for Canada, she and I…" He broke off, not knowing what to say. "While I was gone, Eleanor gave birth to a child, a daughter. For reasons I can't comprehend, she chose not to inform me, even though I asked her to let me know through you, Adam, if there were consequences."

"You were correct in your belief that a momentous event had happened to Eleanor during the months you were in North America." When Hugh made no comment, Adam went on. "But this is happy news, isn't it? You told me at the ball you were in love with her."

"I thought I was. But how could I love a woman who willingly gave up her—our—child?"

"What else could she have done, Hugh?" Cass asked softly.

"Told me, for a start!" He finished his brandy in a long swallow, and Adam got up to refill it.

"What could you have done from Canada? The Broxtons must have pressured her to give up the child, and she would have had little recourse," Adam pointed out, handing Hugh his drink.

"She gave our daughter into the care of one Jacob Abbot and his wife. He is the man we suspect set the fire. He's also attempting to blackmail Eleanor." He shook his head and laughed cynically. "That is who currently has possession of my child."

"What are you going to do?" Cass shot a look at her husband before asking the question.

"I've been to see Stewart McBride, my solicitor. On his counsel, I'm going to remove my daughter from the Abbots and place her in the care of somebody I can trust, until my house is finished and I can employ a nursemaid. Then I'll bring her home."

"And Eleanor?" Adam asked, narrowing his eyes at Hugh. "What does she think of this scheme?"

"As far as I'm concerned, she forfeited her right to a say in the matter when she gave the child away."

Cass spoke, tears shimmering in her eyes. "That is harsh, Hugh, and unworthy of you."

"Agreed," Adam said.

Hugh finished his second brandy and set the glass on the table. "I suspected you would feel that way. You've a right to your opinion, of course. But mine will not change."

"Hold a moment, Hugh," Adam said, rising. "Have you given her a chance to explain?"

Hugh felt his anger mounting and struggled to keep it in check. This visit was meant to inform, not to discuss. "I have, and I did not find her explanation satisfactory."

"As a man, you cannot possibly put yourself in her place," Cass said. "You can endeavor only to understand. The pressures from Sir William and his wife alone must have been overwhelming."

"I know you mean well, Cass, but this is a matter for me to work out. I simply wanted you both to know you have a niece." He glanced from one to the other and said, "And now I must be off."

"Will you not stay the night with us?" Cass asked.

"No, thank you. I intend to start for home."

"At this hour?"

"I have the carriage. Don't get up. I'll see myself out." He paused a moment on the threshold. "It's not that I don't appreciate your offer of hospitality. I simply don't believe I would be very good company."

"Wait," Cass said. "What is her name?"

"Lili. Her name is Lili."

In the entrance hall, Wesley brought his things and muttered something Hugh barely heard. "I beg your pardon?"

"Your mother is not here. A shame, for I'm sure she would have liked to see you."

Hugh doubted it, but kept that to himself. He donned his hat and gloves while Wesley kept blathering on about something.

"I recall how your mother used to visit Longmere and beg to see you. All the servants were ordered not to let her in. It was a sad state of affairs."

Hugh simply stared at the old man. Perhaps his memory was faulty. "My mother came to Longmere to visit me? Do you mean after she moved to London?"

"Many times." The old man's eyes were rheumy, but still a bright blue. They seemed to burn a hole into Hugh's soul.

"You're quite mistaken, Wesley. That never happened."

"Oh, but it did. Ask Mrs. Godwin or the other servants."

Hugh nodded. "Perhaps I shall. Good night, Wesley. Take care of yourself." He hurried down the steps, putting the man's inexplicable comments from his mind.

They stopped at a coaching inn near Woking for ale and a meal on the way home to Surrey. News of Wellington's victory at Waterloo had trickled down, and the citizens were in a celebratory mood. Except for Hugh. While he was eating roast ribs of beef and potatoes, he imagined his first meeting with Lili. Would she take to him? Perhaps she resembled him in some small way, although he was certain Eleanor's looks would predominate in a female child.

Eleanor. Her anguished face came to the forefront of his mind. He paused, fork halfway to his mouth. It was obvious Adam and Cass thought him cruel. "Harsh" was the word Cass had used. Was she right in that assessment of him? He dropped the fork onto his plate, having suddenly lost his appetite. Because something else was niggling away at him as well.

In the carriage, he realized he'd been attracted to Eleanor from almost the moment he'd met her, and since he'd been back, fallen in love with her. She embodied the qualities he most admired: grace, kindness, courage, pluck. And she was a hell of a beautiful woman. Their passionate encounters had been the best of his life.

And he'd thrown it all away.

He'd threatened her, accused her of deserting her child, and told her she was an unfit mother. He winced when he thought of everything he'd said. Staring out the window into the darkness, he told himself it was all true.

Hugh argued with himself, until, at last, the motion of the coach lulled him into a fitful sleep.

・・・

After dinner, Sir William said he would join his wife and daughter in the drawing room. Eleanor, who had spent the meal pushing food around on her plate and could not have said what she'd eaten if asked, was grateful her father didn't prolong her anxiety.

"Why don't you play for us, Eleanor?" her mother asked. "It is so rare to have you here these days."

"Not tonight, Mama. I have something I must tell you." Eleanor was sitting on one of the Sheraton armchairs, her legs arranged in the genteel manner she'd been taught, her hands folded in her lap.

Her mother's eyes grew guarded, almost as if she possessed some prior knowledge of what Eleanor had come to say. "Very well. If you must."

A footman brought in the tea tray and decanter of port. When they were settled with their drinks, Eleanor began.

"You have asked many times about the identity of Lili's father." She nearly choked on the words. "A situation has arisen, and I can no longer keep it from you. Sir Hugh Grey is Lili's father."

Her mother's eyes narrowed. "I knew it all along," she said, leaning forward.

"You suspected, you mean."

"Don't think I did not notice the way he looked at you, going all the way back to the house party at Deborah Grey's country home. He wanted you from the start."

"He was kind to me when I had no acquaintances there. We enjoyed each other's company, and I considered him a friend."

"More than a friend, apparently."

Eleanor's hands had come unfolded and now grasped the arms of the chair. "Yes, of course, but there is a more pressing matter to discuss."

But her mother wasn't done with the "more than a friend" part. "I saw you, you know, the night of the assembly, right before Hugh Grey went off to North America. He left the assembly rooms, and you followed shortly thereafter. That was when he ravished you."

"Mama! That is not what happened."

"This is not seemly, Kitty," her father said. "It is Eleanor's private business."

This was what Eleanor had expected. Why, then, did it tear at her heart? Even if her mother enjoyed humiliating her, she refused to cede her the upper hand. "If I may get to the point, perhaps we can move on from this. I never informed Hugh of my pregnancy or of Lili's birth. He was unaware until recently that he was a father, and now—"

"He wants to wed you," her mother said almost triumphantly, eyebrows raised, chin lifted.

Eleanor might have laughed if the situation were not so

grave. "Quite the contrary. He wishes to remove Lili from the Abbots and raise her himself, without allowing me to see her. Papa has agreed to speak to him, try to make him see reason, but we have no way of knowing if that will make a difference."

Her mother was quiet for a moment, assessing. Finally, she said, "We have an agreement with the Abbots. Mr. Grey can't simply take the child from them. If he does so, it won't be long before people guess that you are the mother. You've been seen together in Society. At the garden party, and the ball. Conclusions will be drawn."

It galled Eleanor that her mother could never bring herself to use Lili's name. "Really, Mama, is that all you care about?" She rose and stared down at this woman who seemed to have become a stranger to her. "I asked Sir Hugh to let me have custody of Lili, but he refused. That is why I've asked Papa to speak to him."

"What? Raise her yourself? You can't do that. Society is a cruel judge, Eleanor."

"I am aware of that. My intention is to move from Haslemere and situate in another town where nobody knows me. I can restart my dressmaking business there. I'll ask Jane or Minnie to join me. Their families can use the money."

After hearing this, her mother's opinion on the matter did an abrupt turnabout. "If Mr. Grey insists on rearing the child, I suppose that is his prerogative. Your father will ask him to use all discretion. He can invent a story, that the child is his ward. He is her guardian, because her parents were tragically killed in a carriage accident." She paused briefly, apparently sorting out the remaining details. "He has the means and money to care for a child, much more so than you."

"You simply don't understand, Mama. I love Lili and want her with me. That is why I work so hard, why I've taxed myself, given up life's pleasures, so that I could save the money to carry out my plan."

No response. Perhaps she was using the wrong approach. Eleanor went to her mother and knelt in front of her. "Mama, do you not remember what it was like when I was a little girl? Would you have wanted to give me up? Knowing you would not be permitted to see me?"

But instead of drawing her empathy or understanding, this seemed to make her mother angry. Without looking at Eleanor, she said, "Do not be ridiculous. I would never have found myself in the same circumstances as you are in now. Your father and I were *married* when you were born."

Eleanor got to her feet and moved toward the door. "This is hopeless, Papa. I'll get my things and leave. You'll let me know when you've spoken to Hugh?"

But her mother wasn't finished yet. "It doesn't matter where you move, Eleanor, if it's even possible for you to do so. People will discover the truth, as they always do in these kinds of situations. You might as well send an announcement to the papers."

Eleanor simply looked at her father. "Papa?"

"You've said quite enough, Kitty. I'm sure Eleanor understands your feelings on the matter."

"I do not believe she, nor you, does. I had an agreement with Jacob Abbot. He was to do all he could to keep the little girl away from you. This relationship you want to have with her, it simply isn't done."

Eleanor gasped. "You what?"

"You may as well know. It doesn't matter anymore. Not long ago I concluded you would never drop the idea of being a mother to that child. So I paid him to do what he could to hinder your visits. It was for the best." Her look dared Eleanor to protest.

Eleanor felt her legs giving way and found the nearest chair. Her father looked thunderous. "Do you realize what you unleashed, Kitty? Do you know what kind of man he is?

He has attempted to extort money from Eleanor, and he is the one who set fire to Hugh's property."

Her mother's face flushed. She wasn't completely devoid of shame, then. "I did not like doing it, but I wanted Eleanor to face the hard truth of her situation."

With those words, an even more horrifying thought occurred to Eleanor. "You told him of your suspicions that Hugh was Lili's father, didn't you?"

"He needed leverage with you."

"And you provided it. How could you trust such a man? Weren't you worried he would tell the world?"

"It was not in his best interests to do so, and he was quite aware of that."

Feeling steadier now that she'd learned the worst, Eleanor rose. "I've been suspicious for some time that Abbot had a hidden motive for denying me access to Lili. How ironic that it was my own mother who was paying him for it."

"I was doing only what I thought best for you, dear. You must understand that."

Sir William had been quiet during this exchange, arousing suspicions in Eleanor. "What did you know of this, Papa?"

Shoulders stooped, his mouth sagging, he said, "I suspected. I never knew for a certainty. Forgive me, Eleanor. Had I known, I would have put a stop to it."

She spun around and made for the door. "I'll see myself home."

Her father hurried to the door and grasped her arm. "Let me escort you, Eleanor."

She shook him off. "No. I'll ask one of the grooms. Good night.

Chapter Twenty

The following day

Eleanor had lain awake much of the night. She could not recall having ever experienced such acute feelings of loneliness. It was a physical pain, settling around her heart. After losing Lili and Hugh, the knowledge that her mother had betrayed her was devastating.

Sitting on her garden bench the next morning sipping her tea, Eleanor tried to sort out her choices. She assumed her father would talk to Hugh, but she had little faith in his intervention. What could he say, after all, that would change Hugh's mind, if she herself could not convince him? She clung to the idea of removing Lili from the Abbots before Hugh had time to act. Lili had been baptized with the Broxton name. If Eleanor had never acknowledged Hugh as the father in law or in the church, didn't Lili belong to her? It wasn't as if she were destitute and would have to depend on the parish for aid.

Aggrieved and confused, Eleanor rose and strolled

about the garden. Her father may be right. Don't act rashly. Wait to see what Hugh would do. She glanced up to see the glorious sunrise, painting the sky burnt orange and violet and gunmetal gray. The colors matched the violence of her feelings. Hunkering down, she began aimlessly to pull weeds from her flower beds.

For the first time, she allowed herself to think of Hugh without considering Lili. He had always been a gentleman toward her, despite his reputation. She'd never believed him a rake. He'd gone off to war, come home, and become more polished, handsome, wealthy. And he was a man who knew what he wanted, exuding a confidence he'd seemed to lack previously.

And then there was the physical attraction between them. Even though she was inexperienced, she thought him a magnificent lover, skilled, tender, and patient with her lack of proficiency. She would never again experience those joys with him.

He had said he loved her. But if that were true, how could he so easily cast her aside? He'd accused her, among other things, of being exactly like his mother. She'd been right to worry, after she'd learned of his bitterness toward Deborah Grey, that he would likely judge her every bit as harshly.

A large part of the blame rested on her shoulders. She had kept the truth from him far too long. In her mind, she had plenty of reasons for doing so, but Hugh had a completely different perspective. If she put herself in his place, she could understand his anger. But didn't reasonable people, caring people, forgive each other? Hugh seemed uniquely willing to carry a grudge, to nurture it, hold it close, until it became a powerful, living thing, capable of causing unending pain to those forced to endure it. And to himself. It seemed an essential part of him, and he couldn't let it go. Didn't it hurt to blame his mother after all these years? To separate himself from his family and live alone in the world? That should have been a warning to Eleanor to stay away from him. Instead, she'd fallen deeply, irrevocably, in love with him. Feeling the sting of tears, she rose quickly and admonished herself.

Enough. Get to work.

She and the girls were nearly done with the end-of-season apparel. Eleanor needed to travel up to London to deliver the gowns and other items. Perhaps she would call on Cass and Adam. They might be able to advise her.

. . .

Hugh and Ned were in the middle of moving his father's massive desk into Hugh's study when he looked up to see Broxton standing nearby, watching. Oh, hell. He should have expected the man to call. "Ned, can you check on the progress in the kitchen? This will not take long." After they'd lowered the desk, Hugh pulled a handkerchief from his pocket and mopped his brow while he strolled over to Sir William.

"Good morning, Sir William," he said. He was determined to be civil.

"Sir Hugh," the older man said. "Is there somewhere we could speak privately?"

"Follow me." Hugh guided him through the halls to the back of the house and the study. "Mind your step," he said. He hoped there were a few chairs available. As it turned out, there was only one. His father's desk chair. Hugh gestured to it. "Sit down. I'll stand. I assume you're here to talk about your granddaughter."

Sir William appeared taken aback. "That's an odd way of stating it. I'm here on behalf of Eleanor, and Lili, too, because she's Eleanor's child and carries the Broxton name."

"Point taken," Hugh said wryly. It was damned awkward to stand there and stare down at the older gentleman. Before he could excuse himself to find another chair, Ned walked in carrying a tall stool. The man possessed an uncanny knack for anticipating Hugh's every wish. "Ah, my thanks, Ned." He slipped onto the stool, which was a minor improvement over standing.

When Ned was gone, Hugh got on with it. "Did Eleanor ask you to come?"

"Of course she did. She's bereft. Are you determined to carry through with this scheme?"

"By 'scheme,' if you mean my quite reasonable plan to rescue my daughter from the Abbots and bring her here, then yes. I am. It is beyond belief that you allowed Lili to be in their care."

Broxton shrugged, as though this choice held no significance, and that irritated the hell out of Hugh. "At the time, we had no reason to think them unfit as foster parents. And what about Eleanor? Do you intend to carry out your threat to keep her from Lili?"

Hugh sighed deeply. Did he truly wish to do so, or had he spoken those words out of anger and resentment? Despite what he'd said, his gut told him that Eleanor was a good mother. Of course, he had no way to judge, since he'd never even met Lili, nor seen her and her mother together. "That Eleanor allowed Lili to be removed from her care after she was born troubles me greatly."

Sir William raised his fists in the air and shook them. "You can't believe it was what she willingly would have chosen. She fought against it as best she could. Her mother and I didn't know what else to do, and Eleanor was recovering from a difficult birth. No doubt she didn't mention that, did she? She blames herself for everything, including her pregnancy."

For perhaps the first time, Hugh realized how this must appear to the Broxtons: like a seduction. But he had always thought of it as inevitable, the joining of two people who desperately wanted each other. So much so, that all reason had fled. "I asked Eleanor to tell me if there was a child. She chose not to. I've missed out on time I might have had with my daughter, and I resent that."

"It was wrong of her to deceive you for so long, I agree. But now that you know you have a child together, can you not forgive her? It is obvious to me that you care for each other. Why not marry her? That would absolve a multitude of sins."

Sins. A series of one sin after the other. The desiring, the giving in, the clandestine coupling. The secrecy, and the abandoning. If they were together, wedded, how would that redeem them? Make up for the first few years of a child's life? "It's not that simple," he said. "I wish to God it were."

Sir William rose, his posture sagging like that of a much older man. "Very well. I will not beg you. No need to show me out."

Hugh let him go. What more could be said? Just before he departed, Sir William straightened his shoulders and spoke once again. "Marrying Eleanor—that was my idea. She never would have asked it of you. And in case you are in any doubt, she is all that is good and true and fine in a woman. With parents such as Kitty and me, I'm not sure how that came about." With a rueful smile, he turned and was gone.

Hugh lowered his head into his hands. God, that had been torture.

After Broxton left, Ned and Hugh finished moving the desk into Hugh's study. "This thing is a monstrosity," Ned announced. "You know that, don't you?"

Hugh laughed. "When I was a lad, I used to beg my father to let me sit in the desk chair and play steward. On rare occasions, he allowed it. Now I have the unenviable task of clearing out the drawers."

"I'll leave you to it, then."

Much of what Hugh found would go directly into the

rubbish. Other items, such as estate record books, he set aside to examine later. After an hour or so, he lifted a stack of letters from a bottom drawer. Had his parents written to each other, perhaps before their marriage? Wrapped in a blue ribbon, they looked as if they'd never been read, or even unfolded. The writing bore the softer curlicues of a feminine hand, and he recognized it as Deborah's. He untied the ribbon, and, rather than starting at the top, he began with the one on the bottom.

Did he already know what they were? Have a sixth sense about them? His heart was knocking hard against his ribs when he unfolded the first one. "My dearest Hugh," it said. He dropped it as though it were a burning coal and found he needed a moment to regain his wits. Hastily, he sorted through the others. Although the greeting sometimes differed, all were written to him from his mother, dated from June, 1799, and continuing through October of 1805. He would have been over twenty-one by then. The earliest date was around the time she'd left Longmere. He'd never seen a single one of them.

25 June
London

My dearest Hugh,

Leaving you, my precious son, has been the most difficult thing I've ever had to do. It was no longer possible for me to live with your father, and I hope someday you will understand and forgive me. He would not allow me to remove both his sons and insisted on keeping you, his firstborn, with him. I cannot blame him for that. Adam misses you quite as much as I do, although he won't admit to it for fear of seeming "unmanly."

I am in the process of arranging, through a solicitor, to visit you, and for you to visit us in London. Please, darling, write to me. I am looking forward to hearing of your progress with your tutor. My dearest, do not let the pig have the run of the house. I fear your father will neither notice nor care. Animals belong out-of-doors or in the stables. Or the pigpen, in this case.

Perhaps by autumn, matters will be worked out and we shall look forward to a visit with you.

I love you always,
Mama

His mother had written to him. Many times, apparently. And not only that, but she had attempted to visit him and arrange for him to visit her and Adam. Hugh chortled over his pet pig, whom he hadn't thought of for years. Theodora. How had he ever come up with that name? He'd been so resentful of his mother's departure, he *had* let the animal run about the house at will, if memory served.

He read another, later missive. This one was written from her country house.

17 October
Surrey

My darling Hugh,

I have given up on lawyers to gain access to you and am now trying to appeal to your father's better nature.

Adam and I are at your grandparents' home in Surrey, and how we all wish you could be here with us! Adam most particularly, since grouse season is in full swing. It would give me such pleasure to see the two of you tramping through the fields together.

I've been to visit you several times, my dear, to no avail. The servants have strict orders not to allow me entrance to the house. Perhaps you might tell your father you wish to see me and your brother. Whether that would change his mind, I do not know, but please try, for all our sakes.

I hope you will make a renewed effort with your tutor in the coming year. You must study diligently in order to sit for the entrance exams for university. Adam perseveres, and I hope I can count on your efforts in this regard as well.

I have not given up hope of seeing you, my dearest boy.

Your loving mother

The letter was interesting on at least two counts. Legally, she had never been granted the right to see him, though she had continued to try. From the sound of it, numerous times. And appealing to his father's better nature in any situation had been a waste of time. He'd never possessed one. Wesley, his father's elderly butler, had not been mistaken after all. And Wesley, possibly others, had supplied her with information about him. Obviously, one of them had told her Hugh's schoolwork had dropped off.

A heartbreaking letter followed that one, carrying the news of the stillbirth of a child. His mother did not dwell on the tragedy. "The baby, a girl, was stillborn. You and Adam would have had a sister. She looked like you, darling, with dark curls and eyes."

Christ! How had his mother borne it? Hugh clearly remembered finding solace in tramping about the sere countryside alone. He felt the sheen of tears in his eyes merely remembering it, and how isolated he'd felt in his grief. His father, after curtly informing him of the stillbirth, had locked himself in his library, and Hugh had not seen him for days. And Deborah must have had only Adam to comfort her, although her mother and father had still been alive then.

He scanned through the remaining letters, noticing how his mother's resolve weakened with the passage of time. She made fewer and fewer mentions of visits. Her tone, many times, was despairing. "Oh, dearest, am I to be kept from you forever?" Had she any idea he wasn't receiving her letters? Hugh had always known his father was a pathetic excuse for a man, but how could he have been so cruel as to separate him from his mother? To not even allow them to correspond?

As a youth, Hugh had been stubborn, wounded, and had never brought up the matter with his father. And he'd hidden when Adam visited Longmere, so he wouldn't be forced to see him.

He regretted that now, bitterly.

Hugh rested his head in his hands. Through the lens of years, he could see he bore some of the responsibility for keeping them all apart. What a fool he'd been! He'd mistakenly blamed his mother for abandoning him and had heaped guilt on Adam as well, even though he was the younger brother.

This must be rectified.

He would make another trip to London and meet with his mother. To beg her forgiveness. She'd had reasons, insurmountable reasons, for acting as she had. Deborah had done all within her power to see him, to remain a vital part of his life. Hell, she'd probably stayed with his father long after any sane woman would have left.

And now he could only hope it wasn't too late.

Chapter Twenty-One

A few days later

Eleanor, Jane, and Minnie were packing the remaining pieces of apparel in bandboxes, wrapping them carefully in lengths of cloth.

"How are you going to deliver these to Town, miss?" Minnie asked.

"I'll ask my father if I can borrow the carriage. It would be too risky to go by mail coach—I can't be sure the dresses wouldn't be jostled off the roof of the conveyance somewhere along the way. Imagine all our hard work lost because the coach hit a particularly deep pothole."

The girls laughed, except for Eleanor. In the quiet, Jane said, "Miss, are you all right, then? It's just that you've been ever so quiet the last few days. And you look tired."

Eleanor had been dreading their questions, but she supposed they were inevitable. If she looked one quarter as bad as she felt, they must be appalled. "I am tired, as you both must be as well. I can never thank you sufficiently for your efforts these past weeks."

"You worked as hard as we did, miss," Jane said, giving her a sidelong glance. "We all could use a rest, I'll wager."

"And we shall have it, as soon as these boxes are filled and delivered. No more work for a fortnight. I shall pay each of you during your time off."

"Oh, miss! You can't afford that," Minnie said.

Eleanor laughed. "It's true I can't afford much, but I'd intended to give you each a little something to thank you for the extra effort you put in on these orders."

The door banged open, and three heads swiveled around. "Papa," Eleanor said. Everything from his disheveled appearance to his flushed, agitated countenance signaled trouble, as did his labored breathing. "Do sit down and tell me what has happened. Jane, bring him some water."

Her father eased himself into a chair, and the three women fussed about him. Eleanor dabbed at his face with a wet cloth, Jane handed him water to drink, and Minnie simply wrung her hands.

Tugging at his cravat, he spoke at last. "Jane, Minnie, I must have a private word with Eleanor."

If she'd known intervening with Hugh would cause her father such distress, she never would have asked it of him. She dropped the cloth and turned to her assistants. "Thank you both for everything. I shall see you when I've returned from London."

"But miss, you might need us," Minnie said, protesting their abrupt dismissal.

"If I do, I shall send for you immediately. Trust me to do so." She mustered a smile while ushering them out the door. In seconds she was back at her father's side.

"Now, tell me, Papa. Did your talk with Hugh cause this?"

He waved a hand through the air. "No, no. It is worse than you can imagine. The Abbots have run off with Lili."

Eleanor felt the blood drain from her face. She forced herself to breathe deeply, to maintain her composure. Nothing would be gained by hysterics. "Tell me all you know."

"Tom Vickers, the Abbots' nearest neighbor, brought the news. Said Abbot told him he was taking his wife and the little girl and heading for Portsmouth to find work."

Eleanor, who'd been kneeling on the floor in front of her father's chair, now sat back on her heels. "But why? What does he gain by taking Lili?"

"I don't know. Vickers couldn't get much sense out of the man, to hear him tell it."

"How did Mr. Vickers know to come to you?"

"Apparently, Abbot told him so, which makes me think Abbot has a plan. Make no mistake, he wants money."

"We must go after them, Papa. He has Lili."

"Yes." Leaning forward, her father grasped her by the shoulders. "Eleanor, we need to inform Sir Hugh."

Her first inclination was to say no. But if she'd learned anything over the last few days, it was that secrecy and dishonesty hurt everybody in the end, and in this instance could do irreparable harm. She'd no doubt that Hugh would be their best ally in bringing Lili home safely. After the cruel, baseless things he'd accused her of, she hated having to ask for his help. And after this, his low opinion of Eleanor would worsen. But that mattered little given the circumstances.

"Why don't you rest here for a time and then return home? I'll find Hugh. I'm certain he'll have an idea of where to start, what to do first."

"Very well. But don't be long."

Eleanor patted him on the shoulder on her way out the door.

When she arrived at Longmere, Eleanor spotted Ned conferring with some laborers near the front door. She dug her nails into his arm, and that got his attention.

"Miss Broxton, may I help you?"

"I need to speak with Sir Hugh. It is urgent."

She'd gotten her point across, because without any hesitation, he said, "He's inside somewhere. I'll find him. I'll be just a moment."

Eleanor waited, pacing, and in the promised moment, Hugh appeared. Her head shot up, and their eyes locked. That cold look he'd bestowed upon her during their recent meeting flickered briefly in his eyes before he seemed to sense her distress. Grasping her arms, he said, "Eleanor, what is it? I was upstairs packing for London."

"Oh, Hugh." Tears welled in her eyes, but she blinked them back. "Abbot and his wife have left Haslemere and taken Lili with them. We must go after them. I don't know how long they've been gone, but they have an excellent head start by now."

"That villain has absconded with my daughter?" He glanced about. "Come inside. You must explain everything to me." Taking her by the hand, he led her down the hall and into his library. After she was seated, he walked into the passage and hollered at one of the workers to ask someone called Mrs. Foster to provide tea. "And for Christ's sake, find another chair!"

A second chair was quickly brought, and Hugh placed it across from Eleanor's, before the windows. "Tell me what you know," he said.

"There isn't much."

When her account was complete, he said, "You're right, it's not much to go on. Abbot, his wife, and our daughter are gone to Portsmouth. But we don't have a direction, or any idea where they might be." He seemed lost in thought for a moment. "Before we race after them, we must make inquiries here to see if we can find out anything that might help us. I want to speak to this Vickers fellow myself."

Mrs. Foster brought in the tea and set it on the desk. Hugh thanked her and poured it himself. After handing Eleanor a cup, he said, "I agree with your father. Abbot wants money." He swallowed the contents of his cup and poured more. "I want Ned to talk to the other laborers. Abbot may have revealed things to them, even if inadvertently, about his intentions."

"But this is all going to take so long," Eleanor said. "Are you sure it's worth the time to talk to these people?"

"I understand your frustration. But if we head to Portsmouth without any idea of where or how to find them, it will take much longer in the end." He placed the palm of his hand against her cheek. When she flinched and drew back, he jerked his hand away. "I understand how worried you must be. I am, too. Now, drink up. We have work to do."

"I am coming to Portsmouth with you. You do realize that, don't you?"

He didn't argue with her. "I'll be at your parents' home within an hour."

• • •

After he'd seen Eleanor off, Hugh found Ned supervising the unloading of materials and motioned to him. They were well out of earshot of anyone else. He kept the tale brief. Ned showed no shock, or even surprise, that Hugh and Eleanor had a child together. In truth, Hugh was beginning to believe there was nothing that could rattle the man. Ned's one question concerned what explanation to give the others as to why they needed to find Abbot.

"Put them off," Hugh said impatiently. "Tell them we

believe he knows something about the fire. No need to say we suspect him."

"Some of the men may have guessed. I took a few of them aside and made some inquiries. Didn't learn anything useful."

Hugh pulled his watch from his pocket. "I'm going to ride out to see Thomas Vickers. He may know more than what he told Sir William. Meet me in an hour at the Broxtons', by the stables. If you've any extra clothing here, you should pack a few things," Hugh said.

Ned turned to walk away, but Hugh stopped him. "One more thing. Can you see to sending an express to my brother in London? Tell him Lili's been taken, and ask him to meet us where the London Road meets the Portsmouth High Street, tomorrow morning at ten o'clock."

The other man nodded, and both went off to their respective tasks.

Hugh found Vickers's farm easily enough. The man he sought was in the stables, checking on a horse with a sore hock.

"Thomas Vickers?"

"That's me," Vickers said. "You'll pardon me if I don't shake hands." He'd been rubbing liniment on the sore spot and hadn't cleaned up yet. "What can I do for you?"

Hugh introduced himself and explained he was trying to help Sir William track down the Abbots. "Can you tell me anything else? Anything you may have neglected to tell Broxton?"

Vickers lowered the horse's leg gently and motioned Hugh outside, wiping his hands on a rag. It was late afternoon, the hottest part of the day. "Like what?"

"Where does Abbot intend to find work, for one thing?"

"Shipbuilding. He heard they're looking for men to help

manufacture the wooden blocks used in riggings."

"Ah. A block mill, then. With his skills, that makes sense."

Vickers shrugged. "I suppose so."

"Does he have friends there, or family? There are any number of places he could find work as a carpenter without going all the way to Portsmouth."

"But maybe no place else he can be so well concealed," the other man said, giving Hugh a sly look.

Hugh held an advantage in both height and weight over Vickers, who was a little too smug for Hugh's liking. He stepped closer to the man and said, "Did Abbot pay you to bring the news to Sir William?"

Vickers dodged the question. "I've told you all I know. Now, if you'll excuse me, there's work to do around here."

Hugh sensed there was nothing else to find out from this source. He'd gotten the man's back up, and even if there were more to the story, Vickers wouldn't be of a mind to reveal it.

· · ·

While her father saw to readying the mounts and making other preparations, Eleanor bathed and changed into a traveling dress. She had no illusions about riding all the way to Portsmouth—it was upward of thirty miles—and she didn't need to be told she wasn't up to it. She would travel in the carriage with one of the maids while the men rode.

When she descended the stairs, her mother awaited her. They hadn't spoken since last night's revelations, and Eleanor had no wish to speak to her now. As far as she was concerned, her mother bore some of the responsibility for this turn of events. She had conspired with Abbot to keep Lili from her; indeed, had paid him to do so. Her actions had encouraged Abbot in the belief that he could blackmail Eleanor with impunity. With disastrous consequences.

"I asked Mrs. Simpson to pack some sandwiches for you to eat along the way." She held out a basket, and Eleanor accepted it. She wouldn't turn down food, for the sake of the others, if not for herself. "Sarah has packed your things and will accompany you."

"Fine. Thank you." Eleanor attempted to brush past her mother, but the other woman wasn't ready to yield.

In a flat tone, her mother said, "Forgive me, Eleanor. I should never have had any dealings with that man. It was very wrong of me."

As apologies went, it was less than heartfelt. "Mama, I've no time for this. As I'm sure you understand, I am only concerned with one thing right now. Lili's safety and welfare. Your actions have put her at risk, as you're aware." Carrying the basket, she shoved her way past her mother.

"Don't you think you are exaggerating the danger?" her mother asked, infuriating Eleanor.

Halfway to the door, she slid to a stop. Trembling with anger, she said, "If any harm comes to Lili, I will never forgive you. And make no mistake, that's not an exaggeration." Eleanor couldn't help gloating over the shocked look on her parent's face.

Out back, her father awaited her, his horse shuffling nervously. "What kept you?" he said.

"I apologize. Mama wished to say a word to me." Eleanor recognized Hugh's horse, and the other animal must belong to Ned. In a moment, the two men came around the corner of the stables.

Hugh spoke first, the unacknowledged leader. "Ah, I see we're all here now, save one. My brother will meet us tomorrow morning in Portsmouth. Ned and I need to inform you of what we've learned. Ned?"

"I questioned the men Abbot worked closest with, the other carpenters and woodworkers, but I'm afraid I didn't learn much. One of the men said Abbot once brought up Portsmouth and the opportunities to be found there. This was after the fire, apparently, but none of the others had an interest, so Abbot dropped it."

"Did they think that was odd?" Eleanor asked.

"As far as I could tell, they didn't think much about it one way or the other. Sir Hugh, tell them what you learned."

"I paid a visit to Thomas Vickers. He said Abbot specifically mentioned wanting to work in the block mills. If Vickers knew more, he wouldn't say."

"But that's a good lead," Sir William said. "We can inquire at the manufactories."

"Do we have a plan?" Eleanor asked. An urgency clawed at her to be under way.

Hugh shook his head. "Not a very well formed one, I'm afraid. Once we get to Portsmouth, we'll stop for the night and discuss how to proceed in the morning. We know where Abbot might seek work, which is in our favor. Traveling with a child, they can't be too far ahead of us." He glanced around at them, and Eleanor thought he paused particularly long to study her. Did he expect her to change her mind about going?

Hugh gave a brief nod. "It is late, but the days are long. We should be able to make it to Portsmouth before night falls, barring any unforeseen disasters with people, carriages, or horses. We'll stop once to refresh ourselves."

He was all business, and she was glad of it. Everybody nodded their assent, and a groom helped Eleanor up the carriage steps. In another moment, they set off toward the London Road, heading south to Portsmouth.

Chapter Twenty-Two

Hugh let Ned take the lead so he might think unimpeded. He had debated asking Eleanor not to travel with them; indeed, he'd thought about forbidding it. She would slow them down. But he couldn't bring himself to do it.

Her countenance was pale, and from the looks of her, she hadn't been eating. He blamed himself for that. If only he'd waited to speak to her about their daughter until after he'd had a chance to calm down and consider the matter from her point of view. He should have been more understanding. She'd deceived him, and he had a right to be angry. But he was beginning to comprehend her reasons, one of which was to shield him from scandal. And she'd apologized. Most sincerely. But no, like the resentful, judgmental man he was, he had barged in and accused her of everything from lying to neglecting and abandoning her child. He'd said she was exactly like his mother, and she hadn't even flinched. She carried too much on those slim shoulders as it was, and he'd added to her burdens. And now this.

Could Eleanor possibly have believed he would not

want Lili? She had said she did not know the kind of man he was and had no idea what to expect from him. At the time she had learned she was with child, their acquaintance had been of short duration. It wasn't until he'd returned and they'd become close—more than close—that he'd confessed his feelings about his mother. She could not have known he would never, ever, willingly give up a child he'd fathered. She'd stated, and she was right, that in such a circumstance, men usually ask to be informed if there are consequences. It was de rigueur. Most men wouldn't have meant it sincerely, though Hugh most certainly had. But she hadn't known that at the time they'd made love atop some hay bales on a freezing November night.

Eleanor had said she wished to start over posing as a widow with a child, in a new location. Perhaps she believed that was the only way forward. Such a lonely, isolated existence that would be.

• • •

They broke the journey at a coaching inn near Petersfield. Ned opened the door of the coach and let down the steps for Eleanor, and they joined her father and Hugh, who were waiting in the yard.

"We haven't much time," Hugh said. "I'll have them bring out a tankard for everybody. Eleanor, I understand your cook provided us with victuals?"

She'd forgotten about the basket, since food was the last thing on her mind. "Yes. Sandwiches. The basket is in the coach." She turned to retrieve it, but Hugh stopped her.

"Leave it. We'll congregate there in a few minutes."

Eleanor nodded and went off to locate the privy. When she'd finished, she found a barrel of water nearby for washing up. While she was rinsing her hands, something caught her eye. A bit of white fabric, which she initially assumed was a lost handkerchief, lay beneath a scraggly yew tree. Out of curiosity, she drew closer to investigate. It was then that she noticed the vivid red fabric, now torn and soiled, attached to the bit of white. Her heart rioting in her chest, she squatted down and picked it up.

It was Lili's doll.

Eleanor didn't know if she possessed the strength to stand up again. If her legs would hold her. But at length she stood, and they did. Clutching the doll to her chest, she made her way back to the front of the inn and found the others gathered around the carriage. Her father had opened the basket, and he, Ned, and Sarah, Eleanor's maid, were all munching on sandwiches. Hugh stood alone, drinking from a tankard. Eleanor stopped before she reached them. Hugh looked up and saw her, tossed his drink to the ground, and came to her at once.

He grasped her arm. "You must sit before you fall down," he said. "What is this you're holding? What have you found?"

She felt the stares of the others. Somehow, Hugh shooed them away from the carriage and helped Eleanor inside, then climbed in and sat next to her. He started to speak, but before he got any words out, a great, racking sob burst from her. She dropped the doll and covered her face with her hands.

"Is this Lili's doll, Eleanor? It looks like countless other dolls to me, but I can see you've recognized it, and most likely made the dress. You've taken such pains with it. It's beautiful. Is that right?"

She nodded. "And the doll." His voice was soft, almost crooning, and it soothed her. When she uncovered her face, Hugh handed her his handkerchief. "Lili loves her doll. She sleeps with it, carries it about. She would never leave it or throw it away. Someone took it from her. Maybe hurt her. Oh God, Hugh."

Now he clutched her shoulders and gave her a slight shake. "Look at me. They were probably in a hurry, and Mrs. Abbot took her to the privy. When they dashed off, Lili dropped the doll. It was most certainly an accident. Nothing more."

"But what if—"

Hugh gave her a stern look. "I forbid any 'what-ifs.' Try to see this in a positive light. Now we know we're on the right track. We know for certain they were here, at this very inn, which means there is no longer any doubt as to where they are headed. This is the proof we needed."

Eleanor dabbed at her face with the handkerchief. "Very well. I'll try to look at it that way."

"Can you eat something, Eleanor? You need your strength for tomorrow. That is when we shall find our daughter, yes?"

She couldn't help smiling. "Yes."

"I'm not leaving this carriage until you've bitten into a sandwich." He fished one out of the basket for her, then opened the carriage door and shouted to Ned. In a minute, Ned passed Hugh a tankard of ale.

She supposed she would be holding them up if she did not try to eat, so she dutifully took a bite and washed it down with some ale. After she'd repeated the process a few times, Hugh seemed satisfied.

"Well done," he said, smiling. When he turned to climb out, Eleanor laid a hand on his arm.

"Hugh." He paused and looked at her, eyebrow cocked. "I will always regret keeping Lili from you."

Did his expression harden? He nodded and was gone so fast she could not judge his frame of mind.

The remainder of the trip flew past in a blur. Eleanor sat and stroked the doll, remembering her last visit with Lili, how she'd helped her to dress it in the ball gown. Her little hands had not quite been up to the task. Sarah, perched on the opposite seat, was knitting. Eleanor didn't know how she could do so in such dim light.

Hugh was being quite kind. She could almost forgive him for his harsh words and his grim determination to remove Lili from her. But he hadn't asked for her forgiveness, nor had he said anything about a change of heart. This whole episode further called into question Eleanor's fitness as Lili's mother.

It was of no consequence. Nothing mattered right now except finding Lili.

When they neared Portsmouth, the traffic increased. Eleanor glimpsed the cobalt blue of the sea shimmering in the distance and spotted riggings of some of the ships. The coach slowed and stopped, and she heard the men conferring. After a moment, the carriage door opened, and her father, after putting down the steps, motioned to her to descend. "Come, Norrie."

For the first time, Eleanor swiveled around to take in her surroundings. The London Road had given way to the High Street in Portsmouth. The garrison, a looming fortress built of limestone, stretched in either direction. Hugh said, "Are you up to a short walk? The coach must be conveyed to the livery, and given the volume of traffic, we don't want to attempt to drive it through Town." Hugh offered his arm, but she pretended not to see.

"Of course," she said, eyes seeking her father. He smiled at her, and she grasped his arm. She could not allow herself to want Hugh, to trust him, to lean on him, ever again. Depend on him she must, to find Lili. But there was no sense in pursuing an artificial closeness with him. After they'd secured the safety of their daughter, their relationship would become adversarial. He, the instrument of her loss, would become her enemy. She must not forget that, even temporarily.

After passing through the Landport Gate, they set off walking, jostled by the crowds. Naval officers in their blue coats with gold buttons, seamen in varying dress, all of them wearing cocked hats. Women of questionable virtue, dressed in their evening finery, strolled about. Eleanor tried not to gawk. Fishmongers, costermongers, and flower vendors were all hawking their wares, striving to be heard over the cacophony. Even at this hour, the road was heavily trafficked with drays, carts, and coaches jockeying for position, and in some cases, narrowly avoiding accidents. Eleanor's confidence began to ebb. How could they ever find one little girl amid all this chaos?

After passing the Customs House and crossing a bridge, they took East Street to Broad Street, until they found the area where the hostelries were located. Her father explained they were at the Point, home of the vast dockyard. This was the part of Town in which they were most likely to find the Abbots, and thus Lili.

They secured rooms at the King's Tower Inn, a reputable-looking establishment. "I'll request a private dining parlor," Hugh said. Although he seemed composed, Eleanor saw signs of exhaustion in the lines around his mouth and the tension in his expression. "Shall we meet here for supper in, say, a half hour?"

Eleanor and Sarah found their room. After the maid had helped her bathe and change, Eleanor flopped down on the bed. "I want to close my eyes for just a moment," she said.

"But, miss, you hardly have time for that."

Nonetheless, she fell into a deep abyss, and when Sarah roused her a mere fifteen minutes later, her mood was black.

• • •

When the group met for supper, Hugh realized they were all somewhat worse for wear. The deep grooves around Sir William's mouth seemed more pronounced, and even Ned appeared haggard, while Eleanor's eyes were puffy.

It was late, past ten o'clock now. Hugh had ordered a light collation. A servant brought in cold mutton and fowl, vegetables, bread, and cheese. And wine. Plenty of wine. He'd borrowed a map of the Point from the innkeeper and spread it out on the table. While they ate, he suggested a starting point for running Jacob Abbot to ground.

"We should start at the shipbuilding yard." He tapped the location on the map. "That's where the block mills are located, as well as any other labor that would involve carpentry."

"Agreed," Ned said. "But how do we approach them? We can't simply wander in and look around for Abbot. There must be hundreds of men employed in the yard."

There was general agreement with Ned's statement. "Surely they have offices," Sir William said. "We can start there."

Eleanor's voice cut into the self-assured ones of the men. "You do realize that Edith Abbot will be the one looking after Lili? And she won't be anywhere near the dockyard. She'll be somewhere in this maze of streets, in lodgings. Or perhaps in a park."

Hugh winced. Leave it to Eleanor to get to the heart of the matter. "Of course, you're right. But, unless we find her husband, how will we find her and Lili? I had thought to locate Abbot and follow him."

"While two of us are pursuing the lead at the block mills, others can be checking on the most likely areas where they might have taken rooms," Ned said. "And visit parks, the quay, anyplace a mother might take a child." He swept a hand over the pertinent areas of the map.

"Eleanor, can you give us a description of Mrs. Abbot?" Hugh asked.

"Of course." She smiled. "Look for a woman who is heavy with child. She would be approaching confinement if she were in normal circumstances. But keeping a child Lili's age in rooms all day would be difficult, so I don't believe the usual rules would apply."

Broxton chimed in. "She's a small woman, brown haired. Unfortunately, no truly distinguishing features."

"One thing," Eleanor said. "She has a mole, just here." She pointed to a spot above one corner of her mouth, by her nose. "The left side."

Hugh hated to ask the next question in front of the group, but it couldn't be helped. "And Lili. Describe her, if you will." He heard the coldness in his voice, and so would everybody else.

Tears welled in Eleanor's eyes, and a faint blush colored her cheeks. If he weren't so deuced angry with her, he would wrap his arms around her and try to comfort her.

Looking at him straight on, she said, "Lili has your coloring, Hugh. Dark hair, dark brown eyes. She is nearly two years old and is quite lively."

Hugh held Eleanor's gaze. He'd been so sure Lili would resemble Eleanor, not him. He couldn't help what burst out next. "She doesn't look like you, then? I had expected she would."

The others had gone quiet, but after a moment, some judicious throat clearing interrupted the private moment between Hugh and Eleanor. Ned said, "Is she talking?"

"Oh my, yes. She's making sentences, quite coherent ones. She knows my dog, Bobby. If you should find her, ask her if she would like to play with Bobby. And see her mama." She blushed and lowered her head.

It struck Hugh then that Eleanor must see a good deal of Lili. In the throes of his anger, he had imagined she visited the child rarely. But he was wrong. She knew things about Lili that she couldn't possibly know unless she saw her regularly. "She is close in age to my nephew, then," Hugh said.

"Yes." He could see that Eleanor was on the verge

of weeping, and he wasn't feeling too well in control of his emotions, either. He cleared his throat. "The hour grows late, and we should all get some rest.

"If we agree, in the morning Ned and I will take the dockyard, since we can both identify Abbot. Sir William, Adam, and Eleanor will divide up the streets and be on the lookout for Mrs. Abbot and Lili. You can ask the innkeeper about parks or other likely places small children might be taken by their nursemaids or parents before you set out."

Wearily, they agreed to the plan.

"One thing we haven't discussed," Sir William said. "What do we do with Abbot when we find him? Turn him over to the magistrate?"

"I've been debating that," Hugh said. "He's guilty of several serious offenses. Arson. Extortion. And now, kidnapping. And we've yet to discover his motive for it, since there have been no demands for money."

"As much as I despise the man," Eleanor said, "I have sympathy for his wife. What will happen to her if he's transported, or hanged?"

Hugh nodded, looking her in the eye. "I've thought the same thing. But perhaps arrangements could be made to offer her aid." He pushed his chair back and stood. "We have time yet to think on it."

It was after eleven o'clock when they began to wander off to their beds. Hugh asked Eleanor to remain behind for a moment. She nodded, although she didn't seem happy about it. He was not sure why he wished to speak to her, but he wasn't ready to let her go just yet. For the first time, the vague abstraction of a child seemed more real to him. He was father to a two-year-old child, and she was that child's mother. Despite everything, he loved her. God, how he loved her. For the last week, he'd been denying it to himself, but it was no use.

"I know you are tired, and I won't keep you long," he said. Guiltily, he noticed the dark circles under her eyes.

She resumed her seat. "What is it, Hugh?"

Not a good beginning. Especially when he wasn't sure what he wished to say. "I wanted you to know that I…perhaps… that is, I may have spoken too hastily and too harshly when I confronted you about Lili. I should have waited until I'd had time to sort matters out. Instead, I rushed to judgment and said some unforgivable things." He hesitated, because Eleanor's expression hadn't softened one iota. He couldn't blame her. He sounded weak and tentative.

When she made no response, he bumbled on. "I can see you are an excellent mother, in the circumstances. I've recently learned that mothers oftentimes cannot do as they might wish where children are concerned. And I've come to believe they should be forgiven for it."

"What do you mean? How did you learn this?"

"I found some letters my mother sent me after she left Longmere. My father had never given them to me. All these years, I've thought she didn't give a damn about me." He laughed softly, shaking his head. "And one night when I was at Adam's, Wesley, my father's old butler, mentioned that my mother had tried over the years to visit me, but Father had forbidden it. I never knew any of this."

"So you've forgiven your mother and now believe you should forgive me. I do hope, for both your sakes, that you can reconcile. However, my life will carry on, even if you never forgive *me*. As I tried to explain, I did the best I could for Lili. I love my daughter more than my life, and at present, my chief concern is finding her."

Hugh sighed. He seemed unable to say what was in his heart. Her words, her feelings, confused him. He'd meant this to be an apology, but he'd ended up sounding like God doling out absolution.

Abruptly, Eleanor pushed back her chair and stood. "What about seeking custody of Lili? Are you going to carry on with that plan?"

Because of his confusion, and her coldness, and the fact that he was weary to the bone, he said, "Yes."

She spun on her heel and exited the room, leaving him bewildered.

Christ. How could things have gone so wrong? He slammed his wineglass into the hearth. The shards glowed like hellfire.

Chapter Twenty-Three

Eleanor avoided any direct contact with Hugh in the morning. She, her father, and Adam Grey, who had arrived while they were eating breakfast, conferred with the innkeeper before setting out. He showed them on the map where most of the dockyard laborers resided and pointed out a few parks. Eleanor, who had spent a restless night rehashing the conversation she'd had with Hugh, was desperate to do anything to end this nightmare. To see Lili safe, most of all, but also to confront the future and consider how she would learn to live with it.

"I will head toward the quay, back the way we came in. I recall seeing a few green areas as we walked toward the inn, where a woman might take a child," Sir William said.

"Are you sure, Papa? I can pair with you if you'd rather."

"No, no. You and Mr. Grey will cover more ground without me. What should our approach be, if we happen to find them?" Sir William asked. Both men looked at Eleanor.

"I don't think it would be wise for any of us to approach Mrs. Abbot alone. She'll be frightened. With at least two of us there, we can be more…persuasive. If you should find her, Papa, send word of where you are, and we will come to you."

"Might she try to bolt?"

"In her condition, and with a two-year-old in tow, she wouldn't get far." What else to tell them? "It's been my impression she doesn't entirely agree with her husband's actions, but I believe she may be afraid of him. One of us, probably you, Adam, would need to find Hugh and Ned. Papa and I could stay with her until Abbot came home from his shift, if necessary."

"This will all be moot if we don't make a start," Sir William said.

"We'll meet you back here for supper," said Adam.

Before departing, Eleanor kissed her father's cheek. "Thank you, Papa."

They walked up and down the cramped streets, with tall, narrow houses blocking the light. A stench rose from the gutters. Cooking odors wafted through open doorways and windows. Bacon, onions, fish. Eleanor hoped, if Lili were here somewhere, it would not be for long. They caught sight of only a few mothers, one with three children, another with a newborn baby. In both cases, Eleanor approached the women and asked if they'd seen anyone new about and described Edith Abbot and Lili. But no, they had not.

After a few hours of fruitless exploration of the streets, Adam found a bench and told Eleanor to sit. They had worked their way toward the sea, and she had a clear view of Spithead, where the ships coming into port lay at anchor. She glimpsed frigates, schooners, even a warship. Now that the war was finally over, where would they moor all the ships? The air was heavy with moisture, and it seemed rain was inevitable.

In a few moments, Adam returned with tea for each of them.

"Thank you. This is most welcome."

They sipped quietly for a time. Adam finally broke the silence and said, "Eleanor, I realize this is not my business, so I'll say only this. My brother was deeply hurt when my mother and I left Longmere, and he has never quite gotten over it. He's making the mistake of equating your situation with Deborah's at the time. I believe he knows in his heart that his thinking is wrongheaded—"

"Does he? Just last night he told me he still intends to take Lili from me and raise her himself. It was wrong of me to not tell him about Lili the minute he returned. He knows how bitterly I regret it, but nevertheless, he is determined to punish me."

"He's as stubborn as they come, the damned fool. Lately, I've noticed a softening in him, but this has been a setback. Allow him some time."

Eleanor didn't comment, merely nodded.

By four o'clock, they had reached the peak of frustration. The rain that had been threatening all day was falling, and they hurried back to the inn huddled under Adam's umbrella. Sir William had also failed to discover anything useful. Adam suggested they remain at the inn and wait for Hugh and Ned. In Eleanor's mind, the fact that they'd heard nothing from them didn't bode well.

"I'll speak to the innkeeper about reserving the private dining parlor for this evening. Why don't you try to get some rest?" Adam said.

But once in her room, Eleanor was jittery. She tried to read but couldn't concentrate. Sarah urged her to lie down, but she couldn't relax. At length, she got to her feet and said, "I'm going out. You'd better come with me, Sarah."

When the maid looked as if she were about to protest, Eleanor said, "Fresh air will do you good. You've been indoors all day."

The rain had let up, but the air remained heavy with moisture. Although she did not do so consciously, Eleanor walked toward the dockyard. She had no plan, no idea of what she would do there. She knew only that she urgently wished to find Hugh and Ned and learn their news, if they had any to convey.

They wound their way over to Otter Street. The dockyard itself was impossible to miss, encompassing factories, storehouses, a vast dry dock where ships were built and repaired, and enormous ponds where the riggings were soaked until the wood was cured. Eleanor had no intention of entering the area; she merely wanted to have a look at it. They ended up at the stairway leading to the ramparts, part of the fortifications surrounding the city. "Let's go up," Eleanor said, gesturing to Sarah to follow her. When they reached the top, the wind blew in their faces, carrying the smell of the sea with it.

Eleanor turned and looked the opposite way, down into the yard. Was she dreaming, or was that Hugh and Ned she glimpsed standing near the dry dock below and looking upward? Had they seen her? No. They were looking at something else. She turned and saw a man racing along the ramparts, headed directly toward where she was standing.

The man was Jacob Abbot.

In mere seconds he would pass by where she was standing. What should she do? Glancing down, she saw Hugh and Ned dashing toward the dockyard exit, probably to locate another access stairway. Should she try to stop Abbot? He'd get away before Hugh and Ned could catch him if she did nothing.

She heard Sarah call to her, but she paid no attention. Abbot hurtled toward her, unaware of who she was. Suddenly, he was on her, and she screamed, "Jacob Abbot!" He slowed, but didn't stop. She gave chase, hollering, "Mr. Abbot! Mr.

Abbot!" To her amazement, he skidded to a halt and spun to face her.

"You," he said. He took a step closer. "You're the cause of all this trouble."

"Yes, it's me. What have you done with my daughter?" Eleanor couldn't believe he'd stopped. Didn't he know that Hugh and Ned were on their way up? A gust of wind nearly took her bonnet, and she clamped a hand on her head to prevent it from flying off.

"If you'd handed over the money I asked for, none of this would have happened. My wife and me, we did our best taking care of your girl. Your father's a rich man. He could've spared the blunt. Grey could have spared the blunt." He drew closer yet. "But no, you had to be a bitch about it, and now see what's happened."

What was he referring to? Unrelenting fear planted itself in her belly as though something were rotting there. "Where is she? Where is Lili?" Now Eleanor became the aggressor, moving closer to him, grabbing hold of his grubby coat. "Tell me!"

He laughed. "Or what? What will you do?" Taking her by the wrists, he pulled her hands off him and gave her a shove. She nearly lost her footing.

Behind Abbot, Hugh and Ned were approaching. They'd slowed their pace, creeping along so he wouldn't hear them or sense their presence. She needed to hold his attention a little longer. "If anything has happened to her, I'll see you hang."

"I'll be long gone before the law gets its hands on me," he said. Hugh and Ned sprang forward at that moment, each grabbing one of Abbot's arms.

"No, you won't, Abbot," Hugh said, panting. "You will take us to Lili, and then we're going to turn you over to the magistrate."

Abbot didn't waste time trying to break free. "You

bastards! Money first, then I'll tell you where to find her."

"Either lead us to her right now, or we'll drag you directly to the magistrate. I don't think he'll show much mercy to a man who's committed as many crimes as you have. Where is Lili? Is she with your wife?"

Eleanor saw something shift in Abbot's eyes. He was working something out. Probably a way to get money and make an escape.

"Money first," he repeated.

Hugh, with a ferocity Eleanor had never seen in him, grabbed Abbot and dragged him to the edge of the rampart, so close that one of the man's legs dangled over the side. Waves crashed against the walls below. For a heart-stopping moment, Eleanor feared both of them would plunge over. But Hugh, his strength seeming almost inhuman, kept a firm grip on Abbot. "I'll shove you off without a single pang. In fact, I'm looking for a reason to do it. This is your last chance. Where is my daughter?"

Eleanor caught a glimpse of Abbot's terrified face and turned to Ned. "Stop him! If Hugh kills Abbot, we may never find Lili."

Ned didn't need any encouragement. "Hugh! Think what you're doing, man! You could hang for murder. Ease off, now." Ned reached for Abbot's other arm, and gradually they pulled him back from the edge.

Hugh, still in a towering rage, said to Abbot, "Need any more encouragement? Let's go." Hugh gripped Abbot by one arm, and Ned took the other.

Eleanor and Sarah hurried to keep up with the three men. Abbot seemed subdued, resigned to his fate. When they turned up a street Eleanor was certain she'd visited earlier in the day, Abbot slowed and finally stopped.

"If you pay me, I'll leave Surrey and never come back. But give it to me now. I've no desire for a wife or babe."

"You bastard," Hugh said in a low, dangerous voice. "You would abandon your wife and the child she's to bear to save your own skin? I should have pushed you off the ramparts when I had the chance." A tense moment passed. "If you take us to Lili right now, I'll consider recommending mercy to the magistrate."

Abbot started to argue, but apparently thought the better of it. He led them into one of the narrow buildings and up a flight of stairs. After rapping lightly on one of the doors, he said, "Edith, it's me. Let me in."

When the door opened, Hugh and Ned let go of Abbot, shoving him inside. Eleanor followed, Sarah on her heels. Edith Abbot stood there, a look of fear in her eyes. Although cramped, the room seemed clean enough. It served as parlor, bedchamber, and kitchen, and smelled of stale cooking odors. Lili was nowhere in sight, and Eleanor's heart nearly stopped.

Hugh whispered to Ned briefly, and then spoke kindly to Mrs. Abbot. "Where is Lili, ma'am? We've come for her."

She appeared confused and looked to her husband for an explanation. "Jacob? You said…what's happened?"

Now Hugh spoke more authoritatively. "Do not consult your husband. You must give me my daughter this instant. If you do not, you may be considered Abbot's accessory, and you could hang along with him."

Mrs. Abbot looked at Hugh, then seemed to notice for the first time that Eleanor was present. Eleanor stepped forward, for it was she who knew the woman best. She had commiserated with her, helped her, given her extra money now and then. And she believed Edith Abbot cared for Lili.

"Edith, your husband has endangered you because of his reckless scheme of blackmail. You must give up Lili or risk imprisonment, or worse. You don't want that to happen, do you? You're soon to be a mother."

Edith Abbot's hand flew to her mouth, and she spun

around and made her way to a doorway leading to a second room. In a moment, she emerged carrying the sleeping Lili. After a hesitant glance at Eleanor, she placed the child into Hugh's outstretched arms.

While Ned kept a close eye on the Abbots, Hugh regarded his daughter with wonder. Lili was slowly waking, and Eleanor feared the child might cry out. But she did not. She seemed to be studying her father as closely as he studied her, her brows knit in concentration. A smile slowly broke over Hugh's countenance. With his thumb he stroked Lili's brow and traced the outline of her cheek. He kissed her forehead and murmured to her. "At last we meet, child. I am your papa." Hugh gave a joyful laugh, then said, "I hope to become well acquainted with you. Oh, what, you're not too sure about that?"

Eleanor watched for as long as her heart could bear it. Then she whispered to Sarah, and they tiptoed from the room.

"But miss," Sarah cried when they'd reached the street. "The babe will want you. You're her mother."

"Never mind that. We're going back to the inn. Don't dawdle." If she must separate from Lili, better to do it in this way. Her daughter was safe. Lili belonged to Hugh now. To her father. He had the money, the clout, the standing to claim her, and there was nothing Eleanor could do about it. Her parents would prefer it this way. Right now, she simply wished to find her father and tell him they must leave. Ironically, the sun was finally breaking through.

As they neared the inn, she heard a voice calling her name. *Hugh*. She didn't want to see him, didn't wish to speak to him. There was nothing left to say, but it was absurd to try to avoid him. Turning to Sarah, she said, "Go upstairs and find my father. Tell him we must prepare to depart right away."

"But—"

"Please don't argue, Sarah. Do as I ask." The girl nodded

and hurried inside. Eleanor wiped at her tear-streaked face with the back of one hand and turned to face Hugh. He was carrying Lili, his face still wearing an awed expression.

"Didn't you forget someone?" he asked.

Eleanor gazed at him in puzzlement. She couldn't bear to look at Lili. But Lili looked at her, twisting herself around and holding out her arms. "Mama," she said. Eleanor took a step back, raising her palms. "Don't do this, Hugh. It's cruel, to me and Lili both."

"You misunderstand, Eleanor." He held Lili out, and Eleanor had no choice but to gather her daughter into her arms. "Lili belongs with you."

"But you said you were taking her. Only last night at the inn."

"I said many idiotic things, too many to count, which I pray you'll disregard. I was an ass."

"You've changed your mind, then?" Eleanor nuzzled her nose into Lili's neck, breathing her in, and then fixed her gaze on Hugh.

He smiled sheepishly. "It bears repeating. I was every sort of fool. I've had many opportunities on this journey to realize how wrong I've been, Eleanor. I've seen what kind of mother you are, and I should never have doubted you. The care you took making the doll clothes for Lili. Your despair when you thought the worst." He smoothed a lock of her damp hair from her face. "And you are familiar with all aspects of Lili's routine. Of her life. The way she talks and walks. What she plays with. What makes her happy. Everything."

"Those are the small details mothers know," she said gently.

"Only the best ones. You were fierce as a wild boar when you confronted Abbot on the ramparts. If you hadn't ambushed him, he might have escaped."

She laughed. "A mother's protective instincts."

"She's a beautiful child, Eleanor. She has your eyes."

"And your everything else."

"Every time an image of her came to me, she was always a little Eleanor."

Eleanor, who'd been completely unprepared for this turn of events, said, "What happens now?"

Hugh shrugged. "That is up to you. I would like the privilege of seeing Lili on a regular basis." Compared to the man who had so boldly led the search for Lili, he seemed unsure of himself. "I hope you'll trust me with her. And if you're still set on leaving Haslemere, let it not be at too great a distance."

"I'll stay with my parents for a time, until I come to a decision. With the end of the Season, my work is over for the present. And you may see Lili whenever you like." Eleanor felt her cheeks flush. "You've missed nearly two years of her life, after all, and I'm to blame for that."

"Not entirely. The British Army had something to do with it, too." He set his hand on Lili's back, stroking gently. She cocked her head at him, as if wondering what to make of this man. "I assume you wish to be discreet about this?"

"You mean, do I want all of Surrey to know I bore your child out of wedlock?" She gave him a wry smile. "In truth, it was always my parents who worried I would be an outcast. That I would never find a husband. I always cared much more for Lili's welfare than I did about my own. But until we make some decisions, I suppose it's best to maintain discretion. For your sake, too. Scandal could ruin your newfound reputation."

"I'll worry about that later. We have much to discuss, but this is neither the time nor the place. When we're home, may I call on you to work out various arrangements?"

"You will always be welcome where Lili is concerned."

"Your generosity overwhelms me." Hugh studied her. "No offense, Eleanor, but you look exhausted. We all need a hot meal and a good night's sleep."

"I'm not offended." And then Sir William and Adam came rushing through the door, and everything had to be explained to them, including a few bits Eleanor didn't know. Ned had taken Abbot off to the magistrate. Mrs. Abbot had packed up Lili's belongings, which didn't amount to much, and Ned would bring them when Abbot was safely in the magistrate's custody.

"What will happen to Mrs. Abbot?" Eleanor asked.

"When I call on you, I'll tell you what I have in mind. I'd like your opinion."

Somehow, Eleanor made it through the evening. Dinner in the private parlor, Lili being passed about from father, to uncle, to grandfather. The child grew fretful early, no doubt as weary as the rest of them. After bidding everybody good night, Eleanor rose to retire.

Hugh got to his feet as well. "May I carry her up?" he asked.

"Of course."

"Let's go, poppet. Off to dreamland." Just as Eleanor had known he would, Hugh seemed to have a natural ease with Lili, almost as though he'd been present every day since her birth.

In the morning, they left for Surrey.

Chapter Twenty-Four

On the ride back to Surrey, Hugh reflected on all that had transpired the day before. In retrospect, it seemed a miracle they'd found Lili safe. In their inquiries, Hugh and Ned had discovered that Abbot hadn't found work at the factories, though not from lack of trying. It was sheer happenstance they'd spotted him, and if Eleanor hadn't intervened on the ramparts, he might have eluded them. He'd seemed to have no real plan for extorting money from them.

Which was why Hugh and Ned had struggled with whether to call in the magistrate. In the end, Hugh decided they must, albeit reluctantly. He hated leaving Mrs. Abbot pregnant and alone. But Abbot's crimes simply could not be overlooked. The man was an arsonist and blackmailer, and he'd kidnapped Lili. If his crimes had been against property only…but they had endangered lives, and Hugh couldn't be sure he would not commit similar crimes again, if the opportunity presented itself.

Ned would remain in Portsmouth this morning until arrangements could be made for Edith Abbot to travel back to Haslemere by mail coach. Hugh had promised to visit her soon. He planned to offer her financial assistance, at least until she remarried or could otherwise find some means to support herself and her child. She had cared for his child for two years, and for that he was grateful.

Seeing Eleanor with Lili had been a revelation. They belonged together. Hugh wasn't certain what he'd expected, but not the closeness he'd observed. He should have known. Known that a woman like Eleanor would never settle for anything less than a true attachment. He wished for that, too, and she had seemed amenable to it.

But was she—could she ever again be—amenable to a close relationship with him? He loved her, and she had said she loved him. But that was before his rash, reckless accusations. Before he'd threatened to take away her child. Before he'd had time to consider her situation when Lili was born. And he knew the reason he'd been so unwilling to see things from her perspective. The chief reason, in any case.

He'd never gotten over his resentment of Deborah. He had blamed her for every misstep he'd ever taken. And before he'd truly thought things through, he had placed Eleanor in the same category as his mother—women who leave their children. What a fool he'd been.

After reading Deborah's letters and hearing the truth from Wesley, he was ready to make amends with his mother. More than ready. And he felt strongly that before he could attempt to get back into Eleanor's good graces, he must make things right with Deborah.

He would never be whole, never be a man Eleanor could truly trust, until he let go of his bitterness.

He and Eleanor would be thrown together often because of Lili. He could only hope to sway her opinion of him once they were more in each other's company. He wanted her back in his bed, too, and he'd lay money on her wanting that as well. Even when he'd been at his angriest, he'd felt the pull, the attraction to her. Though, until now, he'd resisted acknowledging that to himself. To contemplate life without ever making love to her again was as grim as he could imagine.

The truth was, he wished to marry her. He wanted her by his side every day of their lives.

Forever.

He would make a start. Sometime in the next few days, even before he visited Eleanor and Lili, he would travel up to London and see his mother.

· · ·

A few days later

Once back in Surrey, Eleanor and Lili settled in with her parents. Although her mother was subdued, she'd seemed greatly relieved that no harm had come to her granddaughter and had even been helping with Lili's care. Eleanor knew they must eventually have a discussion, but for now she simply wanted to make a home for Lili.

Hugh did not come.

That surprised her. She'd expected him the day after they'd arrived home, or bright and early the following day, but so far he'd stayed away. Perhaps he was giving her and Lili time to adjust to a different life.

Since her return from Portsmouth, Eleanor had been trying to envision what the future held for her and Lili. Looking back on the last few years, she realized her life had been ruled in large part by what others wanted, or demanded, of her. No more. From now on, she would make her own decisions regarding herself and her child. She wanted Hugh to be a big part of Lili's life, but that was the only thing she knew for certain. A daughter needed her father to rely on, as she had done with her own father for her whole life.

With Sir William's help, she intended to carry through with her plan to leave Surrey and settle somewhere else where she was unknown. Somewhere reasonably close to Haslemere, so Hugh could see Lili regularly. It should not be difficult to establish a dressmaking business, and with the money she earned, she could support herself and Lili. She knew her father would not begrudge her the money, and her mother would probably be just as happy to be rid of them.

Her mother had invented a story to explain Lili's presence, but Eleanor was quite sure the household knew the truth, and that was all right. They were good people, and they were kind and helpful to Eleanor and loving toward Lili. Eleanor's mother wanted her to find a nursemaid, but she was not ready for that step yet. When she was gone from this house, she would be occupied with her work. That was soon enough to turn Lili's care over to somebody else. For now, she was determined to make the most of the early morning kisses and smiles, the games they played, the stories they shared at bedtime. These were the most precious moments in her life.

• • •

After a busy few days dealing with matters at Longmere, Hugh had sent an express to his mother requesting a meeting with her. He disliked being so formal, but she and Mr. Cochran were often away, and he didn't want to make a wasted trip. When the time came to leave, however, he found he wasn't quite ready. He wanted to see Lili first. And yes, he could admit it, Eleanor, too. Perhaps Eleanor most of all. He'd wanted to allow them some time to settle in with her parents, but he missed them both too much to wait any longer.

He walked his mount to the Broxtons' home and rapped at the front door. Hugh had never been round to the front of the house; in fact, now that he thought about it, he'd never been inside the house, either. The facade was more London than Surrey, stuccoed and ornamented with a good deal of wrought iron.

The butler accepted his card and asked him to wait in the rotunda, and in a moment Eleanor herself came to greet him. She was wearing his favorite blue dress and, in both looks and actions, she seemed like a different woman from the one in Portsmouth. Her step was lively, her demeanor composed. She had the fresh-faced look of the girl he'd first met at his mother's house party. He watched her come toward him, and God help him, he was smitten all over again. He couldn't take his eyes off her. Her hair was pinned up, although a few locks had fallen free of the arrangement. Her eyes sparkled, and he realized they'd lost that haunted look. Good God, she was speaking to him, and all he could do was stare.

"Hugh?"

"Eleanor. You look…transformed." He took her hand and kissed her fingers lightly.

"Thank you. I think you are paying me a compliment." She laughed. He hadn't heard that laugh in quite a long time. It was sustenance to a starving man. "Come, we are in the drawing room."

By "we," he hoped she meant only herself and Lili. He walked into the room and his daughter, who was playing with bowls that fit one into another, glanced up at him. "Hello, poppet," Hugh said, striding over to her. He hunkered down on the Turkish carpet and planted a kiss on the top of her head. She smiled, but quickly grew shy, getting up and toddling over to Eleanor. Clutching her mother's legs, she sneaked a glance at Hugh.

His disappointment must have registered on his face, because Eleanor said, "She'll grow accustomed to you, don't worry. I believe children develop a certain shyness at her age."

Hugh smiled ruefully. "I mistakenly thought she would

remember me from Portsmouth. She wasn't shy with me there."

"No, she wasn't. They are changeable little creatures. Let's sit down and play with her. She'll be demanding all your attention in no time."

Eleanor was right. They played with the bowls and, after a few minutes, Lili was laughing at him when he pretended to fit a larger bowl into a smaller one. When she grew bored with the bowls, he picked her up, and she allowed it. He noticed then that Eleanor had left the room. He walked with Lili to the tall sash windows, and he pointed out various things outside. He took a ridiculous pride in her saying the names of things, as though he'd had something to do with her learning them.

Eleanor breezed back into the room with a maid. "It's time for Lili to eat. Mary will feed her, and you and I can talk. Is that all right with you?"

"Yes. Excellent." She was certainly being accommodating. He did want to talk. After Mary and Lili had left the room, she beckoned him to the sofa. In a moment, a footman entered with tea, sandwiches, and Sally Lunns, his favorites.

While they ate, he spoke to her of his plans to help Edith Abbot. "That's very generous of you, Hugh," Eleanor said. "In a way, she was Abbot's victim, just as we were. And I always believed she was genuinely fond of Lili."

Silence ensued.

"I wanted to speak to you—" he began.

"Please visit Lili whenever—"

They smiled at each other. Hugh wished things were not so awkward between them. Fleetingly, he wondered if she yearned for him as he did for her. "My apologies. I know we have much to discuss, but selfishly, today I need your advice. I'm riding up to London to talk to my mother, and I'm all at sea about what to say to her. Ridiculous for a grown man, I know, but there it is."

Eleanor had poured the tea and handed him a cup. "Ah. Now I remember. With all the worry and confusion regarding Lili, I barely took note of what you said about her. Letters, and something a footman told you?"

Hugh laughed. "You really weren't listening, were you?"

"Not to that part." She gave him a cynical look, and then he recalled the remainder of their conversation and winced. "I have much to atone for, but I must deal with my mother first."

Eleanor's look softened. She bit into a watercress sandwich and sipped her tea. "What would you like to say? What's at the core of it?"

Eleanor possessed a rare ability to get to the heart of the matter. "Well…I don't want to deny that I was hurt by her leaving. And taking Adam with her—"

"You're not going to say you forgive her, are you?" Eleanor's head was canted, her mouth tilted up at one corner.

"Of course not. Though it may not have been obvious, I did learn something from our talk at the inn."

She continued to study him. "Very well. Pray, continue."

Suddenly, he was weary of the whole thing. Perhaps this was a fool's errand and he should abandon it. If Eleanor thought so little of his ability to humble himself before his mother, maybe it was a mistake. "Bloody hell—my pardon— should I give up this scheme and simply resume a normal relationship with her? She would accept that, I know."

"You mean give up on bringing things out in the open? Yes, do that, Hugh. Much better to pretend none of it ever happened." It took him a moment to see the cynicism in her words and expression.

He laughed, shaking his head. "What, then?"

"Go on with what you were saying. 'You don't want to deny you were hurt, but.' That's where I interrupted."

"Tell her I discovered the truth. That I read the letters, which I'd never received. And the rest of it."

"And?"

"That I'm truly sorry for blaming her all these years. Her and Adam. That I understand now, as an adult, what an impossible situation my father had placed her in." He glanced at Eleanor. Their eyes locked.

"Oh, Hugh, yes. That's exactly it. I'm so sorry I didn't pay attention when you confided this to me at the inn. What wasted years for you and your family! Now you have the chance to make it all right."

Every instinct told him to pull her into his arms, kiss her, and tell her she was a huge part of why he wanted to reconcile with his mother. He'd like to do much more than that, but he knew she wasn't ready and would most likely shove him away. He had to go slowly with her or risk losing her for good. So he ignored those instincts and got to his feet. "I must be on my way."

"Yes. And take the sandwiches and buns to eat on your journey. You'll be starving by the time you reach London." She called to Mary to wrap up the food.

Eleanor walked outside with him. "Your house. Has it always looked like this? With the risk of giving offense, I have to say it resembles a terrace in Town."

She laughed. "My mother insisted on a new facade a few years back. The style was her idea. I'm not offended. I agree with you." She paused a moment, as though gathering her thoughts. "Someday I must tell you of her role in all of this, but not now."

He'd no idea to what she referred, but she was right. It must wait, like so many other matters. A groom brought out his horse. Before mounting, he leaned in and kissed her cheek. "Good-bye, Eleanor. My thanks for your wise counsel."

Her face bore a slight flush. "I shall see you in a few days, then. Safe travels."

• • •

After Hugh left, Eleanor decided a stroll about the park would be just the thing. She felt an odd restlessness she hadn't experienced in some time, and it had to do with Hugh. With herself and Hugh, and what they were to each other.

His intention to apologize to his mother had touched her more than she wished to admit. She was pleased beyond reason that he understood it was he who owed his mother an apology, not the reverse. That was exactly what Eleanor wanted from him. An apology. Oh, he'd indirectly apologized by saying he'd been a fool. That he said idiotic things. But in her mind, those words did not constitute a true apology for wounding her so deeply. For threatening to separate her and Lili.

She sensed in him a desire to revert to their previous close connection, and, God knew, she wanted that, too. But, remembering her anguish, she needed some further proof that he was not the sort of man who was vindictive and spiteful, always laying the blame on the other party. He was repairing his relationship with his mother. Would he ever do so with her? Did he want to?

Until she had proof, she couldn't risk her heart again. It was too painful.

• • •

Hugh made it to London in late afternoon and presented himself at his brother's door. Wesley let him in, took his hat, gloves, and whip. The house was oddly quiet. "Where is everybody, Wesley?"

"Mr. Grey is out on Parliamentary business, and Mrs. Grey—the younger Mrs. Grey— is making calls, I believe.

Your mother said to send you up to the drawing room when you arrived."

Hugh nodded and made his way upstairs. His stomach felt as if grasshoppers were jumping around inside it. He needed to get this right. It was the crucial first step in mending everything wrong in his life.

Deborah must have heard him, because she was standing, hands folded at her waist, when he entered the room. He walked directly to her and bowed. Then he grasped her hand and kissed her cheek. "Hello, Mama," he said.

"Hello, Hugh. You haven't called me 'Mama' in years." Her eyes were bright, but encouraging.

"No, I have not. But that's going to change, I hope." He gestured to the sofa. "Let's sit down."

Deborah smoothed her skirts, a nervous gesture, and waited for Hugh to begin. "I'm not sure where to start. Probably with the letters."

She appeared puzzled. "The letters?"

He nodded. "The ones you wrote to me after you and Adam left Longmere. Father had never given them to me, you see."

Deborah held herself quite still. "I was afraid that was the case."

"His desk is one of the few pieces of furniture I kept from the original house. I had it moved into my study. It was filled with his things, and I found a bundle of letters in the bottom drawer."

"How cruel you must have thought me. To leave you and fail to write or visit."

"You can't imagine…" Choking up, he paused to collect himself. "To read them was a revelation. For the first time, I knew you had cared about me. You loved me and had tried to see me. Before, I'd always believed you'd left without a backward glance."

"Never. I missed you constantly, cried myself to sleep most nights. So did Adam, though he'd probably never admit it."

"You asked me about such mundane things. Was I keeping up with my studies. Barring the pig from the house. Little things, just the kinds of things a mother would concern herself with, if she were there. Through the letters, you wanted me to feel your presence."

"Yes. To think you did not see them when you most needed to…"

"In a way, perhaps I can appreciate them more fully as a grown man. They mean so much to me now, probably more so than they would have when you wrote them."

"And yet I hoped they would comfort you at the time I left."

"You wrote to tell me about the baby. How did you bear it?" Hugh reached out and grasped his mother's hands.

"I held close what I had. My other son. And my mother and father were still living then and were a great comfort to me." Tears welled from Deborah's eyes. "I told myself I would not cry, but I can't help it, dearest."

Hugh was fighting back his own tears. "No matter. I came to apologize for judging you so harshly these many years. Can you ever forgive me?"

There was a silence for a moment, and then she said, "All that matters is that you come back to us. To Adam and his family, and to me. We love you. We've missed you so. There is nothing to forgive."

Hugh pulled out a handkerchief, and after blotting his own face, offered it to his mother. "I want to be part of this family."

"And that is what we want. Hugh, I hope you don't mind, but Adam told me I have another grandchild. May I meet her?"

He chuckled. "Lili. You'll love her. I thought she would look like Eleanor, but miraculously, she resembles me."

"Eleanor Broxton? Do you have plans to wed, dear?"

Hugh sobered. *He* certainly did, but was that what Eleanor wanted? She was keeping him at a distance, and he wasn't sure how to recover what they'd had before he found out about Lili. "I love her, Mama. I intend to propose, but I've wronged her in too many ways to enumerate. I mean to do whatever I can to make up for my sins and persuade her to marry me."

"If you love her, you'll find a way."

"I wish I could be sure."

"There are many ways to show your love, Hugh. You'll sort it out, if it means so much to you."

He nodded. When Adam and Cass arrived home, they found Hugh and Deborah still talking, dark head and light close together, in the drawing room. Kit's nursemaid brought him in, reminding Hugh of Lili. And Pippa, Cass's younger sister, who lived with them, also made an appearance.

But in the main, Hugh's thoughts were fixed in Haslemere. During dinner, he asked Cass about toy shops. He wanted to bring Lili a surprise. He debated whether to do the same for Eleanor, but decided against it. He did not believe he could sway her with trifles.

Chapter Twenty-Five

A few days later

The post brought Eleanor a most unusual missive. After making inquiries, she found out it had not come by post, but had been delivered by a Longmere servant. It was from Hugh.

> *29 June*
> *Longmere*
>
> *Dear Miss Broxton,*
>
> *Sir Hugh Grey respectfully requests the honor of your presence at his home this day, 29 June, in the company of one dark-haired little imp, at four o'clock in the afternoon. Play and conversation are on the schedule, with dinner to be served afterward.*
>
> *Yours,*
> *H.*

Ah. Hugh had returned from London and was requesting

her company at his home. He seemed to have every expectation that Eleanor would dance attendance on him. She sighed.

No, that wasn't fair.

If she were in his position, she would not wish all her visits with Lili to be at the Broxton home. She must tell Hugh he could take Lili away on his own, without her, although he may not be comfortable enough yet in his role as a father to do so.

She supposed they would go. Since Eleanor had temporarily closed her business, she'd been feeling a bit stifled in the daily company of her parents. She'd had so much freedom at her cottage. Now she was required to fit into the customs and habits of the Broxton household. That was not a bad thing for Lili, who needed stability and routine. But it was somewhat constraining for her and reminded her of life before Lili, when she had so craved independence.

That afternoon, Mary helped her pack up some things for Lili—a few toys, books, and a change of clothes. Sarah, who'd accompanied her to Portsmouth, helped Eleanor dress in the primrose sprigged muslin dress she had worn to the Carringtons' garden party. She looked well in it.

Her father insisted on escorting her to Longmere himself rather than sending a footman. Eleanor toted the basket, and Sir William carried Lili. They walked along in amiable silence. After a few minutes, her father said, "Have you sensed any change in your mother?"

Eleanor was a bit flummoxed and had to gather her thoughts before responding. "Are you referring to her attitude regarding Lili?" The child's head whipped around when her mother said her name.

"Just so."

"I have. I'm aware she's making an effort, especially with her granddaughter. She hasn't apologized to me, but in word and deed, I can see she's remorseful. I had told her before we left for Portsmouth that I would hold her accountable if anything happened to Lili."

"I had a long talk with her. I asked if she wanted to be a lonely old woman or one who shared the love of her family. She wept, Norrie. Kitty wept, something I haven't seen for years. She said she would far rather have you and Lili as a part of her life than not. Allow her to make up for her offenses in her own way and in her own time. Apologies are difficult for her."

Yes. Eleanor knew someone else about whom she could say the same. "Very well, Papa. And thank you for everything, for standing by me even though Mama did not approve. You've been my rock the last few years."

He smiled. "What are fathers for, after all?"

Indeed.

Hugh was waiting for them out front. Dressed in buff britches, a pale green waistcoat with gold-thread embroidery, and an indigo coat, he looked devilishly handsome. His hair had been trimmed and was pushed farther away from his face than usual. Eleanor wasn't sure she liked it that way. A servant appeared and collected the basket, and Eleanor took Lili from her father.

After shaking hands with Hugh and receiving his assurances that he would deliver them home himself, Sir William took his leave.

"It looks lovely, Hugh," Eleanor said, gesturing toward the newly planted front gardens. Lili wiggled, and Eleanor set her down.

"It's coming along," he said. "We must wait until cooler weather for certain plantings, but I'm happy with the progress we've made." He wasn't looking at her, but rather watching his daughter. "Will she be all right, just wandering like that?"

Eleanor quelled a smile. "We're here, watching her every move. She'll be fine."

"What do you think she would like to do? If you have no objection, I thought I might take her up on my horse. Just walk around a bit."

"She would love that," Eleanor said. "I trust you with her."

. . .

Hugh took great pleasure at hearing his daughter's squeals of joy when she was placed on the saddle in front of him, his arm firmly holding her in place. He walked the horse down the driveway, but not so far that they would be out of Eleanor's sight. She watched them, smiling, sometimes laughing, while Lili repeated over and over, "horse ride" and "I ride horse," much to Hugh's delight.

Afterward, Hugh carried Lili upstairs, Eleanor following. "I fitted up a chamber for her," he said. "Oh, it's nothing like a real nursery, but somewhere for her to stay when she's here." He set Lili down to explore. When he glanced at Eleanor, her mouth was gaping open in surprise.

"You have gone to a great deal of trouble, Hugh. This is a child's dream."

"It will do for now." In truth, he was proud of it. He'd painted it himself, a bright yellow, and a local seamstress had sewed white dimity curtains. A rocking horse sat in one corner, just waiting for a rider, and a crib in another. Newly built shelves had been hung on one wall, where he'd placed books and toys. Tops, whirligigs, puzzles. Knickknacks she was too young for at present, but eventually she would learn how to manipulate them. Lili went straight for the rocking horse.

Eleanor crossed her arms and tapped her foot. "You must have done some shopping in London. Clearly, you are going to spoil this child. You're aware of that, are you not?"

He smiled sheepishly. "Isn't that a father's prerogative?"

"I suppose it is," Eleanor said, laughing. "Now, didn't your invitation mention food? I'm starving, and Lili will soon become cranky if she doesn't eat."

"Of course," he said, picking up the child before she could climb on the horse. There was a washstand with a pitcher and bowl in the room, and after Hugh washed his own hands, he helped Lili with hers.

Once downstairs, Hugh said, "My new cook, Mrs. Foster, said she would feed Lili if we wished to dine alone. To talk about everything." How transparent was that? Would she guess he simply craved the opportunity to be alone with her? While he adored his daughter, that did not detract from the pleasures of her mother.

"Yes, fine," Eleanor said. "We do need to talk."

When they were seated at the dining room table, an array of food before them, Hugh dismissed the footman. He served the soup himself, and managed not to spill any of it.

"I've been wondering, Hugh. Did you and your mother... reach an understanding?"

He set down his spoon. "More than that. I did what you advised. I told her exactly how I'd felt those many years ago, and that my discovery of the letters had changed everything. Then I apologized."

Eleanor, too, had lowered her spoon and had fixed her gaze on his. "And did she accept your apology?"

"She did."

Unexpectedly, she reached out and grasped his hand. "I'm very glad for you, Hugh. It's high time you reconciled with your mother and brother." Just as he was poised to press her hand against his cheek, she removed it.

"I'm very pleased, and I believe Deborah is, too." He paused a moment before going on. "She wants to meet Lili. Would it be all right with you if I invited her—and perhaps Adam and his family as well—for a weekend?"

Her face flushed. What had he said to upset her? "That is entirely up to you. You may have Lili as much as you like for that weekend, or any other time, for that matter."

She may as well have said, "It's nothing to do with me." And she would have been right. This was not her home, and the way he'd worded his question made it sound as though it was. "Thank you for that. I appreciate your willingness for me to be a part of her life." *Christ.* Now they were back to the stilted formality again.

They ate in an uncomfortable silence, and afterward Hugh suggested they sit in the library for tea. Eleanor went in search of Lili first, and after settling her upstairs for a nap, joined him. A footman brought in the tea, and Hugh poured for her. "You're quite lovely in that dress, Eleanor. You wore it to the garden party."

"Yes, I did. Thank you." She changed the subject. "Your library is every bit as comfortable and cozy as I envisioned. Are you enjoying it?"

"I haven't had much opportunity yet, but I expect to spend most of my time in this room."

Unless you were here, and we would instead do wicked things together in the bedchamber.

Her eyes darted away from him, as though she couldn't bear to look at him.

That was enough. He could stand it no longer. "Eleanor, is there no chance for us? Can things between us never be as they were before? I miss you to distraction." They'd been sitting across from each other, he on an upholstered chair, she on the sofa. He pushed the tea tray away and moved to sit beside her. He did not attempt to touch her.

"You don't look like yourself with your hair brushed back like that," she said.

Her response was so surprising, he laughed. "Very well, I'll fix it. No, better yet, you fix it." She was studying him closely, as though he were a dissected puzzle she must put together. Then, just when he'd concluded she would not, she lifted her hands and began rearranging his hair. Her touch was electrifying, and he closed his eyes from the pure pleasure of it. She was lifting tendrils of his hair with her fingers and smoothing them into place. He could feel them, and her fingers, lightly brushing his face. Good God, how was he meant to withstand this? He caught her hands in his, opened his eyes, and looked directly into hers.

And then he kissed her. Softly at first. But soon his overwhelming need for her possessed him, and he intensified the kiss, enticing her mouth open. Pulling her close, he moaned her name. "Eleanor. Oh God, Eleanor." He could kiss her for hours, if she'd allow it. Kiss her back to him. The sweet taste of her, the feel of her satiny tongue sliding into his mouth, the sound of her soft moans drove him to the brink. He wanted her. Oh God, did he want her. His cock was throbbing, and he was tempted to lay her hand against it.

Abruptly, she drew back, placing her hands on his chest and pushing. Leaving him in no doubt of her feelings. "No, Hugh."

Bloody hell. "You want this, too, Eleanor. Don't deny it."

"That may be, but what I want and what is good for me aren't the same thing."

"I can make it good for you." He tried to drag her back to him, but when she resisted, he ceased.

"You know that is not what I meant. What we had before was enjoyable, but—"

"Enjoyable? *Enjoyable?* That is all it was to you?"

She rose and moved away from the sofa, apparently not trusting him to keep his distance. "Very well. It was more than simply enjoyable. But in the end, it hurt us. *Me.* I'd rather not go down that path again."

Losing the tenuous grip he had on his temper, he said, "It

wasn't sleeping together that hurt us. It was the fact that you kept Lili a secret from me. You didn't trust me enough to tell me about her. You chose a life of endless labor over the one I could have given you and our daughter."

"Oh? I don't recall receiving a proposal of marriage from you."

He got to his feet and raked a hand through the hair Eleanor had just rearranged. "I intended to propose." *Christ, that sounded weak.* Why was he so tongue-tied whenever he tried to express his feelings to her? If she'd told him she was expecting his child, he would have proposed immediately. Upon his return to Surrey, if she'd come to him with the news that he was a father, he would have proposed then. Nothing, in fact, would have made him happier. He damn well should have offered Eleanor marriage by now. He should have bloody begged her to marry him, but his rage and resentment had prevented it.

She threw her arms up. "There, you see? You continue to blame me for a situation that was largely beyond my control. We will never agree." She turned for the door. "It's time for Lili and me to leave. And I would prefer it if a footman, or Ned Martin, if he is available, walk us home."

"Damn it, Eleanor. Don't run off."

She paused at the door. "I want you to know I am proceeding with my plans to quit Haslemere. I've written to my cousins in Devon and asked them to check on cottages available to rent there."

He must have misheard. "I beg your pardon. Did you say 'Devon'?"

She placed one hand on her hip in obvious defiance. "I did."

"But that's miles away, too far for me to see Lili regularly. Why Devon?"

"My cousins can help spread the word about my business."

"Hell, handbills can spread the word. Besides, I will be supporting Lili. You won't need to work as hard as you once did. It feels as if you're doing this to spite me."

She looked on the verge of tears. "No, I'm not, I swear. It will simply be easier if I'm not completely alone. I need a few people to rely on."

Stay here and rely on me.

"Why not somewhere closer? Far enough that you would not be recognized, but close enough for me to visit."

"I'll consider it."

Would she? He supposed that was all she was willing to concede for now. Feeling defeated, he walked over and opened the door for her. There was no point in further discussion of this tonight. "I'll find Ned. He's about somewhere."

"And I'll fetch Lili. She must be awake by now. These late-day naps are usually of quite short duration."

Hugh nodded and went in search of his steward.

· · ·

Once at home, Eleanor played with Lili and dressed her for bed. After listening to a few fairy tales and looking at the illustrations, the child's eyes grew heavy, and Eleanor laid her in her crib and covered her.

The elder Broxtons were out for the evening, thank God. Eleanor didn't think she could have faced them after the disaster at Longmere. She had come dangerously close to giving in to Hugh, because her attraction to him was so consuming. Was she being a fool? He had not proposed, nor said he loved her; instead, he had brought up what she'd hoped they'd laid to rest. Indeed, she had apologized to him more than once. Eleanor thought he'd gotten over the fact that she had kept Lili a secret for so long.

He'd offered no apology to *her*, choosing instead to

continue to blame her for their impasse. Look how many years it had taken Hugh to reconcile with his mother. Eleanor refused to spend her life continually worrying that the past would rear its ugly head once again and come between them.

He said he'd intended to propose to her. Then why hadn't he?

It was best that she carry on with her plan to move, and the sooner it could be arranged, the better.

• • •

Hugh was reclining with his feet on an ottoman, drinking his second brandy and staring into space, when Ned entered the room.

"Help yourself to a drink."

After Ned had poured himself a finger of brandy, he claimed the chair facing Hugh. "You and Miss Broxton had a falling-out, did you?"

"Yes." Hugh was in no mood to discuss it.

"I see. She was very quiet on the walk to the Broxton home. In case you were wondering."

"I was not."

"Ah." Ned took a swallow. To Hugh's consternation, the man was apparently willing to wait him out.

Oh, what the hell. "I can't… She won't listen to reason."

"I see."

"What is that supposed to mean, 'I see'?"

Ned set his glass down. "Nothing. You haven't given me enough information to form an opinion."

"Oh, for Christ's sake. Eleanor doesn't want to stay here in Haslemere. She's determined to take Lili and move to blasted Devon, of all places."

"Why would she do that?"

"To start over where she's not known. Evidently she

has cousins there upon whom she can rely." He paused momentarily, rubbing his forehead with both hands. "When I asked her if she would consider somewhere closer, she agreed. But she was just trying to appease me."

"You don't wish her to leave Haslemere at all, then. If you don't mind my asking—"

"It never bodes well when a sentence begins with those words," Hugh said, casting his friend a baleful eye. "But by all means, continue."

"What do you want, Hugh? With Eleanor?"

Taken aback by the question, Hugh got to his feet and walked over to the sash windows. Gazing into the darkness, he mulled over a response. "I want to marry her. Not just for Lili's sake, but because I love her. I love them both."

"Have you told her as much?"

"Not since I found out about Lili, damn it. I never seem to say the right thing. And then we both become angry, and any chance of telling her how I feel vanishes. And I don't even know if she loves me." Perhaps if he hadn't been so damned vindictive and stubborn, this wouldn't be the case.

"Maybe you should help her achieve whatever it is that will ensure her peace of mind. Her contentment. If it is leaving here, commit to it. If you dedicate yourself to her happiness, she'll see how much you love her."

Hugh made no answer. After a while, he heard Ned leave the room. His steward's advice made no sense. And yet it made a great deal of sense. By the time Hugh climbed the stairs to crawl into bed, an idea had taken root.

Chapter Twenty-Six

A few days later

When Hugh didn't reappear promptly, Eleanor began to worry. Yes, she'd been angry with him. But that didn't mean she never wanted to see him again, despite her determination to move to Devon. Damn the man, she missed him exceedingly. Apparently, he was so exasperated with her, he'd decided to stay away, even from Lili.

And then when she was out front playing tag with Lili, he was there. She must look a fright, her hair coming loose from its pins, her face flushed from dashing about. When she caught sight of him, she slid to a stop. Lili ran right to him, and he hoisted her up and spun her about.

"Hello, my little scamp," he said.

He set Lili down and walked over to Eleanor, bending his tall frame to the side so he could hold Lili's hand. "Good morning, Eleanor."

"We've been running around," she said, feeling idiotic.

He laughed. Well. He was in a good mood, which made

her unaccountably annoyed. "It's put some color in your cheeks," he said, eyeing her. "Could we talk for a moment?"

She nodded, and they walked toward the stone bench situated underneath a linden tree. Earlier, Eleanor had asked for water to be brought out. She poured some for Hugh and herself, then called Lili over for a drink.

"We haven't seen you," Eleanor said after Lili ran off to chase Bobby.

"No. I've been away." Then, suddenly, he looked at her and said, "I think I've found the perfect spot for you, Eleanor. That is, if you're still intent upon moving."

She fiddled with her hair, not making eye contact with him. "I am."

No. That was a lie. She wanted him to take her in his arms and proclaim his undying love. And propose to her.

"Where is this spot?"

"A seaside town called Bognor. Are you familiar with it?"

She shook her head.

"It's close to Chichester, and should you move there, you could likely gain a clientele from that city. Especially when the Society matrons see some of your creations."

"And where is it? How far from here?"

"About thirty miles, as compared to one hundred and fifty to Devon. I freely admit to having a vested interest in keeping you and Lili closer, and you said you would consider a different location."

"I didn't recall that Devon was so far." Eleanor set her palms on the bench and leaned into them, stretching her shoulders. Her enthusiasm for leaving had suddenly withered up and blown away, like so much ash. It now seemed a terrible idea, and yet, unless Hugh proposed, how could she remain? She could not live with her parents forever, without all the neighbors, and ultimately the whole of Haslemere, getting wind of the fact that she had a child. She sighed unhappily on a deep exhalation.

"Did you say something?" Hugh asked.

She regarded him, trying to gauge his feelings on the matter. "Tell me more about it. Where would we live?"

"I found a pretty little cottage. It's at the end of a lane with a few other houses. No view of the sea, I'm afraid, but it's only a short walk away. And it has plenty of windows. There are two front parlors, and your sewing room could be in one of them." He hesitated, then said, "Of course, it must meet with your approval."

"Bedchambers?"

"Four, all upstairs. Small, naturally. You could use one of them for storage of your dressmaking supplies, and there would still be one for you, one for Lili, and a third for a companion. Because you cannot live there alone, of course."

"No, I suppose not. Would Lili be happy there, do you think?"

Eleanor felt close to tears. Carrying out her plan of moving would mark not only a new beginning, but the end of something as well. Hugh would be Lili's father, and nothing more, and they would see less of him. She didn't want that, but she did not see a way to change things. Achieving her goal of leaving Haslemere was a bittersweet victory.

"I don't know why not, provided you're there. You're her world, Eleanor," he said softly. "Would you like to see it? It's called Rose Cottage."

She should try to muster some enthusiasm. "Yes," she said over a lump in her throat.

"Excellent. I hope you don't mind, but I've worked out some arrangements with Sir William. He will see you safely to Bognor and return for you in a sennight. This will enable you to judge how you like the cottage and the Town, and find out if Lili will adjust. And you may wish to spend a day in Chichester while you're there."

He certainly sounded bloody excited about it. Eleanor lifted a corner of her mouth. "You've been quite busy. It seems you've taken care of everything," she said.

"I want you to be happy, Eleanor. Isn't this what you want?"

Miserable, her heart leaden, she nodded. "Of course."

· · ·

A week later

Hugh had not done justice to Rose Cottage and its surroundings. The cottage was immaculate, fitted up with comfortable, sturdy furnishings, including a crib, chest of drawers, and shelves for the nursery. And from its perch at the end of the lane, it was picturesque enough to be part of a painting. The front garden was planted, appropriately, in roses, and, in the moderate climate of the seacoast, they were still flourishing.

Light streamed into the front windows, which faced south, toward the sea. Every day since they'd arrived, mother and daughter had walked to the beach, Eleanor carrying a bucket and spade and a basket of sandwiches and jug of water. Their stretch of shore was deserted, so she had no qualms about shedding her shoes and stockings and wading and allowing Lili to do the same. Because Lili loved the waves and did not seem to fear the pull of the sea in the least, Eleanor kept a close eye on her.

In the afternoon, they walked back to the cottage and Lili slept. Sometimes Eleanor used the time to sketch new designs, but more often than not, she slept, too. She was gripped with a lethargy, and rather than fight it, she surrendered to it. All things considered, she felt she deserved a respite after all her hard work and the ordeal of Lili's kidnapping.

Eleanor was not sure who was assuming the cost of their

stay at Rose Cottage, and who would pay going forward. Her father was vague and circumspect about it on the way down, but she had a feeling it was all Hugh's doing. There was no doubt the sea, the leisure, and the time spent with Lili were rejuvenating. She barely had to lift a finger. Jane had agreed to accompany them, and a woman from the village came in each day to do light household tasks and cook dinner.

One afternoon, Eleanor was drifting off when she heard somebody outside. Lili was sleeping and Jane had gone for a walk. Hastily, Eleanor descended the steps, not wishing to wake Lili. A messenger stood at the door holding a letter. "For me?" she said.

"Are you Eleanor Broxton?" he asked.

"I am."

"Then it's yours, miss." He waited while Eleanor fetched a coin, and after he'd left, she took the letter into the parlor and tore it open. She recognized the bold writing as Hugh's.

10 July
Longmere

My dearest Eleanor,

If you are reading this, you are safely at the seaside with Lili. I hope it is all you dreamed it would be. In the drawer of the worktable in the kitchen, you will find another document from me. It is the deed to Rose Cottage, which now belongs solely to you. I pray this will remove the sadness from your eyes, finally and irrevocably.

My wish is for you to have the freedom and independence you so crave. I pray you will be happy there, but in all honesty, I would rather you were here, where I could see you every day. I speak only of you now, Eleanor, because I love you. Adore you. Worship you. And have since I first met you at my mother's house party.

I believe I may have wounded you too gravely to ever be forgiven. A thousand apologies would probably not make up for what I said to you after finding out about Lili. Nonetheless, I do most sincerely apologize. You cannot imagine how many times I have wished those words back, wished fervently I'd never spoken them. I feel ashamed every time I recall them. You are a loving mother to Lili, the best a father—and daughter—could ever want. And I've come to understand your dilemma at the time of her birth. Had I been in your shoes, I would have done the same as you.

I rode to the Haslemere assembly on that miserable November night with no expectation, no plan, other than to set my eyes on you just once before I departed for Canada. I don't believe I ever told you how the memory of our night together sustained me through my time away, during the endless cold, the loneliness, and the fear. You gave yourself to me so unselfishly, so ardently. I knew if I could somehow make it through the war, I would see you again and perhaps persuade you to marry me. I have not given up that dream.

You have my heart, Eleanor. And it is left only to say, I wish I might have yours.

Hugh

Eleanor raised her head, tears sliding off her face and onto the letter. The golden light of the waning day bathed the room like a radiant watercolor wash. It was so lovely here, but without Hugh, it was nothing more than a place she was staying for a few days. She missed him with a visceral longing. Missed his smile, his dark eyes, his sensual touch. His kindnesses to her. What they might have together—she did not want it to be a thing she *almost* had. A supreme happiness within her reach, but she let it slip from her grasp because of her own willfulness.

When Jane returned, Eleanor informed her they would be leaving as soon as she could arrange for a private coach to convey them home.

• • •

Two days later

Hugh had just come in from a long day of riding out to visit tenants with Ned. He was washing up, shirtless, clad only in a pair of buff britches. Although he was glad he'd taken the trouble to make the visits, he hadn't been truly listening while Ned and various tenants pointed out improvements to land and buildings.

He seemed to see Eleanor everywhere he looked and spent most of his time wondering what she and Lili were doing. Playing on the beach? Tending the rose garden? Or perhaps visiting Chichester. With time, these thoughts would probably taper off, or at least not be so distracting. Grabbing a linen cloth, he dried his face and hair. And then he heard a voice. It sounded like Eleanor. *Perfect*. Now he was hearing her as well as seeing her.

"Hugh."

He swiveled about, and there she was, standing in the doorway, gazing intently at him. "Eleanor?" He fumbled with the drying cloth, finally tossing it aside. "I thought I was imagining things."

"No, you're not. I'm here."

A piercing joy pulled hard across his chest. "I'm afraid

you've caught me in the middle of my ablutions."

Eleanor moved toward him. She was wearing the blue dress, and it looked as though she'd forgotten her stays. "Why are you here?" he asked. "Was the cottage not to your liking?"

"The cottage is perfect. But it was missing one thing." Her smile was sweetly seductive.

Now he took a tentative step toward her. "Oh? What was that?"

"You," she said, right before throwing herself into his arms.

• • •

She felt the rise and fall of his chest as his arms came around her.

"My darling," he said. "My love." And then his lips settled on hers in a kiss that called her back to him. His soft, sensuous mouth devoured hers, and when his tongue slid along her lips, she opened her mouth to him. His fingers threaded through her hair, pulling pins out and dropping them to the floor. In another moment, he'd spun her around and was undoing the buttons marching down her back. Meanwhile, Eleanor explored him with her hands. His sinewy thighs. His rigid flesh. He kissed her nape. "What are you doing, minx?"

"*Mmm*. You feel so good."

Hugh finished with the buttons, and the dress fell to the floor. With a soft chuckle he said, "Did you dress in a hurry, darling? Or did you leave your stays off deliberately?"

"What do you think?"

In a trice, he lifted her into his arms and carried her to the bed. He laid her down gently and slid her chemise down to her waist. Then he began to kiss her all over. Her world was distilled down to the essence of this place and this moment. The feel of him covering her body with his. The warmth and strength of him. She wanted to devour and be devoured.

"You came back to me," he said.

"Yes." With his longed-for touch and intimate caresses, all the tension drained from her.

"I was afraid you might not. That I'd lost you forever." Her skin was hot, burning for him, and he continued to kiss and caress her even while whispering to her. He paused to run a finger around her navel. "I don't think I can live without you, love. Marry me. Please, Eleanor, marry me."

"Yes. Yes, of course I'll marry you. Your letter…"

He slid her chemise over her head, and she wrapped her legs around him. "It was from my heart."

"I know. Hush now, dear Hugh," she said, pulling him down to her. She would have a lifetime of this joy. She would fall asleep beside him and wake up next to him. Oh, they were not perfect. They would argue and make up again. But they would have love and trust, and Lili would bind them always, and other children, if they were so blessed.

And then she thought of nothing. She simply let herself be carried away to a place that was all sensation, a place where she could love him with her body, and her heart and soul.

Later, they dozed in each other's arms. When they woke, she cradled his face in her hands and kissed him. "I love you, Hugh Grey."

"You are my life, Eleanor. Don't ever leave me again."

She smiled. "No."

The slant of the sun signaled late afternoon. Hugh stretched and then asked, "Where is Lili?"

"With my parents. And they know I am with you." She grasped his shoulders and kissed him soundly. "Thank you for the cottage."

"You approve of it, then."

"Being there is like living in a dream world, its perfection marred only by the fact that you weren't there."

"We'll keep it, in that case. Our hideaway."

"Your letter was so perfect."

"I could never seem to say what was in my heart when I was with you. I thought perhaps writing would do the trick."

Eleanor pressed her forehead against his. "I was beginning to think you would never be more to me than Lili's father." Then, hastily, "And that would have been wonderful, of course."

"Yes. Except we both would have been miserable."

Later, much later, they dressed and made their way to the Broxton home. It was deep twilight now, darkness falling over the land. Eleanor felt a quivering in her stomach when she glanced at Hugh. She hadn't known it was possible to be this happy.

"Is something wrong, love?"

She squeezed his arm. "No. Quite the contrary. Everything is perfect."

Epilogue

Three months later

Flambeaux lit the stone gray facade of Longmere, casting shadows on the arriving guests. There was a prodigious number of them. Eleanor thought perhaps they'd invited the whole of Haslemere. Carriages lined the driveway, the coachmen warming themselves with flasks of their favorite spirits. Ned had hired extra grooms for the evening to help stable the mounts of those who had ridden.

Eleanor and Hugh, rather than making use of the traditional receiving line, had chosen to simply circulate and greet people, and they had encouraged their families to do likewise. In the three months since their marriage, most of the gossip had died down. Some among the citizens of the area had decided the newlyweds were too scandalous to associate with, but no matter. Now they knew who their true friends were. Tonight's soiree was to celebrate the completion of the rebuilding of Longmere rather than their nuptials, although many were offering their congratulations for those as well.

Eleanor, sipping champagne, stood with Cassandra Grey, her new sister-in-law. Unashamedly, they were eyeing their husbands, deep in conversation nearby. "If Hugh hadn't fallen in love with you, Eleanor, I'm not sure he would ever have reconciled with Adam and Deborah. Thank you for that."

Eleanor laughed. "My pleasure. It's good to see them so comfortable with each other. Becoming close, as brothers were meant to be."

"They are a handsome pair, aren't they?" Cass said.

"Adam favors Deborah, and Hugh favors his father. But if you watch them together, you begin to see similar mannerisms. And expressions."

"And how are your parents handling things?" Cass had been aware of the difficulties between Eleanor and her mother, especially, and had lent a sympathetic ear when necessary.

Casting her gaze about the room, Eleanor finally spotted them. They were talking with old friends from Haslemere and, on the surface at least, they appeared to be in a celebratory mood. Eleanor wasn't certain her mother would ever forgive her for creating such a scandal. But both her mother and father had grown very fond of Lili and had been spending a great deal of time playing with her and sometimes taking her on small jaunts.

"Much better than I could have hoped for."

Just then, Hugh glanced up at Eleanor, and a slow smile spread over his face. She smiled back. He spoke briefly to his brother, and they made their way to their wives. "Will you dance with me, Cassie?" Adam said, holding out his hand.

When they left, Hugh said, "Well, Lady Grey, what do you think of our party?"

She grasped his arm. "It is a rousing success, from the looks of it. Given our reputation, I'm amazed so many graced us with their presence."

"Some of them will dine out on our scandal for years to come."

"I don't mind, if you don't," Eleanor said.

Hugh gazed at her lovingly. Sometimes she fancied she still saw stars in his eyes. "Shall we dance, darling? It's a waltz, and we practiced."

Eleanor smiled. "By all means. I'm sure everybody will be in awe of our grace and skill."

They joined the dance. After Hugh had taken her into his arms, he said, "Are you feeling quite well, love? You seem a bit out of sorts."

"Only a little tired. I am so grateful your mother and Cass came down to help us with the final preparations."

The musicians had set up in the upstairs gallery. The staff had set out food in the dining room, and guests could eat whenever they pleased. Some of the men had chosen to play cards. Meanwhile, those who wished to dance, or simply observe the dancers, indulged themselves.

The corridors off the gallery led to the bedchambers. Eleanor had told Jane, who often helped with Lili, to bring her to them before putting her to bed. As Hugh twirled her around, Eleanor caught sight of them. Jane waved, trying to get her attention.

"Oh, look, Hugh. There's Lili. Let's sneak off and kiss her good night."

They quit the dance floor and made their way toward their daughter, whose second birthday they'd celebrated in August. Hugh held out his arms, and Lili went to him. "Jane, why don't you sneak downstairs to the kitchen and have some refreshments. We'll put her to bed," Eleanor said.

"If you're sure, ma'am. She's had a story and I've rocked her. She's sleepy."

Lili had made the switch to a real bed. She was indeed sleepy, her eyes closing as Hugh laid her down and covered her. Her long, dark lashes brushed her cheeks. Eleanor sat on one side of the bed and Hugh on the other. "I feel like the luckiest man in England," he said, glancing at Lili, then over at Eleanor.

"Hugh," Eleanor whispered, leaning toward him. "I believe I am expecting another child."

He laughed softly. "I believe you are."

She pulled back, shocked. "What? How did you know?"

He came around the bed to her side and raised her up. "You are looking quite voluptuous, my love. Did you think I would not notice?"

"You scoundrel!" she said. "Are you glad?"

"As I said, I'm the luckiest man in England." He drew her into his arms.

And she was the luckiest lady.

Acknowledgments

As they say, it takes a village. Sincere thanks to my editor at Entangled Publishing, Erin Molta, for her insights and thoughtful comments and suggestions. *A Lady's Deception* is a much stronger book because of her guidance. Thanks as well to Alethea Spiridon for taking a close look and to Nancy Cantor for her astute copyediting. I am most grateful to Holly Bryant Simpson, my enthusiastic and energetic publicist, and to everyone at Entangled involved in the design and production of the book. I would be remiss if I didn't thank my critique partner of twelve years, Lisa Brown Roberts, who, despite her hectic schedule, always makes time to read my books. And last, huge thanks and hugs to my husband, Jim, my first reader and critic, and the person who never tires of listening to my book ideas, helping me work out plot problems, and bolstering me when I've lost my way.

About the Author

Pamela Mingle is a former teacher and librarian who made the switch to writing as a third career. She loves to create romantic tales that play out against historical events and always includes a bit of humor in her books. She and her husband enjoy walking in the UK—even though she's done her share of whining on those fifteen-mile days. The walking trips have proved to be an ideal way to discover new settings for her books. Pam is the author of *A False Proposal*, *The Pursuit of Mary Bennet, A Pride and Prejudice Novel*, and *Kissing Shakespeare*, winner of the 2013 Colorado Book Award for Young Adult Fiction. Learn more about Pam and sign up for her newsletter at www.PamMingle.com. She enjoys hearing from readers and would love to meet you on social media.

Also by Pamela Mingle...

A FALSE PROPOSAL

Discover more historical romance from Entangled...

MY HELLION, MY HEART
a *Lords of Essex* novel by Amalie Howard and Angie Morgan

Lord Henry Radcliffe, the sexy Earl of Langlevit, is a beast. The only way Henry can exorcise the demons of his war-ravaged past is through physicality, in and out of bed. Intent on scandalizing London, Princess Irina Volkonsky is a hellion and every gentleman's deepest desire...except for one. Irina knows better than to provoke the forbidding earl, but she will stop at nothing short of ruination to win the heart of the only man she's ever loved.

THE IMPORTANCE OF BEING SCANDALOUS
a *Tale of Two Sisters* novel by Kimberly Bell

Nothing she does scares off bookish but strong-willed Amelia Bishop's stuffy, egotistical fiancé. The only thing left is to entice childhood friend Nicholas Wakefield into a truly engagement-ending scandal. The Wakefields are the height of propriety, and Nicholas's parents have made it clear a wife from the neighboring Bishop family would be unacceptable... But Nicholas would give up his family *and* his fortune if Amelia would ever see him as more than just a childhood friend. He'll go along with her scheme, even if it means ruining them both, because he's got a plan that will change her mind about him being merely the boy next door.

WHEN A LADY DECEIVES
a *Her Majesty's Most Secret Service* novel by Tara Kingston

In Victorian London, reporter Jennie Quinn goes undercover seeking justice for a murdered informant, only to be drawn into a criminal's seductive game. Matthew Colton is a dangerous man with secrets of his own, but the mystery in his eyes and the temptation of his touch prove too powerful to resist. Forging an undeniable passion, Jennie and Matthew must risk everything to destroy the web of treachery that threatens their love—and their lives.

ONLY A DUKE WILL DO
a *To Marry a Rogue* novel by Tamara Gill

On the eve of Lady Isolde Worthingham's wedding to Merrick Mountshaw, the Duke of Moore, a scandal that rocked the ton leaves her perfectly planned future in a tangle of disgrace and heartbreak. The duke loathes the pitiful existence he hides from the *ton*. With a scandalous wife he never wanted, life is a never-ending parade of hell. When the one woman he loved and lost returns to London, he can no longer live without her. But vows and past hurts are not easily forgotten. Love may not win against the *ton* when a too proper Lord and Lady play by the rules.

CPSIA information can be obtained
at www.ICGtesting.com
Printed in the USA
BVHW031741290719
554589BV00001B/5/P